INFLAMMATION

L. J. Blume

In memory of my wonderful, larger than life cousin David Amstel, with whom I grew up like a brother; who died suddenly from a heart attack aged 52, when I was halfway through writing this book. You really never do know - seize the day.

For Rachel, whose suffering and incredible fortitude in a failed system, was the original inspiration for this story.

For all the women and girls who are murdered by someone in their own family or household, at a consistent yearly average rate of one every eleven minutes*; and those they leave behind.

*Source - The United Nations Office on Drugs and Crime.

Psychosis - A severe mental disorder, with or without organic damage, which may be chronic or transient, characterised by derangement of personality and loss of contact with reality, causing a deterioration of normal social functioning.*

*Source - Oxford Reference Dotcom

Chapter One - 14 years, 11 months, and 19 days until *his* release

Adam looked over his shoulder and stared out across the sea of hats and faces, barely able to discern those he should recognise, from those he couldn't, from those he didn't care to. He had not expected quite such a number of people, although after an existence of spiralling agony for the previous 12 days; he knew his judgement was hardly to be relied upon.

He vaguely heard some hymns being sung, then the Priest's voice rolling out the standard sentiments, of some comfort to those with varying degrees of belief in such things, but of none whatsoever to him; not that he could have absorbed them properly anyway. He awaited the Priest's indicative nod, and approached the pulpit with a distant, glazed stare, and a fixed, blank expression.

- "Those of you who really knew Lorelei, already know what a gentle, loving, loyal, kind, feisty, wonderful person she was. Those of you who didn't, and are here for any other reason; will have to take my word for it. Either way, I cannot do her justice. She didn't deserve to die…....certainly not like that."

He returned to his seat and felt the abrupt, unsympathetic hardness of it. Anyone expecting a more fulsome and ringing eulogy, clearly had not the vaguest idea of the turmoil buffeting around Adam's mind. It was a wonder he had been able to say anything at all, but in any case; it was not his primary concern.

On cue and as requested, Colorblind by Counting Crows rang out tinnily across the church's PA system, which was also unable to do justice to either the beauty of the song, its significance to the former couple, nor the aptness of the lyrics at that moment.

- "I am covered in skin, no one gets to come in. Pull me out from inside. I am folded, and unfolded, and unfolding, I am colorblind."

At the expense of immense effort, Adam managed to accompany the coffin and the rest of the congregation to the graveside. If the term accompany can be used for one who felt so utterly alone on a planet. He kept a steadying hand on the coffin the whole way as it trundled along on the trolley over the rough ground, in one last hopeless attempt to keep her from any more harm.

The Priest uttered some more obligatory sentiments, before Adam felt the seismic shudders run through his entire body, as each shovel of earth thundered down upon the wooden lid of the coffin. As he watched it gradually disappear from view, feeling like Lorelei was being obliterated from history in an attempt to hide all the failings; he felt a gentle squeeze upon each arm. He would not turn away, could not turn away, but knew regardless who they were.

The congregation gradually filtered away, to leave three figures in a shaking, sobbing embrace, observed from a polite distance by two gravediggers waiting to fully complete the task. He had not known how long it had lasted, when he said:

- "I have to go now."

- "Where are you going?"

- "I've no idea."

Kelly and Debs watched on through blurred eyes as he walked away, and gradually disappeared into the distance.

Chapter Two

At 05:16 the following morning, a dishevelled, vacant Adam, walked into the all-night diner at the fruit and vegetable market in Brighton. It had been over seventeen hours since he had left the graveside in London. Despite the absence of any notion as to where he was going, he had arrived on familiar ground via the use of that hidden auto-pilot that can guide even the most paralytic of drunks home.

There was a time during his Psychology Degree at the University of Sussex, when ending up in the all-night diner at an unearthly hour, signified a very good night out. This time though, he saw no familiar faces through drunken eyes, nor felt any compelling urges for chips; instead he was at once in utter anguish and utterly numb, exhausted yet wired.

Shortly after 07:00, he found himself at another familiar spot. Whilst most of his Uni friends had long since departed Brighton, a handful had remained; drawn to stay by the memories and the vibrancy of the place. He rang the doorbell, and sat down on the step. When a bleary-eyed Sarika opened the door, she was not in the least surprised to find Adam sitting there, if rather alarmed at the state of him. This was hardly the first time he had arrived unannounced at a random hour, seeking solace of one kind or another; but that was all pre Lorelei.

No words were exchanged. After a very long embrace in the hallway, she gently guided him to the sofa, made and brought him a chamomile tea, and went off to run him a bath, with every soothing thing she could find in it. Once soaking his weary, blistered body; he stared at the ceiling in much the same way he had stared at everything since he received the news - with eyes holding back a torrent of mixed emotions, like a fragile dam holding back a whitewater river.

After some time, he saw that Sarika had come in, and was standing next to the bath holding up a towelling dressing gown. He hauled himself out, and into the gown, and was once again left alone. A few minutes later she returned, this time with some jogging bottoms and a t-shirt, before returning for a final time, when he felt her gently guide him to her bedroom. Still without a word exchanged, they got into her bed. She lay on her back, while he curled up next to her and rested his head on her soft chest, feeling her arm around him pulling him in closer. A far cry from the movie scene passions of their past; this was more akin to a mother comforting her distressed child, as Adam began to weep.

Chapter Three - Six years before her funeral

In the morning, shortly after he had left for work, Kelly received a message, which simply read "I really am ready now."

She was not taking any chances this time. She hurried round to Lorelei's and his flat, and as soon as she was inside, she simply said "Mobile off, let's go!" She could clearly see that Lorelei had applied even more makeup than usual, but there would be time to learn of those gruesome details later. Lorelei appeared hesitant but Kelly, having anticipated that, ushered her out of the door on the basis that a taxi was waiting.

Nothing was said during the journey to Euston station; nothing really needed saying. Upon arrival they headed to the ticket office, with Kelly keeping Lorelei close at hand, and always in sight. Kelly bought and paid for two tickets to Bromsgrove, via Birmingham New Street, one way. It was by no means as far away as she would have liked to get her; but crucially he had no knowledge of her cousin in Bromsgrove, and nor up until this point did Lorelei.

The 35 minutes until the next train seemed like an eternity, but as like Lorelei, it was to start a new journey from there; they were able to board it 15 minutes before it was due to leave. "Just bloody pull away will you!" Kelly implored internally, as they both anxiously looked out down the platform, on guard for any unwelcome passengers. Finally the train strained itself and slowly pulled away. As it did so, she saw the tears stream down Lorelei's face, smudgingly revealing some of its hidden secrets; but this was no time for questions, just a big Kelly hug.

By the time the train pulled out from Watford Junction, Kelly began to feel the first pangs of achievement of something she had wanted desperately to accomplish for a long time. As they headed further away from London, she found it hard to gauge which of the many emotions she knew to be thundering through Lorelei was the strongest.

There was certainly no shortage of questions in Lorelei's head. How would *he* react when *he* got home? Did *he* already suspect anything from calling their landline and getting no reply, and then finding her mobile switched off? Was *he* already in pursuit? Could *he* somehow have any idea as to where they were going? Would *he* already? Surely not? Even she didn't really know yet. Is she really finally free of *him*? What would *he* do to her if *he* did find her? What would she tell her family? For how much longer could she live like this? Did she even want to? How will *he* react? Does *he* already know?

Kelly had messaged ahead to her cousin to meet them in the car park at Bromsgrove station, and having received the okay, she too kept her phone off. That part should be straight forward enough, but first there was to negotiate a very tearful and nervous Lorelei through the chaos that is Birmingham New Street station. She kept an arm firmly around her in the guise of support, as she guided her through the throng of people towards the local platforms for a train to Bromsgrove. As she fumbled for their tickets at the barrier, giving one to Lorelei, she was forced to let go so that they could pass through in single file. Just as Kelly made the seemingly innocuous move of going through first, she saw that Lorelei had waited for the barrier to close before sprinting off and away. By the time Kelly had found someone and frantically persuaded them to let her back through; Lorelei was completely out of sight.

Chapter Four

Kelly's search for Lorelei had an increasing sense of desperation. Her first instinct was to head for the platform for the next train back to Euston, which was due in 15 minutes. Whilst Lorelei did not have a ticket it was perfectly plausible that she could talk her way through the barrier, if not sneak through it. There was no sign of her there though, so next she tried the toilets, still nothing. Then she looked in all the shops she came across one by one, then the cafes; still not a trace.

Whilst Kelly continued her impromptu tour of the station, Lorelei had already left it. She had anticipated all of Kelly's moves in search of her, and was heading along Edgbaston Street, having asked for directions to the coach station, with only one thing on her terrified mind - get home before *he* did.

Upon successful arrival she headed for the ticket office, and could see on the screen that a coach to London was due to depart in 11 minutes. She cursed sod's law that there was a large queue at every window. She tried to plead with various people in those queues to let her go ahead to the front, but was met with a frosty reception. One man though, who was in second place in a queue, whether from instinct or attraction or both, took pity on her.

- "Susan there you are! I've been waiting for you, I thought we were going to miss our coach!" as he beckoned her over to him.

Lorelei needed no second bidding, rushed over to him just as came to be served, and ordered her ticket to London.

A further obstacle then appeared in the form of her being £8 short of the fare, which was about to see her burst into tears, when the man simply ordered his ticket to Edinburgh, and paid for it adding in her shortfall. As he handed her the ticket, she tried to say something about paying him back, but he stopped her in her tracks and told her not to worry about it. She could not thank him enough as she rushed off in search of her coach. She just made it in time; it was about to pull away. As she went to show her ticket to the driver, she realised that the man had slipped something inside it. Just as she went to look at it as she took her seat, she saw a frantic and flustered Kelly appear by the bay with a rapidly searching look. As the coach pulled out they met each other's eyes. Kelly's were crying and looking imploringly into Lorelei's. Lorelei's too were crying, she just had time to mouth;

- "I'm sorry; I'm too scared." as the coach took her away.

A little while into the journey, Lorelei looked down at what she had been clinging to since getting on; it was a business card, and along with an email address and a phone number, it read:

Adam Cole
Trainee Psychologist

Chapter Five

Lorelei sat on the coach helplessly pleading it on through its last few torturous miles to Victoria Coach Station. In a bid to try and preempt matters, she had long since turned her phone back on as the coach headed down the motorway back towards London, and received a text message from *him*:

Where the fuck are you?

Hi babe, I'm home, my battery died that's all and I hadn't realised my phone had gone off. See you soon x

Once the coach finally pulled into Victoria after what felt like an ice age, Lorelei was poised at the door. As it opened she hurtled through it and ran as fast as she could, along the seemingly three times longer than ever before route to Victoria Station, pulling, dragging her small case behind her. She almost jumped down the stairs towards the tube concourse, trying to get ahead of anyone she could pass en route to the ticket barrier, then down the escalator on the left hand side, pushing past the stragglers who should have been on the right, and towards the Victoria Line northbound platform. She could have screamed as she saw the doors closing and her train pull away. *He* would be home at any moment, could already be home waiting for her. Next train 2 minutes. She tried to hold herself together, using the time to position herself at a good point ready for her exit at Euston in four stop's time. The tube finally came, she got on and stayed near the door. At each stop she internally begged everyone to hurry and get the fuck off, and then to get the fuck on, and then close the fucking doors and pull away. An impromptu extra stop, an announcement that they were just waiting for the train in front to clear the platform and they'd be on their way again shortly, heard by an increasingly desperate and hopeless Lorelei. Finally at Euston, she came up to street level as quickly as physically possible, in a huge crowd with a suitcase via three escalators and two long tunnels. More running. *Don't be home yet don't be home yet don't be home yet don't be home yet......* As she turned the corner into their street, there were no lights on in their flat. She ran up the stairs, fumbling for her keys as she did so, into their flat, threw open the suitcase, mashed its contents back into its usual spots in drawers and wardrobes, hurled the case back on top of the wardrobe, ran into the kitchen, grabbed a small screwdriver from a drawer, ran into the lounge, undid the screw from the landline connection box with great difficulty as it had been painted over, loosened the wire to the bell, closed up the box again, and put the screwdriver back in its place. Then she heard the downstairs door open and close. She looked around her, all seemed normal as she heard *him* coming up the stairs. *The flakes of paint! The flakes of paint!* She fell to her knees and swept them under the sofa with her hands, and had just fallen onto it ready to appear feverish, as she heard *his* key in the door.

Chapter Six - 9 years, 9 months, and 24 days until *his* release.

Adam had been carrying his torment around with him like an oversized anchor. It infiltrated his every thought, his every movement, his every action and inaction. He felt overwhelmingly full, yet simultaneously, utterly empty. He had so many tortured thoughts and emotions that ultimately led nowhere, but always returned. It was exhausting.

He had attempted a return to his clinic, to his patients, to his life; but neither his head nor heart were in it. In addition, he felt it hypocritical to be someone giving out psychological advice on coping strategies and mechanisms, while failing so completely to successfully implement any for himself.

He could not even make eating or sleeping anything more than a sporadic, random event. His only exercise took the form of incredibly long walks, wherein he lost all sense of time and direction, whilst convincing himself beforehand and afterwards that he was at least doing something. On those occasions when he happened to turn back at some point, he eventually found himself back at home; but when he did not, he could find himself almost anywhere, and had to find somewhere to stay once he could walk no further, if indeed it was not already the next day. That aspect did not bother him. Fewer and fewer things seem to matter, when one's focus starts to narrow.

Chapter Seven - 7 years, 11 months, and 3 days until *his* release

Adam had managed to return to work, but his level of interest in most things was still at a minimum, if it registered at all. He had however started to feel drawn to certain news topics, when they involved any form of violence, and especially to the length of any prison sentences handed down.

This was no great surprise under the circumstances, especially to himself; but this went a little deeper. He found himself measuring the term to be served versus his own idea as to the scale of psychological damage caused. The physical damage was there for all to see, but the psychological consequences for the victim, assuming they lived to tell the tale, and those who cared about them, was not. Did the prison sentence outlast the damage, or vice versa? Who will have suffered the most by the time the sentence is over? If it's a tie, is the debt paid? What if there is a deficit on one side? Who decides? What if the suffering never stops?

In one particular news story, across various forms of the media, a man from London by the name of Terry Stevens, was set to be released on parole from prison ahead of time, having served 12 years of an 18 year sentence. Whilst he would be under certain restrictions and reporting requirements to the Probation Service; he was essentially regaining his freedom. Terry Stevens had brutally murdered his wife.

The sister of the murdered woman had been interviewed by a news crew, to allow her to express her distress, feelings of injustice, and horror at the notion that this man should again be unleashed upon society; whilst her sister Daniella had not taken a breath in 12 years, and would never do so again. A protest organised by family and friends was to be held outside the prison the next day, to coincide with his release.

At 10:00 the following morning a sizable gathering was in full swing. A gathering swelled further by the attendance of Adam. He soon recognised the victim's sister from the television interview, and noted that she was looking at him inquisitively, just as he accepted a homemade placard that was offered to him saying 'Justice for Daniella', and did his best not to look too conspicuous as various chants began to ring out.

The protest appeared peaceful and dignified, yet passionate. Although at the moment when there came the shuddering clunk of the huge gates being unlocked, followed swiftly by the appearance of Terry Stevens flanked by two prison officers; he watched the designated police line having to stand very firm to contain those bent on getting closer. They were not required to stand firm for very long as Terry Stevens was swiftly whisked away in a waiting police van, leaving the crowd with all its heightened emotions, and nowhere to direct them.

Suddenly a reporter from one of the several TV stations covering the story, thrust a microphone under his chin, and began asking him as to his connection to the victim and how he was feeling at that moment?

Startled by the reporter, Adam stumbled over a simple "They call this justice?" as he scurried away as swiftly as he could, leaving the placard to its fate upon the ground.

Chapter Eight - 7 years, 10 months, and 28 days until *his* release

Whilst the media furore surrounding the release of Terry Stevens had died down, replaced by the next sensations in waiting; it was very much still a live event for Adam, and no doubt he imagined, for the family of his victim. He found himself pounded by waves of emotions that simply crashed into the cliffs of his mind, and with nowhere else to go, could only gather and return again relentlessly. He needed to find an outlet.

He called an old friend, Peter, and invited himself round for dinner. He and Peter had been at University together, and although Adam had not exactly been sociable since Lorelei's death; they always could simply just pick up where they left off regardless of timescales. Peter had a son called Daniel, who had the Autistic Spectrum Disorder, Asperger's Syndrome. Like many with this particular diagnosis, Daniel was highly intelligent and very focussed on his particular special interest. In Daniel's case, this special interest was all things IT.

Adam bided his time until he and Daniel were left alone in the dining room, and out of character though it was….

- "Daniel I need you to do me a favour, a secret mission, just between me and you."

- "I like secret missions, I get in trouble sometimes when people find out what I've been doing."

- "No one needs to find out. Do you think you could hack into an intranet system for me?

- "That's easy, which intranet system?"

- "Her Majesty's Probation Service."

By the next morning, Adam had received an untraceable link from Daniel. For the next few days Adam did nothing but ponder, as he wrestled with his professional conscience, his moral compass, his fears, his repeating thoughts, until finally; he clicked on the link.

There it all was at his fingertips - criminal records, court reports, psychology reports, prison reports, parole plans; everything. It did not take Adam long to find the file he was looking for, and he began to read through the information of interest. His history of domestic abuse, his relatively low number of charges faced and convictions, his moment of taking things that one step further, his attempts at evading capture, his conviction, his good conduct record in prison, his conditional early release; his address.

Three days later Adam found himself on a customary long walk around London; four days later just near Farringdon Station; five days later along Columbia Road; and six days later walking slowly past the 'halfway house' that was home to Terry Stevens. He repeated the latter every day for the next week, and each time that he did so, he could feel himself becoming more fraught, increasingly pent up with the frustration of one who was desperate to make a change, to do something; yet paralysed to do anything at all; and then he saw him.

As Adam turned the corner onto his street, there he was, clear as day, walking straight towards him, a matter of metres away. He had imagined this possibility on an abstract level, but had no plan of action formulated, nor any idea of exactly how he would feel. What he actually felt was nauseous, as he felt the nervous, strong sensations grip his stomach like a vice. By the time he had even computed this, it was over. Terry Stevens had walked right past him, turned that same corner, and disappeared from view. The only coherent thing Adam did at that moment was check his watch.

Chapter Nine

At the exact same time the following day, Adam was already near Terry Stevens' house, but this time at a rather less conspicuous distance. As anticipated, Terry Stevens soon appeared from his house and headed off out. Adam had planned to follow him, but as the moment arrived, he found himself frozen to the spot, and instead merely watched him disappear around the same corner. Frustrated with himself, he headed off in the opposite direction for a long evening of self-reflection.

He repeated the same exercise the following day, and at the crucial moment felt the exact same paralysis. This time however, he had prepared himself for the eventuality, and forced himself into movement. He had not gone far when from his distance of around 60 metres, he saw Terry Stevens enter a pub - The Forlorn Hope. Around two hours later, he followed at a similar distance and watched as Terry Stevens walked home again. This pattern repeated itself for the next four days.

On the following day, by the time Terry Stevens entered the pub, Adam was already inside, nursing a pint of lager whilst reading a book in a quiet corner. After around an hour Terry Stevens left his seat at the bar, went to the toilet, and returned 87 seconds later. Half an hour later, he did the same thing, this time returning 91 seconds later. Half an hour after that he left the pub. Adam remained where he was.

The next day events panned out very similarly, only this time Adam left during the second toilet break and went home. The following day he only waited for the first toilet break, before getting up to leave. As he passed by the bar, he slowed his pace just near Terry Stevens' stool. The barman was closeby as the seconds ticked away, Adam feigned to look at the adjacent fruit machine, feeling his stomach tighten all the while. Finally the barman headed to the other end of the bar. With barely a discernible motion, Adam dropped something into the unguarded drink of Terry Stevens, and headed straight for the door. It closed behind him just as the toilet door opened. He returned to his stool to find his ¾ of a pint awaiting him, as he began to drink, it turned blood red. He slammed it down on the bar with a start and called the barman over. In the time it took him to finish serving a customer and come over, the beer had returned to its usual colour.

Chapter Ten

Adam stayed well clear of the area for the next week, itching though he was to do something, anything. He still kept a close eye on the Probation Service's outbox though, and in doing so, saw an email go out to Terry Stevens to remind him to report to Holborn Police Station the next day at 10:30, as part of his parole conditions.

Just as Terry Stevens set off for his appointment, Adam appeared from around the opposite corner, and walked slowly along the road, biding his time. The front door of interest had an automatic closer fitted to it, which he had timed at taking 6.3 seconds to function fully. As the halfway house consisted of 12 bedsits, there was a fair degree of activity at the front door. One person came out just as Adam was nearby enough, but took their time checking their coat pockets as the door closed behind them. Shortly afterwards another person appeared, only to go straight back inside again, appearing to have forgotten something. Adam awaited their return as he slowly walked past the door. This time they did set off, and helpfully in the direction from which Adam had just come from. He just had time to stop the door closing fully with his foot, and slipped inside.

Adam knew he did not have long, and his heart was pounding in his chest as he quickly searched for the door marked number 4, which as it turned out was up a flight of stairs on the first floor. He was just about to approach the door, when he heard the door to number 5 begin to unlock. Adam darted upstairs to the next floor, just as its inhabitant emerged, and down again once he heard him descend and leave. He had to get out of there, he had already taken longer than planned just to get to this point. As he approached number 4 again, he pulled something from his coat pocket, remained there for 30 seconds, before heading down and out into the street, deliberately in the opposite direction from which Terry Stevens would be coming. He jumped on an approaching bus, went upstairs and sat down just in time to watch as he came around the corner and approached his front door.

One minute later, Terry Stevens let himself into his bedsit, threw the key down on the table, and went to put the kettle on. As he returned with a cup of tea, he saw that the key was dripping tiny drops of blood.

Chapter Eleven - 7 years, 10 months, and 8 days until *his* release

Adam was on one of his customary walks. He neither knew where he was heading right then, or in general. He had been castigating himself over his last move where Terry Stevens was concerned. He had acted in too risky a manner, been too unsubtle, crass even. Surely he could do better?

A phone call the previous evening to Daniel, had resulted in his gaining access to all Terry Stevens' emails, not just those sent to him by the Probation Service; which opened up any number of possibilities, not least that he could start to monitor his interests. One in particular caught his eye; Terry Stevens, it transpired, liked horror films.

For the next week, a nightly film was ordered and downloaded. Adam kept himself busy studying each main character and their traits. He also spent a little time in Terry Stevens' neighbourhood. He observed that the films tended to be watched at around 10pm, and that lights out was usually around 1am.

Once Adam was satisfied he had established a reliable pattern, he prepared himself for the week ahead. On the next Monday night, he set off at midnight in the direction of Holborn with a rucksack upon his back. Once in the right street he ensconced himself at his carefully chosen vantage point, hidden from view, but in sight of Terry Stevens' window which overlooked the back of the house. He unpacked his rucksack, set up his things, and waited in the darkness.

As expected just after 1am, Terry Stevens turned in for the night, and turned out the light. Just as he did so there came a bright flash at his window and then an image of Hellraiser suddenly appeared. One second later it was gone. Adam watched as the light came back on in the room, and thirty seconds later Terry Stevens appeared at the window. Even though he was out of sight, Adam tensed in the darkness. After another minute the light went off again, Adam waited a few moments, silently packed up his rucksack, and slipped away into the night.

Adam repeated this exercise at random intervals for the next three months, varying only the character in the image, and the time of night. He stopped just in time for Terry Stevens' next appointment with his Parole Officer.

A few days later, Adam saw an email confirming his urgent appointment for a review with the Probation Service's Psychiatrist, and a week later, he was able to see the subsequent report:

Mr Stevens appears to be suffering from hallucinations relating to, and perhaps triggered by, the films he has been watching. He is adamant that these are not nightmares, on the grounds that on each occasion, he was fully awake, and indeed had not yet been to sleep. As these hallucinations are beginning to disturb Mr Stevens, I have prescribed him a course of Olanzapine, and recommended that he stop watching horror films. I will see him again in six week's time to monitor his progress.

Chapter Twelve

As successful as Adam's actions had been, and aside from the risk of discovery; they were very labour intensive. His sleep patterns were being disturbed almost as much as those of Terry Stevens. However he was not for letting up.

He could see from his email activity that Terry Stevens had indeed stopped ordering horror films, but that he continued to watch a film every evening before going to bed. Adam arranged to meet up with Michael, another old, trusted University friend he had not seen in a while. Michael was a wonderful illustrator. After some light catching up:

- "How have you really been since, you know?

- "I'm getting there, slowly but surely. I need you to do something for me."

- "Of course I will, if I can."

- "You can. I'm going to send you a message each night, which I'd like you to copy on a plain piece of paper, put it in a plain, unsealed envelope addressed to Terry Stevens, Flat 4, 68 HOLBORN ROAD, and then post it to me at my house. It must all be in this exact handwriting though." he said, handing Michael a piece of paper.

- "Er okay…..can I ask why?

- "It's for a highly confidential project I'm working on. Something experimental."

Michael looked at Adam searchingly for a few seconds before answering:

- "Okay, I'll do it, as it's you. How long is this to go on for?"

- "About six weeks."

Chapter Thirteen - 7 years, 6 months, and 21 days until *his* release

That morning, Adam received the first of many letters from Michael. Upon inspection, it came as no surprise that the handwriting was a dead match. Terry Stevens himself could not have done it any better. He sealed the envelope and set off for a walk, making sure to head in the direction of Holborn. He could have simply asked Michael to post the letter directly, thus saving a day in the process; but he did not wish to directly incriminate Michael in any way. Besides, this way, he always had the option of adding in a little flourish. Once close enough to Terry Stevens' home, but not too close, he slipped the letter innocuously into a pillarbox as he passed by, and then set off to go about the rest of his day.

The following morning when Terry Stevens returned from a trip out to buy a newspaper, he was rather perplexed to find the letter on the doormat. He took it upstairs to his bedsit, opened it, and sat down to read it.

Dear Terry,

I was interested to hear about your case. As you know, I too was convicted of brutally murdering my wife. The difference is of course, I was completely innocent, whereas you are a violent lowlife scumbag, who isn't fit to breathe clean air, who should never have seen the light of day again, and doesn't deserve a single second of joy after all the pain and suffering you've caused.

Worst wishes

Andy Dufrane
The Shawshank Redemption

Three days later he received another letter:

Dear Terry,

I thought the American slave owners were bad enough with their savage brutality; but hearing about you I've realised that they were a picnic by comparison. You are a disgusting excuse for a human being who should have hanged following your castration.

Yours in hate

Django
Django Unchained

Chapter Fourteen

Adam continued to send messages to Michael, and receive his perfectly written replies. Terry Stevens continued to receive the resultant letters. When at any point Adam felt any pangs of conscience, he only needed to reread the Probation file, to remind himself of the brutal regime and murder suffered by Terry Stevens' wife; to reinvigorate himself anew.

Dear Terry,

You thought you were going to get away with it didn't you? I'm way too clever for you though, I was always going to catch you in the end, and I'm glad I did you vile scumbag. I'm only sorry to see you back out in society again, but I'll be watching you,

See you real soon

Willy Beachum
Fracture

Terry Stevens took this letter, along with numerous others, along to his six week follow up appointment with the Probation Service Psychiatrist. Adam awaited the appearance of the subsequent report in his file:

> I am becoming increasingly concerned regarding the mental health of Mr Stevens. The nightly hallucinations involving characters from horror films he has just watched, do appear to have ceased,

commensurate with the ceasing of his watching such. However, these have been replaced by the physical and regular appearance of letters sent to Mr Stevens, purporting to be from characters in other films he has just watched; yet clearly written by Mr Stevens himself as a form of displaced self-castigation.

Of somewhat greater concern, is the fact that Mr Stevens is absolutely adamant that he is not the author of these letters; claiming to have not even left his home on some of the days on which they were posted. This is in spite of the facts that upon examination, there can be no doubt that they are in Mr Steven's own handwriting, and indeed that he is the only person who has knowledge of the films he has just watched. Mr Stevens does not refute these last two points yet remains adamant as to his lack of involvement and any recollection.

I have doubled his initial dosage of Olanzapine, and have requested to see him again in four week's time.

Chapter Fifteen - 7 years, 4 months, and 16 days until *his* release

Dear Terry,

Did you really think we wouldn't notice that you're trying to watch comedies now? Trying to amuse yourself are you? Do you think that's what you deserve? Maybe you could take your wife to the cinema, just like you probably did when you first met her? I'm sure she'd love to enjoy a funny film with you, you know, have a really good giggle, maybe enjoy a nice Japanese whiskey as a nightcap afterwards? Oh no, hang on a minute, I remember now, she can't go because you spent 20 years physically and mentally abusing her, until one day you finally killed her.

Perhaps next time?

Yours in loathing

Charlotte
Lost in Translation

Adam wanted to judge for himself the effect he was having on Terry Stevens, and so decided to risk a couple of visits to The Forlorn Hope that week. He was careful to give off a different demeanour this time, lest there be the slightest risk of any memory associations. He neglected to shave for 3 days beforehand, dressed in a more casual manner, and paid attention to the television rather than read.

On the first of two planned visits, he sat a fair way away from the bar, but in good sight of it, making sure he arrived first. When Terry Stevens arrived at his regular time and sat at the bar, Adam kept up his feigned interest in the television, but took any and every opportunity for subtle observation. There could be no doubt about it, Terry Stevens appeared agitated. His eyes never stayed in the same place for long, like he was constantly scanning the room, and each time the door opened for a departure or an arrival, they darted nervously to see who it was.

On the second visit, Adam decided to be a little bolder. This time he waited until he knew Terry Stevens would already be inside. As he walked in, he noted Terry Stevens' stare as it hurriedly landed upon him, but ignored it and headed to the bar, a couple of stools away from him. Adam made a point of exchanging a few light pleasantries with the barman, before ordering a pint of Guinness, in the knowledge that the pump was a few metres away, and that Guinness takes longer to pour. As the barman turned away to fulfil his order, Adam casually turned to Terry Stevens and said:

- "Alright mate, good day?"

Terry Stevens turned to him, appearing surprised by the question, and to wonder if he knew the person who had asked it. Seeming satisfied that he did not, he replied:

- "Not really, I've had better."

- "Sorry to hear that mate, shit day at work? Bloody traffic? Missus giving you grief?"

Terry Stevens' eyes seemed to flash as he reached for his drink to take a distracting sip. Adam noticed the slight shaking of his hand as he brought the glass to his lips.

- "Yeah, something like that." he replied quietly.

- "Oh well, here's to a better day tomorrow."

Adam raised the glass the barman had just put in front of him, before heading away from the bar to sit down at a table near the television, to continue his furtive observations. One such observation being that Terry Stevens stayed beyond his usual time in order to drink more.

Chapter Sixteen

Adam deliberately reduced the frequency of the letters, in the time remaining until Terry Stevens' next appointment with the Psychiatrist. He wanted him to keep hoping that it was over, to keep thinking that it was over, with the relief that would bring him; only for another letter to then arrive. It was becoming clear from some nighttime observations of the lighting in his room, that Terry Stevens was not sleeping too well. Adam keenly awaited the next report:

I saw Mr Stevens today, four weeks after his last appointment as requested, and my concerns continue to mount. Far from improving following the increased dose of Olanzapine; he is undoubtedly deteriorating further. Whilst appearing to be orientated in time and place, he continues to write and receive the aforementioned letters, albeit with a little less frequency, and remains adamant that he is not the source of them.

Moreover, he presents as agitated and is visibly shaking. He appears withdrawn relative to previous visits, and has clearly lost weight; 8kg to be exact. He reports an increase in his intake of alcohol, and a decrease in his food intake, and in both quantity and quality of sleep.

I have decided to increase his dosage of Olanzapine from 10 to 15mg and add in 20mg Fluoxetine as an antidepressant. I have repeated my advice to Mr

Stevens to avoid alcohol, and have made him another appointment in four week's time.

Chapter Seventeen - 7 years, 5 months, and 27 days until *his* release

As Adam wandered past the WellBeing Clinic in Harley Street, he saw the nice shiny plaque bearing the name: Dr Anthony Faring.

The following day, he happened to be walking along Harley Street just as Dr Faring was leaving the clinic. He easily recognised him from his profile picture on the website as he came out onto the busy street, already in focus from its artificial lightning, that managed to make it appear less dreary in the grey evening. As Dr Faring headed off to his unknown destination, Adam followed from a safe enough distance given how many people were milling about.

After ten minutes Dr Faring entered Great Portland Street tube station. Adam had to shorten the distance between them quickly, so as not to lose sight of which platform he headed for through the maze of tunnels and escalators. He just about managed it through the crowd that seemed to be heading in every direction at once. Dr Faring headed for the Metropolitan Line casually enough, but then suddenly quickened his pace as he turned onto platform one, so that he could just jump on a train as its doors were closing. Frustratingly this sudden manoeuvre caught Adam out, and he was left standing on the platform like a fool as the train pulled away.

The next day around the same time, Adam repeated the exercise, but with a little more foresight, was not to be thwarted twice. He boarded the same tube carriage as Dr Faring, but made sure to be as far away as possible. After just two stops he could see that a departure was being prepared for the third, Wembley Park, so Adam readied himself too. He followed amongst the crowd as Dr Faring headed towards the Jubilee Line, and boarded a train to Stanmore. As he left Stanmore station, Adam had to extend the distance between them as the crowd thinned, but not so far that he could not see as Dr Faring walked down the driveway of 23 Royal Gardens, to be greeted by two excited red haired children, and a smiling dark red haired wife, akin to a scene from a 1950's latest mod-con advert; before he continued on his way.

Three days later, just as Dr Faring arrived home around the same time; the look on his dark red haired wife's face was rather different.

Chapter Eighteen

Dear Mrs Faring,

I couldn't help noticing what a lovely nuclear family you make, with your successful husband and your two delightful children. Your life together really must be as wonderful as it seems. Tell me though; is it? Does he beat you like he ought to? Does he punch you in that beautiful face of yours, or kick you in the crotch whenever you talk back to him? Or do you always keep quiet, have his dinner ready for when he walks in, and fuck him whenever he wants, so that he doesn't have to?

I look forward to getting to know you all a lot better, and finding all this out for myself.

Best wishes

Terry

- "How is the letter writing currently?"

- "I'm still receiving letters that I haven't written, if that's what you mean."

- "Tell me about the last letter you sent Mr Stevens."

- "I haven't sent any letters."

- "Oh come now Mr Stevens, you must remember?"

- "I've not sent any letters!"

- "Maybe less so to yourself, but what about to other people?"

- "Like who?"

- "Oh I don't know, perhaps to many people, but to my wife for example?"

- "Your wife? I didn't even know you had one!"

- "An interesting answer. What do you make of this then….?"

- "I've never seen it before."

- "It is in your handwriting though is it not Mr Stevens?"

- "Yes, but I didn't write it though!"

- "I see. Are you completely sure about that?"

- "Positive! How would I even know where you live?"

- "How indeed Mr Stevens? Would you excuse me for a moment?"

Dr Faring got up and opened the door to his office, to reveal two Metropolitan Police Officers and a Psychiatric Nurse, who promptly entered the room.

- "Some of your actions constitute a breach of your parole conditions Mr Stevens, for which you could be returned to prison immediately. However, I am sufficiently concerned about your mental health that for now at least, I am sending you to a secure psychiatric hospital for a minimum of 28 days for further assessment."

As the officers and the nurse took him away, Dr Faring could still hear his vehement protestations of innocence all the way down Harley Street.

Chapter Nineteen

Terry Stevens found himself ensconced in a secure ward at the South London and Maudsley Hospital. He was surrounded by people disturbed enough to qualify by modern criteria, as needing to be held under a Section. The ward was noisy, hectic, and under-staffed. He was one of 24 patients being cared for/supervised by just one Psychiatric Nurse, and two auxiliary carers. Half-hearted attempts were made at offering daytime activities, but most patients stayed on or near their beds. Therapy such as it was, came in the form of group therapy sessions held in a large meeting room.

He reluctantly attended such sessions, and was given a chance to speak his mind each time. Whenever he tried to explain how he had come to be there, he was laughed at by many of his fellow patients, which increasingly infuriated him. By the 5th such incident, as a young woman called Maria began to laugh, he flew at her, knocking her off of her chair. By the time help and restraint arrived via the therapist's emergency alarm; Maria had been badly beaten. He was placed in a solitary confinement room, from which he was only let out once per day under strict supervision.

By the time his initial 28 days were completed, and with still no sign of any acknowledgement of his letter writing; Dr Faring via liaison with the hospital, extended his stay for another 28 days. This second bout was spent back on the ward, with group therapy and further violent incidents avoided.

Adam maintained a close eye on the situation from afar. He had felt mortified by the suffering inadvertently caused to Maria, and was racked with self-reproach. A few days later he saw that Dr Faring was due to visit Terry Stevens at the halfway point of his extended detention for a review, but at an unspecified time.

On the morning of the appointment, when Dr Faring arrived at Stanmore tube station, Adam was already there. He kept a good distance but just kept Dr Faring in sight for what became 15 stops to Green Park, and made sure not to lose him as he changed onto the Victoria line for one stop to Victoria. At Victoria, a little more discretion was needed as they boarded the less crowded overground train towards Dartford for one stop to Denmark Hill. Once at Denmark Hill, Adam let Dr Faring go about his business alone, and went to get a coffee in a nearby cafe.

One hour and twenty minutes later, as Dr Faring arrived back at Denmark Hill station, Adam was already on the platform awaiting the next train to Victoria, which they boarded together. At Victoria, they headed back down to the tube towards Walthamstow and got off together at Oxford Circus. On the busy escalators up towards the street with time running out, he seized his moment. Feigning to adjust his shoe, with the cover of many legs and bodies around him, he slipped something into the side pocket of Dr Faring's briefcase. At the top of the escalator, he let Dr Faring continue on his way towards Harley Street, as he casually joined the throng heading the other way back down to the tube, vanishing like he was never there.

It was only several days later when Dr Faring went to put something into that side pocket, that he found a letter addressed to himself:

You doctors think you're so fucking clever don't you Dr Faring? Think I'm mentally ill do you? As if I wouldn't know about the letters! Course I fucking knew! I was just taking you for the mug you are, that's all! How's that missus of yours doing? Given her a slap yet or do you want me to do it for you? I know you probably don't have the bottle, so I guess I'll have to do it.

See you soon

Terry

Later that day, a bemused and very angry Terry Stevens had his Section revoked, and was returned to prison to serve out the remaining six years of his sentence, with an extra two added on, once the conviction for the assault on Maria had been processed.

A few days later, Amanda, the sister of Terry Stevens' murdered wife Daniella, received a postcard from Brighton. It was anonymous, and it simply read "You're welcome." For a split second something flashed across her mind from that prison protest, but then it was gone.

Chapter Twenty - Five years before her funeral

Kelly had long since returned alone from Birmingham, saddened, worried, and feeling like a total failure; but never angry with Lorelei. They continued to spend time together whenever it felt safe to do so, or whenever *he* allowed it.

Lorelei had been prescribed Diazepam for her bouts of anxiety by her GP. She had picked her moments carefully before each appointment to ensure no bruises were visible, and had convinced the Doctor that her anxiety stemmed from recurring and terrifying nightmares that had been plaguing her for a while, rendering her unable to sleep.

Rather than taking her Diazepam only in moments of heightened anxiety, she had come to depend upon them daily. Her intake was far outstripping the supply via her prescriptions, and with her GP not for increasing them; she had taken to sourcing them through less official channels. She had also been prescribed antidepressants and sleeping tablets, on which she had equally become dependent, and on evenings when *he* was there, would take the latter as early in the evening as she thought she could get away with, both to shorten her day, and in the hope that *he* would then leave her alone. On the evenings when *he* was not there, she weighed up the gamble each time - would *he* be more or less likely to attack her for already being asleep when *he* got in; relative to her being awake and saying or doing something to displease *him*? Sometimes she calculated correctly.

She lost weight from barely eating, until *he* complained that she was 'too skinny to be attractive to *him* and didn't even want her near *him*.' She gained weight from overeating in a bid to please *him*, until such time as *he* complained that she was 'a disgusting fat bitch who *he* didn't even want to touch.'

She was hanging on by the thinnest of threads. Soon she reached the point where she could barely bring herself to get out of bed in the mornings. As soon as *he* had left for work, complete with the packed lunch she had just made *him*; she took herself back to bed and remained there until there was just enough time to make herself presentable enough for *him*, to avoid *his* vociferous complaints, or worse.

She had not told *him*, but she had long since returned to taking the pill, despite how ill they made her feel. If she could control nothing else, she was at least going to control that.

Lorelei's GP was becoming increasingly concerned with how she was presenting, especially in the absence of any apparent causes. She had her suspicions of course, born out of instinct and experience; but no concrete evidence, and Lorelei was always extra careful not to supply any. She tried her on different medications and doses, different combinations of medications and doses; but Lorelei only continued to deteriorate. Eventually she referred her to Community Psychiatric Services, to see if she would respond to any therapy, and perhaps even open up, at least somewhat.

Despite the referral being an urgent one, it was 3 months before an appointment arrived in the post, and even then, it was for 5 months hence. Unfortunately the letter arrived on a Saturday morning, when he was there to see and open the post.

The fact that it was addressed to her and marked 'Private and Confidential', was not going to hinder him.

- "What the fuck is this?" *he* said, as *he* threw the letter at her on the bed.

- "My doctor is worried about me, that's all."

- "Oh yeah, been telling her stuff have you?"

- "I've not said a word about you, nor would I, ever."

- "No that's right, best not to, or something like this might happen."

She saw *him* grab a pillow with both hands, and felt the pressure of it being held tightly over her face, and its remaining presence. She did not move, not even a flinch, not an ounce of resistance came forth.

When she felt pillow's release, all she could feel was disappointment, bitter disappointment. She heard the front door slam as she turned over onto her side and curled herself up, in a bid to become as small and insignificant as possible.

She waited until she was sure *he* was not popping back for anything, then dragged herself up. She headed for the drawer in the kitchen where she kept her medication, and removed her bottle of sleeping tablets. She emptied them out onto the table, and counted them. Eleven; was eleven enough? Figuring there was only one way to find out, she took them as quickly as she could, lest she change her mind, disposed of the bottle in the recycling bin in one last favour to the planet, and went back to bed to see how much time she had left to feel.

When he returned from the pub six hours later, very much the worse for lager, he shouted out towards the bedroom demanding immediate food. Upon receiving no reply to his increasingly loud and threatening demands, he headed to the bedroom in search of retribution.

- "Didn't you hear what I fucking said you stupid lazy bit…!"

There she was, laying flat on her back, motionless, just as he had left her that morning, but something was different; perceptible even to someone in his state. She was not normally one for drooling for a start.

Panic set in; drunken, sobering panic. He paced around the room with his hands on his head. "Fuck fuck fuck fuck" was all he could express. Thoughts, though, were racing around his head.

What the fuck am I gonna go now? What the fuck! Say I just got home and found her like this? Better get rid of that fucking pillow! Call a mate round to help me get rid of her body, and say she's just disappeared, upped and left me, with all her stuff? Who though? Who could I trust enough for that? And how? How the fuck could I get her out of here without anyone seeing? It'll have to be tonight, really late tonight. But could I dump her? Bury her somewhere maybe, where no one ever goes? Think! Think! Think for fuck's sake!

Then he heard the faintest of murmurs. Oh thank fuck thank fuck!

- "Wake up you stupid bitch, wake up, wake the fuck up!"

Nothing.

- "Fucking wake up will you! What's the matter with you!?"

Nothing.

- "Fucking wake up!" *he* yelled, shaking her by the shoulders and slapping her round the face.

Nothing.

He looked at his phone, hovering over the emergency call button. Then he looked at the pillow. He stayed in that state, calculating, for several minutes, until finally, he picked up the pillow.

Chapter Twenty One

Returning from placing the pillow safely in the large dustbin in the next street, *he* called an ambulance. His story was to be as simple as he could make it, based on as much truth as possible. He had left her in bed, gone to the pub, and had been unable to rouse her once home.

Upon its loud arrival, he watched as Lorelei was quickly connected to an oxygen supply, with her levels of such were dangerously low, and stretchered inside. He once again, did a marvellous job of making his own concerns look like ones for her, stroking her hair, holding her hand, kissing her forehead, imploring her to wake up, telling her everything would be okay, until finally they burst through the doors at A&E in movie scene style.

- "Twenty year old woman found unconscious by partner, oxygen and heart rate low, possible overdose of as yet unknown substance, suspected to be Zopiclone as it's prescribed but was not found at the property."

- "Thank you Steve." said Debs to the Paramedic, "We've got her from here." as she rushed Lorelei through to an urgent care room, ushering *him* to the waiting area as she did so.

With help from a colleague, Debs quickly wired Lorelei up to breathing apparatus, and heart rate and blood pressure monitors. Based upon the readings, she calculated that the overdose was thankfully not as severe as it might have been, meaning that powerful antidotes and invasive interventions should not be necessary on this occasion; although she had her colleague have them on standby just in case. In a further take no chances measure, she stayed with Lorelei personally rather than delegate to a less senior and experienced colleague, as she would normally have done, with a patient not deemed to be critical.

It was 5am the following morning when Lorelei began to come to. She opened her eyes flickeringly, trying to take in where she was, if she was. She felt something holding her hand, so she turned her head slowly towards it expecting with dread to find *him* there. To her relief, she instead found Debs dozing in a visitor's chair at her bedside, seven hours after her shift had finished. At the sudden needle-sharp recollection of what she'd done, and the realisation that it still wasn't over; she began to weep silently.

Instinctively, Debs woke up, and crossing over the many leads and cables, along with her professional boundaries; gave Lorelei a close and long hug. After several minutes she said:

- "I know, I know, we'll find a way, it'll all be okay."

Chapter Twenty Two

Debs was beavering away behind the scenes, using every trick in her book to keep Lorelei under her care for as long as possible to buy time. This entailed thwarting some of her colleagues' attempts at having her either discharged to home, or into local psychiatric care as a suicide risk. With funding thin on the ground, any alternative placement was proving hard to find, but she was not about to simply give up and wave Lorelei off. In the meantime, she also found any and every excuse to enter the room during the visiting times when *he* deigned to show up to give a performance as a deeply concerned partner. It was always time to update the notes with the latest monitoring figures, fiddle with the equipment, or flush through a drip with saline.

After many a fruitless phone call and email rejections of favours she had attempted to call in; Debs finally found a residential placement in a drug rehab unit in Sussex, having gone overboard on Lorelei's medication dependence as a major contributing factor to the whole scenario. It was far from ideal and carried its own risks, but it was infinitely preferable to sending her back home to her life with *him*, and it would provide some respite at least.

When Debs broke the news to Lorelei, her relief and gratitude were tangible to the point of being overwhelming. The placement was initially at least, to be for three months, and Debs promised to stay in touch in any way she could.

He was rather less pleased at the news of her forthcoming absence, however this was more than tempered by his relief at the absence of any mention of a pillow.

Debs maintained her tactic until and at the point of Lorelei's discharge into rehab. She arranged for a community ambulance to facilitate the journey down to Sussex, lest *he* should be the one doing the transporting. *His* objections were met with a firm "It's hospital policy." It was no more hospital policy for Debs to accompany the patient in the ambulance and see her safely admitted into the rehab centre, many miles from her job; but she did it anyway.

Whilst Lorelei could technically discharge herself, all the while that she was there without a formal Section; Debs knew her achievement of the placement had two things in its favour. The voluntary basis could be made involuntary if Lorelei looked like leaving ahead of time; and being a rehab unit, visiting was very restricted, and highly supervised when it did occur.

Lorelei's room was basic but comfortable enough, and the rehab unit itself was a former grand stately home, surrounded by the green, leafy rolling hills of the Sussex Downs. At the tearful parting embrace, Lorelei struggled to express her gratitude, but Debs eased her struggle:

- "It's okay sweetheart, your being out of harm's way for three months is more than thanks enough for me. I just hope that it's time enough for you to rest and then gather your strength for a big change."

- "I hope so, I'll try"

- "I know you will. Direct contact will be tricky, but I'll keep in touch with the Staff Nurse here to see how you're getting on, okay? Good luck!"

- "See you soon Debs."

- "I bloody well hope not sweetheart!" replied Debs with a rye smile.

Lorelei watched from the grand front entrance as the ambulance passed through the security gates, and disappeared around a bend in the long driveway, before she was gently led inside.

Chapter Twenty Three

It took a couple of weeks, but gradually Lorelei started to find some of the mist clearing, to reveal the woods rather than just the trees. She had been in a heightened state of alert and emotion for so long, that she had only been able to think accordingly.

However, with increased clarity comes realisation. A view of the bigger picture whose parameters do not end in the unconsciousness at the end of each day, but stretch far beyond to see what lies ahead. As the late great American Football writer Chris Wessling used to say: history is instructive. As she began to realise what lay in store for her unless something drastic were to change; she felt the deeply suppressed emotions from the traumas she had already suffered, rising to the surface.

Nurse Tom found her in her room in a fit of sobbing so uncontrollable that he had to call for help and an urgent sedation by injection. Within a few days, the diagnosis of Post Traumatic Stress Disorder was added to her notes, with the previous loss a baby in a car accident, cited as the antecedent.

Since Lorelei's arrival at the rehab, a date had been looming large on the staff room calendar, and even more so in her mind - her first visitor. A delay of at least two weeks from arrival was the strictly enforced rule, to allow for new patients to settle; but time was all but up.

He had been on the phone to the staff at regular intervals, playing the well-rehearsed role of concerned partner, to inquire as to how she was getting on, and to ask that the message that he couldn't wait to see her, be passed on. Officially, the staff only knew that which was in her notes. Unofficially, they knew plenty more besides.

The night before the impending visit, Lorelei was talking with nurse Tom:

- "How are you feeling about having your first visitor?"

- "Nervous. I'd have much preferred it to be my best friend taking the slot."

- "Why haven't you allocated it to her then?"

- "My partner wouldn't have liked that."

- "I see, okay, but I think you need to be thinking about what's best for you here Lorelei."

- "Maybe it is best for me."

- "What do you mean?"

- "Nothing, don't worry."

- "But I do worry, it's my job to worry."

- "Yeah, I know."

- "Might I suggest something? If you were to cancel the visit, it could be the first step towards your exerting a little control."

- "It's not quite as simple as that, Tom."

- "I know, I really do, but even the longest journeys start with a single step and all that."

Lorelei sat and stared out of the window without speaking. Tom let her think a while before saying:

- "How about I call him and say that you're not up to receiving visitors, and that we'll let him know when you are?

Lorelei pondered upon her response, so tempted by the thought of relieving the anxiety, for now at least, before finally saying:

"Okay. Thank you Tom."

Tom was not about to hang around lest there be a change of mind, and so headed straight to the office to call him. He sensed it was all he could do to contain his rage at the news, and that he just about managed to stay in character for the duration of the call.

Once it was finished he screamed "Fucking bitch I should've finished you off!" as he threw a pint glass against the wall, before cursing her again for not being there to clear it up.

Chapter Twenty Four

With the relief of not seeing *him* came the anxiety of how *he*'d be taking the news, and the feeling that all she had really done, and all she could ever do; was delay the outcome.

She tried to think back to the very beginning, which felt like the last time she'd made any kind of active choice in her life, and wished that she could warn that 15 year old version of herself, and send her off down a very different path. She knew such thoughts were futile, but she thought them anyway, over and over again, until it was all she thought.

The staff gently tried to coax her into the daily group talking therapy sessions, and sometimes they succeeded, but Lorelei was always reluctant to speak, and when she did, she felt horribly judged despite the emphasis on the non-judgemental ethos. Whether in fact anyone actually was judging her, she could never get away from her own judgement of herself, which was harsher than even the harshest of critics could have arrived at.

The clock was ticking on Lorelei's three month placement. Debs was again beavering away behind the scenes trying to have it extended, but funding for such and availability were equally thin on the ground, whilst there was no shortage of demand. She went to visit Lorelei, who appeared particularly distant.

- "How are you feeling hun?"

- "Oh you know, I've been better, and a lot worse."

- "I'm still hopeful of getting you an extension, or getting you into a refuge."

- "Thank you Debs, but I think I've made a decision and there is no point in putting it off."

- "Oh…..okay, what decision would that be then?

- "I'm going to leave *him*."

- "Okay, erm good, just like that though? How do you plan to do it?"

- "Well first of all, I'm just gonna tell him to his face."

- "It's admirable certainly, but are you sure that's wise hun?"

- "I'll do it here in front of the staff on a supervised visit, so *he* won't be able to kick off."

- "That's great hun, it really is, but what about afterwards? *He* doesn't strike me as someone who's just gonna accept it."

- "*He*'ll have to."

- "How so?"

- "Because I won't be around."

- "What sort of not around?"

62

- "Just not around."

Debs headed off to report her concerns to the staff, so that Lorelei would immediately be placed on a more intensive 'watch', and end the debate as to whether she needed to be, and was going to be, held there under Section.

On the fourth morning under her new 'formal' status, Lorelei dragged herself along the corridor for yet more group therapy, and took her place in the circle. The therapist running the group was a woman called Jane, who dressed in an informal manner, almost to the point of being dishevelled. Jane, like many therapists in rehab units, was herself an ex-addict.

Lorelei was paying minimal attention to her and anyone else in the room, staring instead out of the window at the wavering trees, as Jane began to speak:

- "Hi everyone, thanks for coming. Before we get going, can I just say please ignore the extra people we have in the room today behind me. They're here purely as observers as part of their training, so they'll not be participating in any way. I hope that's okay with everyone? No major objections? Okay good, let's get going then, who wants to start us off today?"

People began, in turn, to broach the subject of their thoughts and feelings. Lorelei, as was customary, was planning to say as little as possible, and nothing at all if she could get away with it, but with no one else left to speak, Jane was just about to turn her attention to her, when she noticed him; and he was already looking at her.

- "Lorelei, what would you like to share with the group today?"

-

- "Lorelei?" Is there anything you'd like to share today?"

- "Er what? Oh sorry…. erm, er no, not today, sorry."

- "Okay well perhaps tomorrow? Okay moving on then………"

Chapter Twenty Five - 6 years, 9 months, and 20 days until *his* release

Although Adam had felt a degree of satisfaction at having achieved *something*, even if it was a mere drop in the ocean; he could not shake the feelings of restlessness that plagued him on a daily basis.

The only people he saw with any regularity were Kelly and Debs, when he needed to feel close to Lorelei again, and Sarika, when he needed to feel anything resembling human contact again, although any comfort or pleasure gained was quickly dispelled by guilt, if not already prevented or ruined by it.

On one such occasion with Kelly, he decided to tell her all about his exploits with Terry Stevens; because he wanted to tell someone, and because he knew he could trust her with anything. Kelly was rather shocked at learning of his involvement at all, and of the lengths that he had gone to, the boundaries he had crossed; but most of all, she was shocked at the look in his eyes, and the strain in his voice as he talked.

- "Wow you really did a number on that scumbag, didn't you Ad!?"

- "Yeah I guess so, he'll be out again in eight years though, and his poor wife will still be dead, so what good was it all?"

- "Well it will have brought some comfort to her family, and bloody hell I bet that bastard Stevens is as furious as he is puzzled by it all! So there is that at least!"

- "Yeah there is that, let's hope it drives him crazy."

- "Are you sure you're really okay though, Ad?"

- "I'm not sure I know what that is anymore. I relied on Lorelei to know when I wasn't, and to do whatever was needed to put it right. Are you really okay Kells?"

- "I just get through each day as best I can, until the next one. The guilt haunts me, the images haunt me, *he* haunts me."

One week later, Adam met up with someone else for a coffee; someone equally racked with guilt from trying and failing to help Lorelei - Debs.

Debs was still working at A&E, and her efforts had been rewarded to the point whereby she was now the most senior nurse there. They chatted for a while in their friendly way, bonded as they were by experience, by remorse; before Adam asked:

- "So how's life amongst the bedpans and bed baths?"

- "You know how it is Adam, nothing fucking changes, ever."

- "Yeah I guess not sadly."

- "I had another case in today. Usual story, fucking obvious that she'd been beaten up yet again at home, husband claiming that she'd been mugged in the street, and her too scared to contradict him."

A look came over Adam's face, Debs looked at him, somewhat alarmed by it.

- "Give me their address Debs."

- "Don't be daft Adam, you know I can't do that!"

- "Please Debs."

- "Don't be ridiculous, and in any case, what could you do about it?"

- "Something. I could do something."

- "You know I'd love to help the woman, but I can't. I've alerted the police again, but we know how that'll go. That's all I can do.

- "It's okay, I know."

- "Are you sure you're really okay Adam? I know it's a ridiculous thing to say; but you have to move on with your life.

- "I am moving on."

Adam arrived home via a very long walk, and sat staring out of the window at nothing he was aware of, lost in sadness, desperation, and frustration. After what could have been twenty minutes, but was in fact over two hours, he reached for his phone to contact Daniel, but noticed the Whatsapp message symbol. He opened it to find a message from Debs that contained nothing but a file. Upon clicking on the file, it said 'password protected, enter password'.

He stared at his phone screen for sometime, before suddenly typing the word Lorelei. The file opened. There it all was. Accidents, incidents, injuries, x-ray reports, admission reports, discharge reports, contact with the police resulting in no charges ever being brought, phone numbers, emails, names, addresses. Her name was Emily.

Adam spent the next few hours reading through it, digesting it, absorbing it; crying. Ideas and thoughts came flooding in and out of his mind, some alot milder than others. Could he do anything? Should he do anything? Terry Stevens on his own was one thing, but a living, breathing Emily, with a rampaging husband was quite another thing entirely. Could he act alone? Should he act alone? Was it fair to involve anyone else? What about Emily herself? Should he try to befriend her? Would she want his involvement, or would she be terrified by it? Would it make her panic and do something rash? But surely it was for her own good? Shouldn't she decide that? Was she even capable of making an objective decision? Would her liaising with him place her in even greater danger? What would he do to her if he found out? What would he do to him? Perhaps just a little wander along their road, for now? It couldn't hurt, surely?

As Adam meandered towards Emily's neighbourhood, he found himself in Kensington. She lived in St.Martin's Drive, which like the many surrounding it, was a street full of expensive cars, and ludicrously expensive houses with immaculate front gardens and driveways. It quickly induced the feeling in him that an air of wealth, education, success, and polite society, counted for nothing behind closed doors; at least not for Emily.

He spent the next few hours on reconnaissance of all the surrounding streets; or avenues and drives to be precise. Pillar boxes, cul-de-sacs, vantage points where discretion was at a premium in a quieter area, routes to tube stations, bars, restaurants, and potential shortcuts; were all absorbed in the form of mental notes. He was just taking one last wander for now, along St.Martin's Drive, when he saw her.

To any inquisitive neighbour or passer by other than Adam, the scene was a touching one. A husband carefully helping his wife out of their car after a trip to hospital, making sure that she did not bang her head on the doorframe as he did so, lest she hurt herself, before letting her lean upon him as he gently guided her into their lovely home, so that no doubt he could dote on her, with nothing being too much trouble, helping her towards a speedy recuperation at the hands of his infinite, loving care.

Chapter Twenty Six

Adam wasted no time in gathering as much information as he could, in as short a time as possible. Daniel had gained him access to his personal inbox, which greatly cut down on the leg work. Emily's oh so loving husband's name was Jonathan.

Jonathan was a popular, seemingly affable chap. Outside of his often long working hours in the City, in the murky world of corporate finance; sport was his thing, especially golf, cricket, and rugby, playing the first two, and watching the third one.

On Sunday afternoons in summer, he could be found amongst the echoing sound of leather on willow, opening the batting for the Kensington XI, to the acclaim of his teammates and the small crowd, before pausing around 4pm to step into old England, and enjoy a nice cup of tea and a slice of cake, prepared and served with a radiant smile by Emily, and her fellow dutiful wives and partners. With a fair degree of regularity though, Emily was not quite feeling well enough to come and attend to her duties.

On Saturday mornings, come rain or shine, he was to be found at his local golf club for a round with the boys, followed by a long lunch at the 19th hole. He was often there during the week too, fulfilling his various duties on the committee as part of his role as Membership Secretary.

- "Mr Cole, welcome, do please take a seat."

- "Thank you Mr Mills, please do call me Adam though."

- "Adam it is, and in that case, please do call me Jonathan. Now I see from your application that you're somewhat of a golfing virgin? Can I ask why now, and why our little old club?"

- "You can indeed Jonathan, it's just been a question of time really. I've always wanted to play, but what with work and relationships, I've never managed to find the time. There always seems to be something more pressing to do, you know how it is I'm sure?"

- "Oh I do indeed, and why us, you don't exactly live next door?"

- "Well I'm actually in the area quite a lot lately, for one reason or another, and I've rather taken a fancy to your club. Such beautiful, peaceful surroundings, and I've heard nothing but good things about you all."

- "Indeed, and I see you're a Psychologist by profession? I imagine that's a fascinating world to be in?

- "It definitely has its moments. I've certainly come across some characters in the course of it."

- "Ha I don't doubt that for a second! Well we'll let you know in due course Adam, just a formality really, I can't see any grounds for rejection by the committee, bunch of old duffers that they are; it's always good to have new blood around "

- "Thank you very much. Perhaps once I've had a few lessons from your Club Professional, so as not to embarass myself too much, we could have a round sometime?"

- "I can't see any harm in that, in fact I'll look forward to it Adam."

- "Great. Me too!"

His word being his bond, Jonathan quickly facilitated Adam's application.

- "They make this look so much easier on the telly don't they!" said Adam to Tim, his golf coach.

- "They certainly do! Don't worry though, we'll get you there, and soon given the intensive course of lessons you've booked! I do like a keen learner!"

Five mornings per week for the next month, the golf club's newest and unlikeliest member, was to be found out on the course, trying to put into practice that which Tim had just been showing him, to at least a passable degree, grateful to learn of golf's handicap system, whereby he was given a 32 shot cushion each time. He spent his evenings that month, swotting up on cricket and rugby.

The following week, Adam took notice of a poster in the clubhouse, inviting members to bring their partners to a cocktail evening at the club. A timely chance to show his sociable side to Jonathan, and maybe meet Emily into the bargain.

- "Kelly, what are you doing next Friday evening?"

- "Nothing as far as I know, why?"

- "Good, because I need you to be my plus one."

- "Okay sure, what's the occasion?"

- "A cocktail evening at my golf club; wear a nice frock and your blonde locks down."

- "What the actual fuck!?"

- "I'll pick you up at seven, we can go over the details in the taxi."

Chapter Twenty Seven

The evening, by design, had an air of sophistication about it. The clubhouse was dressed as immaculately as the waiting staff, and the cocktails flowed as freely as a waterfall in spring sunshine.

Kelly had been fully briefed. They hadn't been together long, about four months, she wasn't really the sporty type, but she was more than happy to join in the social side of things. She was to be bubbly, the life and soul of proceedings, quick with a smile and a laugh.

They had been in their respective roles for about half an hour, when Jonathan arrived, accompanied dutifully by Emily. She hid it well enough, but Adam noted that Jonathan was definitely the more enthused of the two at being there. They began to do the obligatory rounds of a committee member and his wife, exchanging pleasantries and platitudes as they went. It wasn't too long a wait before they arrived at Kelly and Adam.

- "Emily darling, do let me introduce you to our latest recruit, Adam, our resident Psychologist. Perhaps he might turn to Sports' Psychology one day and sort out my putting!?"

- "Delighted to meet you Emily, and let me introduce you both to my partner Kelly." replied Adam, having not failed to notice the slightest of flinches from Emily at the word Psychologist.

A few moments later, the happy couple had moved on to greet others, and the evening began to roll along uneventfully enough. Kelly felt like she'd been dropped onto another planet, but did a fine job in her role, with the aid of a cocktail or two.

A little later, whilst in the men's toilets, Adam could hear the faint sound of voices, becoming rather less faint for the briefest of moments. As he opened the door, he discerned that the sound was coming from the Member's Secretary's office. He just managed to slip out of sight again into another doorway in the dimly lit corridor, as the office door was flung open and Jonathan came bounding out, closing it behind him. He could hear a quiet whimpering coming from inside. A minute later Jonathan returned complete with a ladie's coat draped upon his arm. There was the briefest of illumination before the office light was extinguished, then he watched Emily being firmly ushered out of the office, along the corridor, and out the back way into the car park. Twenty seconds later, he heard the sound of a car starting up. It had all happened very quickly, but not so quickly that Adam had not noticed the blood streaming from her lip.

Once back in the clubhouse lounge, Adam soon got wind of a circulating rumour that Emily had had to go home early due to feeling unwell.

- "Such a shame about Emily!" said Adam a little later in passing to Jonathan."

- "Yes, isn't it? Her head was throbbing, the poor filly, another one of her migraines no doubt."

- "No doubt. I do hope she'll be okay."

- "Oh it'll pass soon enough. Now, how about another drink?"

Chapter Twenty Eight - 6 years, 6 months, and 12 days until *his* release

- "Hey Kelly how's you?"

- "Not too bad ta Ad, to what do I owe the honour of your call?"

- "You remember that charming couple we met at the golf club?"

- "The one with the wife-beating bastard you mean? Yes I remember them well."

- "Good because I've invited them round to dinner next Friday, 7.30; will you join us please?"

- "What!? Why on earth have you done that Ad?" I can't even bear to look at him!"

- "Me neither, but in middle class golfing society, when one goes to a couple's house for dinner, it's the done thing to reciprocate the invitation."

- "Oh bloody brilliant, so we get to spend two evenings having dinner with them!?"

- "At least two yes. It's the gift that keeps on giving."

- "Looking forward to it already! See you there."

Jonathan and Emily's invitation had come about during the round of golf Adam had managed to wangle with Jonathan, during which Adam had not looked a threat to the professional ranks, but had managed not to disgrace himself either. He was quietly confident of a reply in the affirmative, having followed Jonathan's eyeline towards Kelly at frequent points throughout the cocktail evening, and Jonathan did not disappoint.

The evening passed pleasantly enough, with Jonathan on his best behaviour throughout; as was Emily. Adam's instincts had not proved unfounded, and there were several moments whereby Jonathan's attraction towards Kelly was clear. Kelly did a fine job of not showing her disgust, and Emily an equally fine one of pretending not to notice.

The evening drew to its natural conclusion, and Adam briefly left the dining room to retrieve coats. As he re-entered the room Jonathan said:

- "Well this really has been a most splendid evening, thank you both so much!"

- "It certainly has!" replied Kelly. "We really must do it again soon!"

- "Absolutely we must, but we insist, do we not darling," as he turned to Emily, "that it should be at our house next time!?"

- "It would be a pleasure." replied Emily with her best smile.

- "How about next Friday?" said Kelly.

- "That's fine by us isn't it darling!?"

- "Yes of course."

- "I have a work thing, but blow it, I'll move it to another night, it's not that important. Why let work get in the way of friendship aye?" said Adam.

- "Indeed! Excellent that's settled then, next Friday at our place it is!"

Chapter Twenty Nine

Jonathan and Emily Mills' house on St. Martin's Drive, lived up to expectations. A carriage driveway, a pillared entrance porch, and an attached double garage large enough for both of their cars, and plenty more besides.

Once inside, there was no doubting the taste and sophistication in its furnishing and decoration, which both Kelly and Adam were quick to compliment during the extensive guided tour.

- "Why thank you both, but I'm afraid I can take no credit for it whatsoever; it's all due to the work and great imagination of my wonderful wife."

- "Well she does you proud!" replied Adam. You're a very lucky man."

- "I am indeed, now, who's for a G&T?"

Aperitifs were soon accompanied by canapes, which were soon followed by a lavish dinner in an ample formal dining room, with no shortage of expensive wine being eagerly served and topped up by Jonathan. As the evening wore on, Adam noted his increasing animation was more than equally offset by Emily's decrease in such. On more than one occasion, Adam caught a glimpse of a contemptuous look fired in her direction, which seemingly only served to wither her further. Adam also noted that Jonathan increasingly focussed his attention on Kelly, with a subtlety that decreased commensurate with the amount of wine he consumed.

As the evening was coming to its natural conclusion, Adam started to make 'we'd better be off' noises, but Jonathan wouldn't hear of it:

- "No no no don't be daft old boy! Why fork out for a cab at this time of night, when we've plenty of room to put you up!? Emily'll make you up a bed in one of the spare rooms in no time, won't you darling!?"

- "Yes of course."

- "We really wouldn't want to put you to any trouble…."

- "It's no trouble at all, come on, while Emily gets busy upstairs I'll sort us all out a nightcap. Large ones!"

Whilst this had not quite been part of the plan, Adam was pleased at this turn of events, not least because it decreased the likelihood of Emily suffering another bout of physical abuse at the hand of her drunken husband, as an extra after the emotional kind served throughout dinner.

Kelly on the other hand, at facing the prospect of sleeping with her late best friend's partner, in an impromptu and rather awkward scenario; was somewhat less enthused, but stayed in character impeccably.

When finally it was time for bed, she found herself in an even more uncomfortable situation, when upon leaving the bathroom she found Jonathan in her path, clearly in want of a kiss goodnight, and not wishing to move out of her way until receiving such. He moved right into the intimate personal space of her face and neck, she felt his alcohol laden breath upon her skin, and his hands attempting to pull her even closer. Just then she heard Adam open the bedroom door and call her name, just allowing enough time for Jonathan to take a step back, bid them both a hurried good night, and scurry off to join Emily in their matrimonial bed.

Chapter Thirty

In a guest bedroom at the Mills' house, Kelly spent an extraordinary night in bed with Adam. She swam in an ocean of raw, heightened emotions, fuelled by alcohol, the bonds that tied her to him, experiences she had been through with him, unresolved grief, guilt, yearnings for solace. She could feel his presence, his body heat, feel the gentle rise and fall of each breath, feel every movement however slight, and wondered for a fleeting second whether it was towards her, feeling the pulse of excitement and desire that it was, followed immediately by disappointment when it did not arrive, and then the guilt of that, over and over again in a seemingly endless, unresolvable tension of present versus past, of passion versus conscience, of loyalty versus betrayal, all the while sensing, knowing, that he was feeling the same; and all at a distance of two inches.

Eventually there was a very slight shaking of the bed as quietly, both began to sob, in a futile attempt to hide it from the other. Their hands touched under the duvet, each desperate to comfort the other, they turned and met in the deepest of embraces, wherein each tried to hold the other ever tighter, to the point where they were emotionally one entity, and it was all there was.

In the meantime, just along the hallway, Emily was also sobbing quietly, having just suffered the drunken, rough desires of a husband's attempts at acting out his frustrations before passing out.

Chapter Thirty One

Adam was keen for another round of golf with Jonathan, and given that he had awoken in his house on a Saturday morning, it was easily brought about with the aid of some borrowed equipment and clothing to save the need for returning home first. This left Kelly alone with Emily for what turned into a long brunch in the garden:

- "I hope you and Adam were comfortable last night?"

- "We were thank you; very much so."

- "Did you make love?"

- "Err...... wow.... I wasn't expecting that! No, we just cuddled up really closely all night."

- "That's lovely."

- "Yeah it was." she replied, trying to hide the lump appearing in her throat. "Did you and Jonathan make love?"

- "No, we had sex, or rather, he did."

The journey to the club in Jonathan's car was somewhat less intimate:

- "You should be fine with my old clubs Adam, they're perfectly good still, it's just that Emily, bless her, got me a new set for our anniversary."

- "That was thoughtful of her, you're a lucky man!"

- "Not as lucky as you though Adam eh? Kelly is delightful!"

- "Yes she certainly is! Now about my swing, perhaps you'll give me a few pointers today? I'm still hooking too much for my liking!"

- "Yes of course!"

Three days later, Kelly and Debs spent the evening at Adam's home, having dinner and drinks, and chatting long into the night. One week and a flurry of text messages later; Kelly arranged to meet up with Jonathan for a surreptitious drink, far enough away from Kensington, so as to minimise the chances of being recognised.

Chapter Thirty Two

The following Saturday Jonathan headed off for his constitutional round of golf, having told Emily that he would be back much later than usual, as he had arranged to spend the day with some of the chaps from work. One of them had a corporate box at Chelsea, so after golf it was to be a long catered lunch at Stamford Bridge, football, followed by a spot of dinner. She shouldn't wait up, as she knew how these things go, and she was fine with that.

Jonathan did indeed play his round of golf, in fact with Adam, but the rest of the day panned out rather differently.

At 2pm he arrived at The Second Serve pub in Wimbledon village, to find a smiling Kelly waiting to have lunch with him.

- "Where does Adam think you are?"

- "Out on a long day's shopping trip with the girls."

- "Excellent!"

They chatted over lunch, whereby Kelly skillfully kept it tantalising, without letting it get tactile. Afterwards they went for a long stroll around Wimbledon Common, during which Jonathan kept hinting, not overly subtly, that perhaps they should go somewhere a little more private, to which Kelly, without completely dismissing the idea, kept saying that they should take things one step at a time, and that she expected to be wined and dined first at least.

The afternoon wore on and became evening, which resulted in a swanky dinner back in Wimbledon village, full of apparent promise. At 9.53pm Kelly said it really was time that she was getting home else Adam would become suspicious as to her whereabouts. Reluctantly Jonathan agreed to drive her home, his disappointment tempered by the promise of another meeting. He went to the bathroom, while she was to wait outside to get some fresh air. When he emerged from the restaurant, Kelly was nowhere in sight. He waited for several minutes by his car, before royally cursing her cowardice, and driving home in a very disgruntled mood, deciding that Emily would have to do again tonight, and had better well be in the mood!

Kelly had in fact gotten into another car, parked out of sight of the restaurant, and was busily having make up applied by Kat, a friend of hers who worked in the West End, before being dropped off at nearby Wimbledon Common and laying down in the bushes, one minute before illustrator Michael came along walking his dog. Upon being alerted by the dog to something in the bushes, he found a woman he had never met before apparently injured from a blow to the forehead, and immediately called for an ambulance. The ambulance was particularly swift in arriving, crewed by Helen and Richard, who applied all necessary first aid to Kelly until their arrival at A&E, where they handed her care directly over to Debs, who quickly tended to her wound in a private room, and left her suitably bandaged to rest there, whilst she went off to attend to the resultant paperwork and obligations.

Two hours later the police arrived to interview Kelly, who was able to describe her day in great detail, right up until the moment she left the restaurant having rebuffed Jonathan's desires to extend the evening further; from which point she could not recall anything until being in the ambulance.

The following morning, with Kelly's entire story having checked out perfectly, and just as Jonathan was preparing to leave to play cricket; the police arrived at his and Emily's house, wishing to speak with him. Jonathan was keen to be as cooperative as possible, confident of having nothing beyond attempted adultery to hide, and so took the officers into the garage to talk. His story too was checking out nicely up to leaving the restaurant, complete with all the messages in his phone he had exchanged with Kelly in the lead up; which was all fine until the point when one of the officers noticed the slightest of gleams coming from his golf bag. Upon closer inspection there was a discernible dash of red on the end of his putter, at which point both he and the putter were taken into custody for further investigation.

After some delay at the Police Station, he had just finished giving his Formal Statement to one of the arresting officers, when another officer came into the room and handed a forensic report to his colleague, which confirmed that the substance found on his putter was blood, and furthermore, that it was undoubtedly Kelly's.

That Sunday afternoon Emily arrived at the Police Station to give her Formal Statement, in which her description of her understanding of the previous day's events, and his arrival time at home; also all checked out perfectly. The only thing she omitted to mention was that Kelly and Debs had popped round for a cup of tea and a chat, the day before.

88

What she very much did add to the statement though, was a detailed account of every violent incident she had suffered at the hands of Jonathan since meeting him, but had been too terrified of reprisals to report, however if the police cared to check her medical records, they would find a complete corroboration, down to the last stitch. Moreover, now that it appeared that he had started to pursue and assault other women as well, she felt it her civic duty to come forward and protect the public for as long as possible by elongating his impending sentence, thus providing further reasons for his bail application to be refused.

The following morning, just as Jonathan's bail application was indeed being refused; Emily went to see her Solicitor to begin divorce proceedings.

Chapter Thirty Three - Four years, nine months before her funeral

Adam's placement was for six weeks of shadowing fully qualified colleagues as they went about their work. He was to gain valuable experience by observing how and why they came to their decisions and recommendations, the issues they faced, and how they interacted with their patients both in group, and one to one sessions. Although he was not especially looking to specialise in addictions; it had been too good an opportunity to decline.

The point when he immediately recognised the frantic young woman from the coach station, was hard to process in the context of the moment. He had long since abandoned hope of hearing from her during the interim 15 months. He was trying not to look at her, but kept finding his eyes drawn there. She was paying little attention to anything anyway, so it began to appear that he was to avoid any compromising, awkward scenarios, which was surely for the best, although he could sense his own disappointment.

Then the young woman finally did look in his direction. The look on her face was not one of vague puzzlement, but of clear recognition, tinged with shock, embarrassment; maybe even a hint of pleasant surprise.

The rest of the group session was characterised by the two of them in a stereotypical scene, whereby repeatedly one looked at the other for as long as they could, until the split second when they were caught doing so; and their roles immediately reversed. At the point where the patients left the session to leave the therapists to it, they shared a sustained look until she had left the room.

It was not until the next day that their paths crossed again, this time in a stairwell, heading in opposite directions. Had there been an observer, the scene would have appeared a rather strange one - two people standing three stairs apart, facing each other with a fixed, intense gaze, verbalising not a word, yet showing no signs of trying to move on.

Two contactless days later, Lorelei arrived for her one to one session with Dr Simmons.

- "Hi Lorelei, this is Adam, one of the trainees, would it be okay if he were to sit in on our session today, just to observe, nothing more?"

Whether Adam was feeling even more awkward than her, she could not judge, but at least he wasn't expected to speak, and share his intimate thoughts and feelings at that precise moment. Lorelei neither wanted to divulge them in front of him, nor ask that he should leave; leaving her sitting there feeling like she was in some form of suspended animation.

After several answerless attempts from Dr Simmons, and at the risk of creating a bad impression by not waiting for instruction; Adam said:

- "I really don't want to make Lorelei uncomfortable, nor inhibit her therapy in any way, so I'll just go."

She watched him leave the room.

When they made eye contact on the first of many occasions in the dining room later that day at lunchtime, she mouthed the words "thank you", and knew that his quick smile in response imparted that it was okay.

The following day Lorelei found him in a quiet spot in the grounds, surrounded by large Oak trees, in the middle of some lunch that he had clearly brought in with him.

- "I believe I still owe you £8?"

- "I regarded it as a gift rather than a loan."

- "A gift that keeps giving?"

Adam could only smile.

- "Is the dining room food that bad here, or is it my looks that you're trying to avoid?"

- "I just don't want to make things any more difficult for you, that's all."

- "Perhaps you should stop making these sudden appearances in my life?"

- "I'll do my best, it's just that you're proving rather tricky to avoid."

- "Maybe it's just inevitable, and we'll have to learn to live with it?"

- "Yeah maybe."

92

Chapter Thirty Four

Somewhat less coincidentally, Lorelei found Adam the following day.

- "This is unbelievable! I've turned up at the exact same spot at the exact same time, only to find you here again!"

- "Yeah it's almost getting spooky now. What brings you here?"

- "Do you mean to this spot, or more generally?"

- "I'm not sure which is the safer question to ask!"

- "I'm not sure which is the safer question to answer!"

- "You really don't have to answer either, it's okay. Maybe you could just lay on the grass, close your eyes, and let the song I was about to play on my phone just wash over you?" he said as he offered her one half of his headphones.

- "Okay thanks."

The distance between them was restricted, but it was just far enough to maintain separation, as the Sade song The Sweetest Gift began:

"Quietly while you were asleep, and the moon and I were talking, I asked that she'd always keep you protected.
She promised you her light, that you so gracefully carry. You bring your light and shine like morning.
And then as the wind pulls the clouds across the moon, your light fills the darkest room. And I can see the miracle that keeps us from falling.
She promised all the sweetest gifts, that only the heavens can bestow. You bring your light and shine like morning. And as you so gracefully give your light, as long as you live. I'll always remember this moment."

After a minute or so, Adam opened his eyes to two realisations. Silent tears were streaming down Lorelei's face from her still closed eyes, and they were holding hands. Several more minutes passed by, bereft of movement, until finally he saw her slowly open her eyes, jump up, and run off at speed, leaving him to berate himself.

The following day, Adam went to the same place, at the same time, with trepidation, but with other feelings too. He attempted to look like someone casually enjoying their lunch in a pretty spot, but was not about to threaten any acting awards for one man plays. A leaf on the move was enough to make him turn his head sharply in that direction, and feel the instant disappointment. The minutes ticked by, and were fast running out. She did not come.

Later that afternoon during the inevitable crossing of paths at some point, Lorelei did a far better job of evading eye contact than previously, although no one was on the verge of calling the BAFTAs for her performance either. By the next day, with rather less sleep than either party might have benefitted from; the scene was again set at the lunch spot. This time, Adam had only been there for ten minutes, when a faint rustling did finally produce the appearance of Lorelei.

- "Oh er, hi, I wasn't sure if I'd see you here again."

- "I wasn't sure if you would either, in fact I tried to ensure that you wouldn't, and yet here I am."

- "Look I'm glad you have come, I really want to apologise for the other day. I never wanted to overwhelm you or upset you in any way, I........."

- "It wasn't your fault, please don't feel bad. I'm sorry that I ran off like that."

- "But I shouldn't have......."

- "But I'm glad you did, it was a beautiful moment, maybe the most beautiful moment."

- "Yeah it was, but even so I......"

- "Can I lay next to you again?"

- "Er well, if you think it'll......"

- "It'll be okay if you stop talking." she smiled, as she reached for the ground.

- "Okay I'll stop now."

- "But you haven't though!"

- "Clearly I have."

Chapter Thirty Five

Two weeks into Adam's six week placement, the furtive lunchtime rendezvous had continued undiscovered, although they felt increasingly risky. Adam was all too aware of the jeopardy in which any such thing would place his future career; yet the only moments when he was not longing to be with her, were those when he actually was so.

Lorelei refused to allow any trainees to sit in on her one to one sessions, so that took care of the possibility of a repeat of that blatant awkwardness; but the group sessions continued with a full complement, and it felt like their feelings would be stripped naked for all to see at any moment. The best, and only solution they could devise, was for her to arrive early enough to be able to select her chair in the circle. She did not want her back entirely towards the line of trainees, that would have been too much to bear, but just round enough so that eye contact was only possible with a deliberate manoeuvre, rather than irresistibly available at every second. She still maintained her policy of saying the bare minimum, feeling excruciatingly uncomfortable knowing that Adam would be obliged to take notes.

- "So how was your evening last night?"

- "Oh you know, I decided to spend it in a secure rehab unit again, surrounded by addicts at varying stages of recovery; so yeah, really good thanks. How about yours?"

- "Not as brilliant as yours by the sounds of it, but pleasant enough thanks."

- "What did you get up to?"

- "I watched American Football for several hours."

- "Sounds great, anything must be better than being here, well almost anything."

- "It wasn't all great, every few minutes the commentator said "We'll be right back after these messages." Then I had to sit through a load of annoying adverts for home insurance or floor cleaner or similar. That's not a message is it?"

- "No I suppose not."

- "No, something like, "Your Mum called, dinner's at 8 and it's your turn again to give the Rottweiler his suppository." That's a message!"

Lorelei laughed more than she could remember doing in a very long time, as much at his words, as at his feigned indignation. By the time she had recovered herself, it was too late, she was kissing him, or he was kissing her, neither could really say for sure who had started it. The classic thing would have been to pull away quickly, awkwardly, and each waited fearfully for the other to do so, but neither did.

Chapter Thirty Six

One week, and several lunchtimes later, *he* came to visit Lorelei. The visit was strictly controlled. All visitors had to leave jackets, coats, and any bags in a locked area, and be subject to a search, lest they be bringing in any untoward gifts for the patients. The visiting lounge was spacious enough to allow for a degree of privacy, but was a well staffed, communal space, layed out for multiple visits at a time.

Lorelei had been in a trepidatious state all week, but found the strength and resolve to go through with it. She arrived early enough to position herself right in the centre of the lounge for maximum visibility. At the allotted time, in *he* breezed. As *he* approached Lorelei was already sure that her galloping heartbeat could be heard by all. *He* had put on *his* best smile and she suffered *his* attempt at appearing to give her a heartfelt, long-lost hug. Her skin crawling was not apparent to anyone but her. *He* sat facing her.

- "It's so good to see you darling! How have you been, how are you getting on?"

- "Fine thanks."

- "What's it like in here?"

- "It's alright, yeah."

- "It's certainly shit at home without you!"

- "Is it?"

- "Course it is, I fucking miss you!"

- "Yeah, I'll bet."

- "You don't seem very pleased to see me!"

- "Really? What were you expecting, cartwheels?"

She could sense *him* bristle, strain to contain *himself*.

- "I thought you might be missing me too!?"

- "Did you? Which parts did you think I'd be missing the most?"

-

-

- "When do you think you'll be able to come home?"

- "Able or willing?"

- "What do you mean by that?"

- "You imagine I want to come home to you do you? To our happy life? To your loving arms, is that it?"

- "I just thought that….."

- "I'm not coming back to you, ever."

- "You what?"

- "We've reached the end, time to move on, adíos!"

She could see that look, hear *his* teeth grind, see *his* fists tense; sense that fury. She knew though that, as vile as *he* was, *he* would not do anything then. They sat in silence for a few moments more, until she beckoned Tom over to her and said:

- "I'd like to go back to my room for a lie down now Tom please, I'm feeling really tired."

- "Okay no worries, I'll see your visitor out. Do you want a minute to say your goodbyes?"

- "No it's okay, we're past that."

Chapter Thirty Seven

The next day, Debs arrived to see how Lorelei was getting on, and they sat chatting for a while. The previous day had seen a momentous step taken, for which Debs was full of nothing but praise; but neither were under any illusions as to the likelihood of *him* respecting or accepting her decision lightly. Debs was still desperately searching for some kind of protective solution.

Just as they were leaving Lorelei's room for her to see Debs to her car, Adam happened past and exchanged the briefest of looks with Lorelei, before continuing on his way down the corridor. Debs immediately led her by the hand straight back inside her room and closed the door again.

- "What was that?"

- "What was what?"

- "That!"

- "That what?"

- "Okay I'll try it a different way. Who was that?"

- "That was Adam, he's just doing some observation training here for a few weeks."

- "Ah huh. Why do I get the impression you've moved past mere observation?"

- "Er, I don't know Debs."

- "Bloody hell hun, that could get very messy, for both of you."

- "Jeez, nothing gets past you does it!?"

- "You should know that by now," she smiled. "Look, if it's given you some hope and the strength to do what you did yesterday, then great; but promise me you'll be really careful okay? It might have to wait a while."

- "I know, thanks Debs."

Chapter Thirty Eight

The end of Adam's six week placement was looming on the horizon, as inevitably as the setting sun. More perhaps by luck than sound judgement, his extracurricular moments with Lorelei had as yet passed undiscovered.

Quite how he would cope without her daily presence, he was yet to conceive. Quite how she would cope without his, was perhaps of greater concern to both of them, but the prospect of uniting fully once she had left there, was to sustain them in their anguish in the interim.

During the last few days of Adam's tenure, several of the staff expressed their concerns as to an apparent decline in Lorelei's mood and levels of interaction; but as she was quiet at the best of times, it did not raise too much alarm.

On his last day, Adam arrived rather more laden than usual, having brought in some thank you presents for certain members of staff who had been particularly helpful throughout his time there. He went about his day as normally as possible, signed out at the usual time, and left by the secured door.

Although he appeared to be about to head off to the gates and up the winding exit lane, he in fact diverted towards the back door of the kitchen and slipped inside, a few seconds after the chef exited for one of her constitutional smoking breaks. Once inside, he quickly left the kitchen via the code he had carefully observed, and headed along the warren like corridors.

- "Are you that reluctant to leave us Adam?" came a voice from behind him.

It was all he could do not to jump out of his own skin like a startled cartoon character.

- "Oh hi Dr Simmons, no I just forgot something that's all."

- "Ah yes, an occupational hazard!"

- "Indeed so, I'll see you again sometime soon I hope, have a nice evening."

- "I hope so, and thanks, you too."

With his heart still beating at a rate inadvisable for even the healthiest of humans, that he was sure would be audible in the next town; he tapped a knuckle on Lorelei's door. She opened it within 0.2 of a second, and within 0.4 of the same second, she had closed it again with him inside.

With the partial security of her locked door, albeit that the lock could be overridden if need be, they kissed like never before, like there really would be no tomorrow, with that fear only intensifying every fibre of their physical beings, and every strand of emotion. They did not have long before Lorelei had to go and attempt to act out a normal evening without drawing any undue attention, leaving Adam to ensconce himself silently somewhere in a room that had the bare minimum of furnishings, although at least he did not have to be around anyone for the snail-paced duration.

Lorelei could barely contain her longing to be with him, the excitement of what could be to come, nor her impatience at every word she had to utter or listen to, or at everything she had to do or see during the following four agonising hours until 10pm. It was like someone had set the time space continuum to frame by frame mode.

Finally, finally, finally, the universe allowed it to be 10pm. It was all Lorelei could do not to sprint down the corridor to her room. Just as she neared her door she was intercepted, and Adam, from the other side of it, with a sinking heart heard:

- "Hey Lorelei, I'm glad I've caught you, I was hoping to have a chat with you. I could really use one."

- "Oh er hey Susie, er look I'm really sorry but I'm really done in for today. Can I make it up to you tomorrow?"

- "Alright, but double chats tomorrow okay?"

- "I promise. Good night."

- "Night hun."

Checking for any further possible interceptors, Lorelei at last entered her room, and closed and locked the door behind her, and there it was; they were alone for the night.

Keeping the lights off, and some music on at a gentle volume to replicate as far as possible a normal night for her there; they could not stop embracing or kissing with a silent but otherwise uncontrollable passion, for the first hour or so, whilst on the other side of her door, things began to settle down for the night.

They undressed each other, terrified of making the slightest sound, before getting into her single bed. The thrill, the joy, of finally being in that so yearned for scenario quickly became overwhelming, and it was several minutes before they could do anything but hold each other so closely it was almost suffocating, until eventually, their mutual desire for each other, to explore and revel in the newness of each other, won through.

She delighted, bristled, as he touched, caressed, searched every millimetre of her, first by hands, then by lips, savouring every second of that never-to-be-repeated first time. She sensed no less delight or bristling from him as she acted out her passion and desire.

Once saturation point had been reached, repeatedly, and there were no new sensations to discover or tastes to taste; the moment arrived.

She lay on her side facing him, her face only centimetres from his, in a deep gaze, feeling him laying on the inside of her right thigh, as she wrapped her other thigh and her arms around him, feeling his arms do likewise, until they were completely entwined. Then incredibly slowly, like the savouring of the world's most divine chocolate as it melts over the taste buds for the first time; she felt him entering inside her. She let out an ecstatic gasp at each sensation of him entering deeper, trying so hard not to make a sound loud enough to be heard elsewhere, until there was no more to enter.

There was no further movement for some time, only the savouring of ecstasy, with her face buried in his neck she breathed in the smell of his skin. Then holding him with all her might, feeling him reciprocate, kissing long, deep kisses, at the slowest, almost imperceptible pace, she began to move, and felt him do so in unison, exercising unimaginable control and restraint, which only served to heighten the intensity of every sensation.

For the first time in Lorelei's life, and in the truest sense, she was being made love to. She sensed, knew, that for different reasons, it was like nothing Adam had ever experienced either. When finally, she could endure not one second more, she felt their orgasms meet like two tidal waves crashing into each other; and wondered if they might drown, but did nothing to try to prevent it.

Chapter Thirty Nine

They passed the most beautiful night together that either would ever remember; not allowing sleep to rob them of even a single second of it. However, as night follows day, day follows night, and Adam still had to accomplish the successful completion of their plan.

At 6am, with the greatest degree of reluctance he had ever felt, he had to leave Lorelei's bed, not made any easier by her holding onto him for all she was worth. When finally he achieved the painful separation, he dressed in the dark clothes he had also brought in in the rucksack.

This time there could be no chance encounters in the corridors or anywhere else, so Lorelei, in her pyjamas, had to go ahead and run reconnaissance along each corridor, and around every turn, beckoning him forward at each clear interval until they reached the kitchen. She left him there with an agonising, beautiful, kiss, before scurrying back to her room.

Adam slipped back through the coded door and arrived out in the open again, but that still left him within the secure grounds of the unit. He used the darkness to creep towards the vehicle entrance which had two sets of electric coded gates to negotiate. Although he had learned the codes, leaving at that point with no car in sight, could have attracted attention, so he hid himself and bided his time. As expected, at 6.33am it was the chef who arrived first. She passed through the first set of gates, before having to wait for them to close fully so that she could put in the code for the second set and drive through. After she had driven off to park, Adam had half a second to pass through just as they were closing again, which he managed, leaving him in between the two sets of gates. He laid down in the ditch at the side of the narrow road, just by the opening point to wait, on what would be the passenger side, to an on-coming vehicle. Next to arrive should be Billy from maintenance, in his transit van and alone.

Sure enough at 6.42am there he was. At the first hint of a gap provided by the inwardly opening gate Adam was through and out onto the public country lane. He walked at a brisk pace towards the main road, darting into coverage at the merest sight or sound of a vehicle, until he was well clear and able to walk freely. He arrived at where he had called home for the last six weeks ready to pack. As he did so, the songs his heart wanted to sing, and the excruciating pain of her absence, competed ferociously for his attention; each having their moments of winning the battle.

Chapter Forty

Adam had returned to Brighton to continue his studies, and to commence the six weeks of agonising, restless, beautiful waiting, for Lorelei's release from her Section.

So much ran through his mind. Would she get out okay, or would a relapse prevent it? If she does get out, would she relapse then? Would she forget about him in the meantime? Was he just a lovely distraction, or was this as real for her? What about *him* that he'd unofficially heard so much about? Would *he* attempt to force her back to *him*? Maybe she'd find her own way back there anyway such are the ties that bind? What would he do about that? What could he do about that? Could he just carry on without her?

Amidst all the doubts, he kept coming back to a faith in the same thing - what they had shared was real.

Lorelei in the meantime was having a similar experience. Would he really wait for her? Was she just a pleasant distraction during his six weeks there? Would *he* really just let her walk away? Could she get away from *him* either way? Was what she felt for Adam real? Was he simply playing some sort of rescuer role in her mind? All those lunchtimes though, that last night……

Contributing hugely to their shared angst, was the inability to stay in contact and provide any reassurances. Under one of the many conditions of Lorelei's placement, her phone was locked away by staff. She could access the internet on a restricted basis, which included blocking email access. Desperate as she was for him to visit, he could hardly just breeze in on some innocent pretext. One person who could though was Debs.

Having confessed all, she knew that it would make no difference to Debs' desire to help. In fact in Debs' mind, whilst not ideal nor coming with any guarantees, and in the absence of success in finding her somewhere safe to go to; Adam represented her best chance.

Two weeks before Lorelei was due to leave rehab; Adam received a call from an unknown caller. Warily, hopefully, he answered:

- "Hello."

- "Oh hi is that Adam?"

- "Yes it is, who's this?"

- "I'm Debs, let's say we have a mutual interest in looking out for someone dear to us."

- "Hi Debs, it's okay I know who you are. Lorelei has told me about you. You already have my gratitude and admiration, you've been wonderful."

- "Let's hope I'll always say the same about you!?"

- "Fair enough, and I certainly think and hope so too!"

- "Okay with that subtle shot across your bows out of the way, any chance of us meeting up very soon? I think we need to talk."

- "Of course we can, as soon as you like."

- Okay well let me talk with Kelly, who I'm sure you've also heard of, and I'll call you tomorrow, okay?"

- "Okay great thanks".

- "Oh one more thing, Lorelei said to tell you she's counting the minutes."

- "Oh god, is she suffering from OCD now too? That could really delay things!"

- "What? No, she just……"

- "Debs! I'm just joking with you, out of joyous relief! Please tell her I can't stop thinking about her either!"

- "You're an arse!" she laughed. "Okay I'll tell her, speak tomorrow."

- "Thanks so much Debs, speak tomorrow."

At 12pm on the following Saturday, Adam was standing on the concourse at Brighton station, looking out for two women who could fit Debs' descriptions. After receiving some odd looks from pairs of women not expecting his friendly greeting; the rendezvous met with success.

After a few formalities, Adam guided them through the North Laines to his postgraduate student digs, where they spent the next four hours chatting. During which time, whilst Lorelei had already told him many things, and he had gleaned much from colleagues and his own observations; the remaining blanks were filled in.

With everything set, Adam then took them on guided pub tour around The Lanes, culminating in an abandonment of the plan to walk them back to the station that evening, and it being replaced with one whereby Debs and Kelly shared his bed, whilst he slept on the couch.

Chapter Forty One

One week later, one day before Lorelei's expected release date, and in the hope of rather more precision; Debs arrived in a community transport vehicle driven by Helen. She waited in the car park, whilst Debs went inside to attend to matters at hand with Dr Simmons. After that, she retrieved Lorelei's phone from nurse Tom, complete with 133 text messages from *him* and kept it.

An hour later she emerged with a happy, if nervous looking, Lorelei. When she asked about her phone, Debs replied:

- "It's time for a new phone, and a new number hun."

Half an hour later they were saying an emotional farewell at Chichester train station, as Kelly emerged from her train onto the concourse. Twenty minutes later, Lorelei and Kelly boarded a train together.

Nine long stops, and 51 minutes later, the people of Brighton there present, witnessed a scene the like of which they had only seen in films; as Adam and Lorelei ran towards each other at a startling pace, culminating in her jumping up and wrapping her arms and legs around him, as he only just managed to stay upright, whilst they kissed each other with a ferocious intensity.

Once Kelly had managed to find a pause long enough to say her goodbyes, complete with heartfelt hugs and thanks; she boarded a train bound for London. As she awaited its departure, she texted Debs:

- "Mission accomplished. Thank you for everything x".

The following day, around the same time as Lorelei awoke in a new life, to the sound of seagulls, and the feel of Adam; a car approached the double perimeter gates and pressed the intercom button.

- "I've come to collect Lorelei,"

- "Oh, I'm terribly sorry for your wasted journey, but Lorelei left us yesterday."

-

-

- "Who picked her up?"

- "I couldn't say, it was my day off."

-

- "Hello? Are you still there? Hello!?"

Chapter Forty Two - 5 years, 10 months, and 29 days until *his* release

Adam had steeled himself, virtually forced himself to do something he had been putting off since the funeral - go to the place where they had shared their happiest memories. He did not feel, could never feel, that he truly deserved to; but he needed to make the memories a little more tangible again. As the flight to Málaga surged from the runway, the stranger next to him asked whether he was sure he was okay?

The airport appeared somewhat different, but the route to his house was not, at least geographically. The short walk from Arrivals to the train platforms, the short three stop ride to Maria Zambrano, the brief walk across the concourse and out across the road to Málaga bus station, the eighty five minutes east hugging the coast looking out across the Mediterranean, sometimes even with waves splashing the windows via a rock, then five minutes inland towards the beautiful, whitewashed, Andalucian, mountain village of Torrox, until the final few minute walk to his house; all traversed with vivid memories of the excitement they felt, the first time he had taken her there, contrasted against, and battling with, the starkness of her absence now.

His house, although unlived in for so long, had not been neglected in his absence. Adam could not have allowed that and in doing so, tarnish the memories it held. As he entered through the front door, went up the stairs, then up another flight out onto the roof terrace, and saw that stunning view again; it all just washed over him until he felt like a drowning man who already knew there was nothing to reach out and grasp.

During the next few weeks, he retraced their favourite walks through the mountains and hillsides, visited their favourite bars, cafes, and restaurants, and attempted as best he could to immerse himself entirely in it all. Occasionally he encountered a member of staff or owner, long-standing enough to remember them, and ask how and where she was. He could only bring himself to reply that he had not seen her in a long time. Somehow though he felt closer to her again, like she was more real, more vivid, and not just fading evermore into the horizon, leaving him with only the torment of her.

He was in absolutely no rush to return to London, in fact he kept postponing his return flight, but then one Tuesday afternoon on the roof terrace, as he attempted to concentrate for long enough to make it worthwhile reading a book; he received a message from Emily.

Chapter Forty Three - 5 years, 9 months, and 21 days until *his* release

It was already mid-evening when Adam got home from his travels, but once he had showered and sorted out a few immediate arrival chores, he headed straight out again to see Emily. Whilst not exactly serene, it was the first time he had ever seen her even towards the description of relaxed; and it was as if another person greeted him at the door. After a long and deep hug, and a much shorter and shallower conversation over drinks, Emily came to the nub of the matter:

- "I need your help again Adam, your wizardry if you prefer. Well not so much me really, as a friend of mine, Ruth.

- "I'm not sure we should always expect things to be as simple as they were with Jonathan."

- "I know, but I know what's going on with her, you can't kid a kidder, though it's worse for her, they have a child."

- "That does complicate matters. How bad is it?"

- "Bad."

- "How is the child?"

- "Well she's ten. Not old enough for the full picture, but plenty old enough for enough of it. She's struggling."

- "Okay, I'm getting the picture. Is Ruth to be in on it, or is this a 'for her own good' type of intervention?"

- "I'm not sure how best to play that to be honest."

- "Well we can figure that out as we go along."

Emily disappeared into the kitchen and quickly returned with a pre-prepared tray of olives, humous, guacamole, and breadsticks, along with a large bottle of Rioja.

- "I thought I'd keep your Mediterranean vibe going a bit longer!"

- "Thank you, I am quite hungry, but I didn't want to trouble you."

- "Nothing would be too much trouble for you, after, well, you know, everything."

- "I really didn't do that much, plus I had some brilliant and willing assistants."

- "You did more than you can know, and I'll….. never be able to repay or thank you enough.

- "That you're okay, and he isn't, is all I need."

They remained chatting, but on lighter subjects, eating and drinking long into the evening.

- "It's really late, I'd better get going."

- "Don't go, stay, please."

- "Er… well… I'm not sure if that's such a ……."

- "Can I confess something?"

- "Erm…..okay."

- "The morning after you stayed here with Kelly, she told me something."

- "What did she tell you!?"

- "She told me that you just held her closely all night in a beautiful way, without trying to have sex with her, even though, well, I expect she would have wanted you."

- "Ah, that. Well it was a little more compli…….."

Emily cut him off with a soft but firm finger on his lips, she stood up, took him by the hand, and gently led him upstairs to the guest room, which was now her room. In the darkness, she stood before him by the bed, then unhurriedly undressed him down to his boxer shorts, and remained there a few seconds until he realised she wanted him to reciprocate. They remained there for a few seconds more, as two faint silhouettes, until she pulled back the duvet, got inside, and gently pulled him in to join her. As he lay on his back she did not so much cuddle up to him, as entwined herself around him, until every millimetre of her bare skin came into warm, soft contact with his, and there she stayed, falling asleep long before he did.

After having just spent so long retracing, reviving the memories of Lorelei, the guilt was horrific. This wasn't Sarika; Sarika was repeating something from before, even with the guilt, it didn't count somehow as a full betrayal. Even the impromptu night with Kelly didn't feel this bad, justified to an extent within themselves by the circumstances and their shared love for her. Yet for all that, right here and now with Emily, Adam relished the comfort, the closeness, the weight of her all around him, the feel of her skin on so many different places of his own, the contours of her curves, her head on his chest, her long hair, the feel of her gentle rise and fall; to hold and be held - a torturous bliss.

Chapter Forty Four

The following morning, each kept their own council on the subject, but there was no discernable sense of awkwardness. They enjoyed a late breakfast, during which Adam requested a summary of everything Emily knew about Ruth, her family, and her family life.

Emily had known Ruth for a few years, since they had met at a yoga class. She was married to Phillip and had been so for 12 years. They had a ten year old daughter called Sally. They lived nearby, in a less salubrious neighbourhood, but nice enough nonetheless. Phillip owned and ran a local estate agency, Jacksons, aided and abetted by his brother Simon, who also served as his doubles partner at their local tennis club, when either of them weren't playing mixed doubles or singles against each other, to test and satisfy their competitiveness. Ruth was an intelligent, confident, and out-going person, with her own career in publishing; although these last two personality traits were steadily but noticeably diminishing in Emily's view, commensurate with an increase in Phillip's violence. Sally was to all outward appearances coping well thus far with family life, but those closer to her, including Emily, were seeing the signs.

Adam left around midday to head home and straighten a few things out after his time away. He would be in touch in a few days, once he'd had time to think.

At 12.45am that night Adam was in bed, but still very much awake. He checked his Whatsapp:

'Emily, last seen at 12.44am.'

'Emily, last seen at 1.07am.'

'Emily, last seen at 1.21am'

'Emily, last seen at 1.28am'

'Emily, last seen at 1.31.am'

"Are you awake?"

"No! Haha yes Adam I am"

"I can't sleep either, I'm wide awake."

"That's probably for the best as I've just ordered you a cab. It'll be picking you up in ten minutes, so maybe put some clothes on?"

Emily, having listened out for the arrival of the taxi, had run downstairs, put the door on the latch, and gone back upstairs to the bedroom.

Adam let himself inside, and had sensed where to head. He entered the bedroom which was all but pitch black, though he could just make out the figure of Emily sitting at the foot of the bed. As he moved towards her, she stood up and slowly, silently, began to undress him, item by item. He went to reciprocate, but only encountered her soft, warm skin, at any place that he sought, even where he had expected to find evidence of one last item. She had reached the point again where all that remained were his boxer shorts, as a last barrier to the prospect of achieving complete skin on skin contact, but this time he felt her slowly lower them to the floor, and he stepped out of them. He then felt her embrace him fully as they stood face to face in the darkness, feeling her softness melt into him for several minutes, then sudden anguish at losing that sensation, just fleetingly, but still for far too long, before it returned to an even greater degree when he felt her pull him into the bed with her, and instantly entwined herself all around him again. As she did so, he let out an involuntary gasp of exquisite relief.

Chapter Forty Five

The following day, Adam decided it was time to have a little peruse of the local housing market. Dressed in a smart suit, he wandered into a few local estate agents, collecting a few printed details of houses of interest along the way, until finally arriving at Jacksons. He was greeted in friendly fashion by Dawn, Receptionist, Administrator, Secretary, sometimes Estate Agent.

- "Good morning, I'm Dawn, welcome to Jacksons, how can I help you?"

- "Good morning to you Dawn, I'm Adam, I'm on a bit of a scouting mission, just to get a sense of what's available in the area."

- "Are you already living round here or looking to move to the area?"

- "Looking to move here, you know, fresh start and all that."

- "I do indeed know, let me see if one of the brothers is free for a chat. I think Simon's out actually, but Phillip's here, just a moment."

- "That'd be great thanks."

- "He'll be free very soon, would you like a drink in the meantime?"

- "Oh yes please, black coffee, no sugar."

By the time she had returned, Phillip was free to see him, and so he and his coffee were led through to his office, situated at the back of the premises.

- "You must be Adam, pleased to meet you, I'm Phillip Jackson, do come in and take a seat."

- "Thank you. I'm very pleased to meet you Phillip."

- "Our wonderful Dawn tells me that you're considering moving to our neck of the woods."

- "Indeed so."

- "Is that for work, or family reasons may I ask?"

- "Well I'm not married..."

- "Lucky you! Do go on."

- "And as for work, well I can do that anywhere."

- "Oh, how so?"

- "I'm a writer."

- "How marvellous! Might I have read anything of yours?"

- "Well you might well have done, but I write under a pseudonym."

- "How intriguing! I can see some upsides though!"

- "Yes, maybe everyone should have an alter ego?"

- "Maybe so. Now what sort of properties might you be interested in?"

- "Two to three bedrooms, perhaps a garden, some outside space certainly, but generally I'm open minded."

- "That's always a bonus, price range?

- "I'm flexible on price."

- "Another bonus! Okay just give me a few moments……..right, I think perhaps this one…..this one…..not that one….definitely not that one….this one certainly…. Okay, coming to a printer near Dawn. I need to head off shortly, but have a browse and give me a shout if and when you'd like any viewings; here's my card."

- "Thank you Phillip, I certainly will."

Having duly collected the printouts from their wonderful Dawn, Adam went for a wander around the area, taking in the relevant roads, and one in particular, which happened to back onto Ruth and Phillip's house.

- "Hi Daniel, how are you all doing?……….That's great, listen I've another email address in need of your special attention, if you'd be so kind please……."

128

Adam had agreed to see some patients later that afternoon, and did so as best he could with an increasingly active mind, before heading home. By 9pm, he had sent a whatsapp message:

"I'm not going to pretend that it's even worth trying to sleep without the feel of you"

"Well I'm glad you've finally realised, hurry up then!"

Adam arrived at Emily's house at 10pm. No one would have been more surprised than him that he was allowing himself this indulgence, but already by just this third night, the desire was becoming a compulsion, and one so strong that it was outstripping even his guilt; which in itself became another source of torment.

Emily greeted him with a long, intimate hug and a glass of wine. He told her that he had set the wheels in motion where Phillip was concerned, and assured her that he would do all he could for Ruth and Sally, and where and if possible, he would keep her out of it. He went to say more but felt that finger on his lips again:

- "I know, I couldn't doubt you, but right now….."

She led him gently upstairs to the darkness, and undressed him in her own way, which he reciprocated. He found himself almost agitated with anticipation for the next moment when she would slowly pull him into bed with her, and entwine her softness all around him, and she did not disappoint. It was like the relief one feels when finally arriving home after the longest, most arduous of journeys. He lay still awhile, utterly consumed by the feeling of her, until silent tears rolled down his face. Within a minute or two he felt a whisper:

- "I don't know what you've been through Adam, but this is okay, it's more than okay, and we can just lay like this every night, I need it as much as you do."

- "I don't just need it though, I want it."

- "That's okay too."

- "I'm not sure that it is."

- "You deserve it Adam."

- "I don't deserve anything."

- "Well from now on I am going to be the judge of what you deserve."

They fell silent again. After a few moments he felt her begin to slowly move her arms and legs, still maintaining that close, firm yet soft, skin on skin contact, so that the entwinement became a soft caress that reached every part of him at once. He could neither keep in his gasps of delight, nor hide his arousal. Emily maintained her caress, but slowly ran a hand down his chest and found him. She wrapped her hand around firmly, and held him there.

Chapter Forty Six

Adam spent his free time for the rest of that week busying himself on his laptop, researching a number of topics. He also wandered into a tennis club in the Kensington area:

- "Good morning, I'm Helen, the club secretary, how can I help you?"

- "Good morning to you Helen, I'm Adam, new to the area, or soon to be. Could I please enquire as to how one goes about joining your lovely club here?"

- "Yes of course, well here's one of our packs with all the information you'd need. Our only real requirement to get the ball rolling is that you're proposed for membership by an existing member, you know, sort of by way of introduction. Might that prove tricky for you if you're new around here?"

- "Well by lucky hap, I may know just the person for the role."

- "Wonderful, well I look forward to receiving your application. Would you like a little guided tour of the facilities?"

- "I'd very much appreciate that, thank you."

No sooner had day turned to evening, the yearning for the feel of Emily all around him, overwhelmed whatever else he was feeling, or had been feeling. On a couple of occasions that week, he had still tried forcing himself to go home in an attempt to both deny himself the satiation of the need, and deny that he needed it satiating; but it was futile. She never applied any pressure, but she knew he would be on his way to her before the evening was out, and no time was too early for her entwinement.

On the Monday morning of the following week, Adam met up with Phillip to see three local properties for sale:

- "Good weekend Adam?"

- "Very good thank you, I trust yours was too?"

- "Yes thank you, nothing special, just at home with the family mostly you know, well, and a bit of tennis."

- "Ah yes on that very subject, would you have any objection to proposing me for a membership?"

- "Of course not, I'd be delighted. Do you play much, usually?"

- "Well I used to, it's been a while you know so I'd need to brush up with a few lessons, but I'd very much like to get back to it regularly."

- "Splendid, well I look forward to clashing racquets with you soon!"

- "Excellent!"

Later that day, Phillip had an appointment to show a couple from Manchester, around a five bedroom house. He met them in the driveway as arranged:

- "Ah Mr and Mrs Dewhurst, how lovely to see you again, do please follow me. Now this one's been empty for a while, so just excuse me for a second whilst I clear a path."

As he opened the door, he quickly gathered up the collection of letters, free newspapers, and junk mail, and placed them in a pile on top of the hallway table. He turned and was just about to commence the tour, with his best sales patter, when he realised that Mr and Mrs Dewhurst were standing transfixed at the table, looking on in horror.

There at the top of the pile was a high definition picture of a woman, lying face up on a white, plush looking sofa, battered, and covered in blood.

Chapter Forty Seven

The following Sunday morning, Adam was in the middle of a series of one to one coaching lessons at the tennis club, when he heard Phillip's voice greeting him as he came up the path from the car park.

- "So glad to see they let you in Adam!"
- "Yes they did indeed, and thanks again for proposing me!"
- "No problem at all. I can see you're keen to brush up your skills, so let me know when you think you're ready for a game!"
- "I am, and I certainly will!"

After his lesson, Adam hung around at the club for a little while, chatting to a few people, wandering around the courts, assessing the playing standards of various players, and enjoying a spot of lunch, before heading off home.

During the following week, not at every viewing, but at around one in three of them, Phillip and his clients discovered the same shocking picture of the bloodied woman on the doormat. By the next week, it had gotten to the point where he would perform a round of checks on his list of properties for that day, on his own, and before going into the office. However the picture kept on appearing at some of the houses.

By the third week, he decided to do a little surveillance. He performed his morning checks, then made it look as though he had driven away from the third one of them, but in reality he had parked up again just nearby enough to still have it in sight. Whilst he was sitting in his car hoping to catch sight of the culprit; Adam, dressed to not look like himself, was visiting the letter boxes of the first two.

Phillip tried again, this time going back to wait nearby house two, only to later discover the picture with clients at houses one and three.

When he had only two viewings, the picture appeared at either the one he had not kept a watch upon, or at neither.

So he told the wonderful Dawn to only make him one morning appointment for the next three days. He checked the doormat, nothing there, and so he parked up and waited, and waited, and waited, right up until the clients arrived for the viewing with no one else having appeared. Phillip repeated this the next day, with the same outcome. At least this way, to his mind the viewings were going well again. On the third of these three days, he let the clients in with some relief and began showing them around. As they reached the kitchen they were all greeted by the picture of the bloodied woman, stuck to the outside of the backdoor.

Chapter Forty Eight - 5 years, 7 months, and 24 days until *his* release

However Adam had spent his day, there was only one place that he could spend his night. The nightly arousal that the feel of Emily's caress all over him induced, could no longer be lived in any way other than making beautiful, passionate love to her. It was impossible to say which he found more pleasurable, comforting, or blissful; her pre and post intwinement or her lovemaking; but when she did both simultaneously, it was too far beyond exquisite to be conceivable.

Adam maintained his policy of not keeping Emily informed as to his actions regarding Phillip. However he was going to need a little assistance to move things onto the next phase, which he made known to her over breakfast, whereupon she was more than willing to fulfil the task. He then set off to meet Kelly for an overdue coffee and warm embrace:

- "It's so good to see you Ad, how have you been?"

- "Likewise Kells, pretty good actually."

- "What's happened? Something's happened!"

- "There's no hiding from you, is there?! Well, er, well Emily's happened."

- "Emily!? Emily Emily!?"

- "Emily Emily yes."

136

- "Oh Ad, I'm so pleased for you both!"

- "You really mean that? You don't hate me for it?"

- "Of course I don't! It's been over nine years Ad, you needed to move on, you deserve to find happiness again!"

- "It doesn't mean I've forgo…….please don't think I've forgot…."

- "It's okay Ad, I know." she said, reaching for his hand.

-

-

- "It's probably just as well we never… you know, that night."

- "Yeah, probably Kells, and because we could've never lived with the guilt."

- "Yeah, and you're probably rubbish anyway."

- "Yeah thanks, you too!"

Chapter Forty Nine - 5 years, 4 months, and 26 days until *his* release

Despite not having bought a property through Jacksons or any other local estate agent; Adam began to fully ingratiate himself at the tennis club. He regularly attended the mix-in club play sessions; thus improving his playing standard as well as his social networking. The latter was further enhanced by his attending some purely social events held there in the clubhouse, such as buffets and film nights. He deliberately did not invite Emily to any of them, but on a couple of occasions, Phillip did bring Ruth, affording Adam the opportunity for innocuous, polite chats.

- "Hi I'm Adam, a bit of a newbie around here."

- "Pleased to meet you, I'm Phillip's wife, Ruth."

- "Oh right, yes I know Phillip, he's pretty good isn't he? I'm trying to improve quickly, perhaps one day soon he'll meet his match!?"

- "That might be harder than you think; he almost always wins."

- "Well one can but try. Do you play Ruth?"

- "No, I used to, but I prefer to curl up with a good book these days, if and when I get the chance. I just come along when His Nibs requires it."

- "Ah got you. Who's your Favourite author then? I'd still have to go for Dickens, all time, but modern day, there's a Spanish writer I love, Nieves Garcia Bautista, I don't know if you've heard of her?"

- "I believe I have, do you read her books in Spanish?"

- "I do indeed."

- "Well get you Adam, quite the surprise package aren't you!?"

- "On occasions."

- "I don't think I could name a favourite from so many; occupational hazard."

- "Oh you're in that profession are you? How wonderful! I'm actually a writer."

- "Really? Under what name?"

- "Oh I never like to reveal that, I'm afraid."

- "Well, you just get more intriguing by the minute don't you? Perhaps I'll be able to deduce it one day?"

- "Maybe so."

His Nibs in the meantime was becoming increasingly concerned about the pictures found regularly at the property viewings. Whilst he had not wanted to draw any undue attention to them, his brother Simon could not help but notice the decline in sales, with no apparent explanation.

- "Your figures have really started to drop off lately Phillip. What's going on?"

- "Look, I hadn't wanted to worry you with it, thinking it'd blow over, but it hasn't."

- "What hasn't blown over?"

- "Some local nutter has been targeting my viewings, I keep finding the same horrible image at many of them."

- "What!? What image?"

- "This image……"

- "Bloody hell that's hideous! No wonder the clients are being put off! Where the hell are they coming from?"

- "I've no idea, a rival firm maybe, although it'd be a pretty extreme tactic!"

- "Have you tried catching them in the act?"

- "Well of course I have! They always seem to be one step ahead."

- "Well we can't be having this, perhaps we should report it to the police?"

- "No! That'd be even worse for business! Imagine the publicity!"

- "Well we've got to do something! Is it happening to Dawn too?"

- "No, just me it seems, for now at least."

- "Right, well send Dawn on as many as possible for a couple of weeks, and we'll monitor the situation. Jesus Phillip, you should have said something sooner!"

- "I know, sorry, I really didn't think it'd last this long."

Whilst Phillip continued playing detective, Ruth began to see an increase in the frequency with which Emily popped round for late morning coffees. She was always pleased to see her though, and glad of someone in which she knew she could confide, as she gradually began to do so.

Ruth was not the only one who felt they could confide in Emily, but in Adam's case it came at a very slow pace; piecemeal and highly selectively. He wanted her to know him, to understand him, to receive more of and from him; but it always came at a great cost, and he felt it always would do. There was that, and then there was the great fear of opening himself up again, to being utterly vulnerable to the whim and occurrences of, and the dependency upon, another.

Emily too was running such risks, but had grown over time to be more perceptive than most people gave her credit for. With each little piece of the puzzle from Adam, small things gleaned from Kelly and Debs, and her own often intimate observations and experiences; she began to build the picture.

More concretely, she wanted, needed his touch, his feel, his protection every night; whilst wanting and feeling the need to protect him, in equal measures.

Chapter Fifty

Adam had no intention of traumatising the wonderful Dawn, and therefore ceased his direct action posters, at least for the time being, to focus on other aspects, including plenty of tennis.

The increased frequency and intimacy in the friendship between Emily and Ruth, began to bear fruit:

- "It's the waiting for it that can be one of the hardest parts."

- "I remember it only too well Ruth. It's a weird thing to say I know; but there's almost a sense of relief afterwards……..like it was building up……..like it was inevitable, so, best get it over with."

- "Oh my god you felt that too!?"

- "Yeah I did, many times."

- "I thought it was just me……..like I was terrible to feel that way……..like I might have even encouraged it as a consequence."

- "You're not the first, and are very far from the last sadly."

- "That's a relief in itself to hear."

- "I imagine so, but it's quite an indictment on the state of affairs. We need to find you a way out."

- "It's not just about me though is it? Sally absolutely idolises her Dad."

- "I don't doubt that, however she's not exactly in possession of all the facts is she? She may well do a lot less idolising if she were."

- "I couldn't do that to her, shatter her illusions like that!"

- "But that's just it though Ruth, they are illusions….. She won't stay ten years old forever, and if you think she hasn't already picked up things, sensed things……well frankly I think you're also under illusions."

-

- "I'm sorry Ruth." she said, hugging her. "I didn't wish or mean to be so blunt. Something has to change, that's all. If you don't divert or turn around at some point along a path, you'll eventually reach the end of it."

- "Who said that line?"

- "I don't know, but I imagine it was someone extremely wise." she smiled.

Despite the optimism felt by Emily, that some progress was being made; Ruth did her best to avoid her over the next few weeks. During such time, Adam played some doubles with Helen, versus the Jackson brothers. They lost every time, but each time they managed to make the battle a little more hard fought.

- "Bad luck Adam, well played!"

- "You'll not resist me forever Phillip."

- "Maybe one day Adam, but not just yet eh?"

- "It may come sooner than you think."

After drinks and lunch in the clubhouse, Adam went home to do some work on his laptop, before finally indulging his immense craving for the feel of Emily.

The following weekend Adam managed to catch Helen for a chat at the tennis club after playing:

- "Morning Helen, how are things with you?"

- "Great thank you Adam, and I must say I'm hearing nothing but good things about you!"

- "Good to know!"

- "Not just your improved play, which I've seen first hand; but the way you're mixing in and getting along with everyone!"

- "That's kind of you to say so, I'm certainly enjoying it. On the subject of the social side of things; I'd very much like to host a quiz night, tennis themed of course, perhaps we could even raise a few pounds for a good cause along the way?"

- "I think that's a great idea, but you know how it is; I'll have to run it past the committee first."

- "Of course no problem, no rush, it's just something I'd like to try, that's all."

- "Leave it with me, I'll let you know if and when I get the seal of approval."

- "Great, thanks very much."

Adam bided his time, but didn't want Phillip getting too comfortable with the delegate everything to the wonderful Dawn policy. On three separate occasions that week, upon opening seemingly innocuous emails, Phillip was confronted with the full screen image of the bloodied woman. By the Thursday, it had turned up again as his screensaver. On the Friday morning, he received an email from a very alarmed client, demanding to know why he had sent such a thing to them amongst some attached property details. No amount of scans, firewalls, or purchases of increased IT security seemed to be enough, whilst he kept as much hidden from Simon as he could.

The seed of wonder began to take root in his mind, which was along the fine line Adam knew he was treading. Had he been naïve to dismiss this as the work of some local nutter? Was it just coincidence that Simon and Dawn remained untargeted? Has Ruth opened her mouth somewhere? She'd damn well pay for it if she has! Surely not though? She wouldn't dare! I don't want to give her the satisfaction of knowing about it, but I'll get it out of her tonight one way or another!

He headed home with an itch in need of scratching. He pulled into their driveway, and was just getting out of his car, when his mobile rang:

- "What the fuck is going on Phillip? That horrible image you showed me has just turned up on my computer!"

Nonetheless, at 10.32pm that evening, ten year old Sally awoke in her bed to the sound of an altercation below. Despite the terror fueled urge to hide under her bed covers, she crept along the landing to the top of the stairs, and just down them enough to be able to see into the lounge. The sight that greeted her was one of Daddy sitting astride Mummy's tummy on the sofa, pinning her arms to her sides with his knees, as he punched her in the face repeatedly. It was only Sally's screaming that made it stop.

Chapter Fifty One - 5 years, 3 months, and 21 days until *his* release

A mortified Adam received the all clear from Helen the following week, and the earliest possible date was set for the tennis quiz night. He made preparations which included drawing up posters to be dotted around the club:

You may be unbeatable on the court, but how much do you really know about tennis?

Be the first to be crowned Club Champion in this field!

Enter individually or in a pair.

Only £10 per person including buffet.

All proceeds to a local good cause.

During the intervening days, Adam decided to hold back with his targeting of Phillip, whilst Emily paid Ruth several visits at times when she was alone in the house, and of course saw through the make up, in every sense.

The Saturday evening of the quiz finally arrived, and preparations were in place. Ruth was unfortunately not feeling well enough to attend, in addition to still sporting a few bruises, and had been told to:

- "Stay at home then you miserable cow, and miss my triumph!"

Any disappointment Ruth may have felt was soon tempered by the company of Emily for the evening.

It was all hands on deck at the tennis club, as buffet contributions were being meticulously arranged on tables at one end of the clubhouse by several volunteers, and others arranged the tables and chairs accordingly. Whilst this hive of activity was taking place, Adam was setting up for his quiz at the other end, which was to go beyond mere pens and papers for the total of 28 entrants. Phillip and Simon Jackson were the only individual entrants, whilst everyone else was in pairs.

- "Welcome along to what I hope will be the first of many of these tennis quizzes! I'm Adam Mills for those of you that don't already know, please introduce yourselves to me afterwards if that's the case. Okay let's crack straight on………"

- "Question One - Roger Federer won five straight US Opens. In what year did he win the 5th of them, and who did he beat in the final? A point for each."

-
-

- "Question Four - Andy Murray famously finally won Wimbledon in 2013, ending the drought by beating Novak Djokovic in the final. Who did each of them beat in the semi final that year? A point for each."

-
-

-
-
- "Question Nine - How many French Opens did Chris Evert and Justine Henin win each? A point for each"
-
-
-
-
-
- "Question Fifteen - This is a video question, look at the projector screen, name the player and the year of their triumph in each of these Wimbledon finals. A point for each, 6 points on offer in total."
-
-
-
-
-
-
- "Question Twenty Two - Who was the last French woman to win Roland Garros, who did she beat in the final and in what year. Three points on offer."
-
-
-
-
-
-
- "Thirtieth and final question - Using the extra sheet supplied, write the name of the player against each of the slightly obscured figures pictured. There are ten in total, one point for each."

- "Okay folks, we've struggled through to the end, please hand your answer sheets into me, and whilst you're all devouring the lovely buffet, I'll be totting up the scores on the doors, and will announce the answers and winners as soon as possible, preferably whilst there is still some dessert left."

Adam beavered away with the scores, stopping only to exchange a quick whatsapp message, or take a bite of something from the plate Helen had kindly put by him. Once he was finished collating them, he performed the classic tap a piece of cutlery against a glass to draw everyone's attention, which did its job:

- "First of all, a big thank you to everyone who entered, we've raised £280 for the local women's refuge. Well, I thought this might be close, despite it being out of a possible 100 points, but you've surpassed yourselves! In third place with an impressive 81% is Ken and Gary!"

- "In second place with an even more impressive 83% is Helen and Claire!"

- "In first place, we have a tie! With a mighty 86% each it's Phillip and Simon!"

- "Now I know neither will be happy with a tie, but fear not, I have prepared a tiebreaker question. So all eyes back to the projector screen, and Phillip and Simon get ready, the first one to shout out the answer is the winner. Tennis has had many famous brothers, but which brother is featured here?"

A video, including audio, appeared on the big screen, 10.33pm, showing Phillip sitting astride Ruth, pounding her face with his fists. As Sally appeared on the stairs and screamed, the video clip ended.

Neither brother had shouted out the answer - a tie it was then. It was only the blue flashing light reflecting around the clubhouse windows from the darkness outside, that broke the stunned silence.

Chapter Fifty Two - Three years, three months before her funeral

It was summer, the greatest summer. Lorelei and Adam were immersed in the bliss of the early stages of their true love. A time when even a moment's separation was an hour too long, when any task to perform or conversation to be had apart, was a painful inconvenience, something to be endured until the immeasurable yearning could be soothed and satisfied by sweet reunion.

When they did go out somewhere together in public, the desire for it to be just the two of them alone again would overwhelm them, until they could do nothing else but give in and hurry home.

On days when they did not have to go anywhere, the only thing that interrupted their post-coital bliss was pre-coital anticipation, and every physical sensation was magnified, multiplied, by the strength of their emotions. No kiss was long enough, no embrace tight enough, no love making deep enough, words almost futile for not expressing enough.

Lorelei awoke from an early afternoon nap on the 1st September, to the sound of a suitcase being zipped closed. She blearily opened her eyes to see Adam smiling as he came over to the bed.

- "Hey beautiful, sorry to disturb you but it's time to wake up. Sit up and I'll bring you a coffee."

- "Eh…..what's going on…….why are there suitcases around?"

- "We're just off on a little trip that's all, an adventure if you will."

- "What……where to……how come?"

- "We don't have time for all that just now, get your gorgeous self into the shower; we've a train to catch."

- "Are we off to Butlins in Bognor?" she smiled.

- "It won't be that glamorous, but let's go anyway."

The night before this conversation, Kelly had been walking home from work via her usual route, lost in her own thoughts. As she opened her front door *he* pushed her through it, and in an instant had closed it behind them, knocked her to the floor, and was on top of her with *his* hand over her mouth.

- "If you scream, I'll knock you unconscious, and when you come round, if you scream again, I'll do it again, and we'll go on like that for as long as necessary. Get the picture?"

- "Mmmmmmm hmmmmmm hmmmmmmm."

- "Where is she?"

As *his* hand lifted from her mouth she tried to scream for help, but it was quickly stifled by the hand returning in the form of a fist. She was groggy and bleeding from the blow, but still conscious.

- "Where is she?"

- "I don't know."

- "Liar!" as *his* fist pulled back again.

- "I'm not lying! I went all the way down there….. to pick her up on the right day….. and they told me she'd left the day before!"

- "They must have told you something more!?"

- "All I could find out was that…..she left on her own…..in a cab, that's all. I've been really worried about her actually!"

- "Are you taking me for a mug? You expect me to believe she wouldn't tell you, her best mate, where she is?"

- "Maybe she needed a new start….a clean break?"

- "Yeah right. I know what she needs!"

- "Why can't you just leave her be? Move on and let her do the same!?"

- "I'll do what I fucking want Kelly!"

Reluctantly *he* got up off of her, and was about to leave, when he saw it there on the mantelpiece; a postcard of the Brighton Pavillion.

Chapter Fifty Three

Kelly's face was throbbing, but that was not the most painful sensation she was feeling by some distance. With the evidence still fresh on her face, she headed into the local police station. The male Desk Sergeant who began to deal with her, was not wholly unsympathetic, but was very matter of fact in his manner. After taking down some basics of the situation, and offering some first aid, which she declined, he asked Kelly to take a seat in the waiting room.

Forty minutes later WPC Whitworth arrived and led her into an interview room. She took some photos of Kelly's wounded face and explained that at first she wanted an informal chat, and then they'd see about taking things further.

Encouraged to take her time, Kelly gave a synopsis of the history of Lorelei and *him*, including the grimmest of the grim details. All too sadly, WPC Whitworth found none of it shocking, and moreover had attended A&E in failed attempts to get Lorelei to tell the whole truth and press charges.

- "I really thought we'd got her away this time, given her a chance at least, but he's relentless, I can't believe I was so bloody stupid in keeping that postcard!"

- "You weren't to know, don't give yourself anymore of a hard time."

- "That's just it though; I was to know!"

- "Okay look, *he* doesn't have her actual address yet does he? We still have time to intervene."

- "Not yet *he* doesn't, but you don't know *him*, *he'll* stop at nothing, we won't have long!"

- "Okay look, I'm going to go and speak with a colleague to see about an arrest warrant based on your assault charges. If we can add in Lorelei's charges at a later date, so much the better. Whilst the warrant is being sorted, I'll take your formal statement."

With everything very fresh in her mind, Kelly went into great detail regarding her ordeal, and *his* motivations behind it. Whilst the evidence was on her face, no witnesses had been present at the scene, so time would be of the essence if any trace of corroborating evidence was to be found on *him*. With no charges ever having been brought, Kelly had little to back up her claims regarding *his* motivations, past actions, and likely intentions for future actions - for that she needed Debs. She tried calling and leaving messages, but to no avail, discovering later that Debs was embroiled in a particularly arduous shift in A&E all that evening and night.

Whether immediate input from Debs would have resulted in a Warrant Officer hastening their visit to his flat, would forever remain unknown. What is known is that by the time one called at the address the following morning, he had already left for the day. With his car out of action, he was already traversing the rail network in a southerly direction.

Chapter Fifty Four

He had no concrete plan when he had set off for Brighton; just a burning desire eating away at him to reclaim what was his. Brighton isn't that big, he figured, if he hung around long enough and often enough, searching likely places; he'd find her sooner or later, maybe even with the help of the one piece of foresight he had brought with him - a photo of her which he planned to hawk around.

He was on unfamiliar territory as he came out of Brighton Station onto Queens Road, but it did not take him long to find the tourist information office, and acquire a map. He wandered around all the main and likeliest areas to run into someone. He walked up and down the full length of the Palace Pier, his eyes drawn like a dagger to anyone with even the vaguest similarity to Lorelei's physique, hair, demeanour or voice. He wandered around the gardens of the Old Steine, the narrow alleyways of The Lanes, the public gardens around the Brighton Pavilion with its popular café and consequent array of people sitting eating and drinking on the surrounding grass, the Churchill Square indoor shopping centre; all the while hoping to see her, expecting to see her, thinking he had seen her.

Next he headed to Brighton Library, centrally situated in the North Laines. With her love for books, surely she'd frequent there? He approached the main information desk, put on his best smile and said:

- "Oh good day to you, I'm so sorry to trouble you, it's just that I'm really worried about my sister. She went missing three days ago and without her medication she'll be incredibly vulnerable. We're all so worried about her. Do you recognize her by any chance?"

- "I'm sorry to hear that. To be honest I couldn't say that I do recognise her, with all the thousands of faces we see in here. Perhaps you could make up a missing poster with that photo?"

- "That's a great idea! I wouldn't know how to do that though."

- "We can help, don't worry. Sarah, could you please help this poor chap, show him how to scan in his photo of his sister and make up a poster?"

- "Thank you so much, you've no idea what a relief this could turn out to be!"

- 'No problem, happy to help, and I hope you find her soon."

Armed with a dozen posters, complete with his phone number, he put one up on the library notice board, before setting off to place the others at prominent and likely places around town. Satisfied that the legwork would now be done for him; he headed back to the train station just in time to board the 1442 train back to London, and sat down on the first available seat.

Lorelei and Adam cut fine figures as they made their way through the North Laines, giving off as they were, nothing but an air of love and happiness as they laughed and embraced their way to Brighton Station. Adam had already sorted out the tickets and so they headed straight for the platform and soon boarded the 1442 train bound for London. Lorelei was brimming with excitement at the prospect of a trip, and of extended, exclusive time together wherever it was to be, although she did keep fishing for clues, which Adam managed to avoid giving, despite his excitement being of equal measure as the train pulled out.

As the train came to Adam's favourite part of the journey, the views of the Sussex Downs from both sides of the bridge just north of Haywards Heath, which for him summed up the beauty of England; he encouraged Lorelei to look and enjoy them too. She began to gaze out from the window trying to take it all in; first one side then the other, then back again, then the other side again, until few minutes later:

- "This is our stop sweetheart."

- "Hhhmm Gatwick huh? Cunning!"

They got off the train. As it pulled away, Adam was just orientating himself as to where the nearest route up to the terminal was, when she saw *him*. Sitting on the very same train, one carriage back from the one they had just vacated, larger than life, performing *his* standard imitation of a decent human being. It was fleeting, but it was definitely *him*. However much she wanted to try to convince herself she was imagining it; she knew. What she could not be sure of, was whether *he* had seen her. She didn't think so, judging by *his* lack of reaction, but she just couldn't be 100% sure. She knew *he* would find her one day, but this soon!?

- "Are you okay sweetheart? What's the matter? You don't look too well suddenly!"

- "Errr…..I'll be okay…..I just suddenly felt extremely sick that's all. Give me a minute, I'll be okay."

- "Okay well maybe it's just as well we got off."

- "Yeah, definitely!"

- "I'll get you some anti-sickness tablets for the flight."

- "Thanks, and where might we be flying to?"

- "Sorry, no clues."

Adam couldn't keep the secret for much longer though as they headed towards the check-in desk for a Málaga flight, and instead just enjoyed the look of realisation on Lorelei's face.

Chapter Fifty Five

Although she had a passport, Lorelei had barely been abroad, and never to Spain. What to him was an oft repeated journey, took on a new excitement, a whole new significance as everything was the first time with her, enhanced by watching the wonder unfold on her face at various points along the way.

His secret was blown as to destination, but she was still to discover the rest. He had booked her a window seat, meaning she could look down at the snow-capped beauty of the Pyrenees, as the plane crossed from France into Spain, and then enjoy the stark but equally beautiful mountainous landscape at gradually closer quarters, as the plane gently made its descent after passing over Madrid.

Once on the tarmac at Málaga and descending the steps of the plane, the jump in temperature from the 15°C they'd left behind to the sudden 35°C, hit like one of those steaming hot towels they give you in some restaurants for no apparent reason. It was gloriously powerful and an instant joy to both of them.

They were quickly through passport control and soon heading to the train platforms, with Lorelei delighting in the slightest thing, happy to let Adam guide her along. They sat in the sideways seats on the train just for novelty factor for the three short stops to Maria Zambrano, a locally born philosopher and author, he proudly informed her. Their walk across the concourse was briefly interrupted by a visit to the Málaga CF shop to buy her a cap, so that she could look the part if necessary, before heading past the huge information boards, enticingly advertising their romantic departures to Barcelona, Madrid, and Seville.

As they crossed the street to the bus station, they stopped again, this time to enjoy Argentina's equivalent of vegetarian Cornish Pasties at one of Adam's favourite little cafés, before heading to catch 'La Ruta', eastbound along the coast. For many, the extra time taken by this bus, going as it does all the way along the coastline, rather than inland slightly and along the motorway, was an annoying inconvenience; but not for Lorelei and Adam.

The whole journey barely strayed more than a few yards from the beach and even the sea itself, with the waves often splashing the bus like a gentle salty kiss. The scene was added to by the sun shining down above its infinite expanse, resulting in large swathes of shimmering, glistening, dancing water, that dazzled the eyes of anyone who cared to look, or could look. Seeing this natural phenomenon would have been incredible enough, but to experience it together, it took on an enhancement which elevated it to another sphere entirely. It was there for everyone lucky enough to be able to see it; but somehow the universe had put it there right then, just for them.

They walked from the bus stop across the pretty village square of Torrox, with its elegant, wrought iron lamp posts, and it's multicoloured, welcome shade-giving umbrellas, through the narrow, undulating, winding streets, up colourfully tiled stairways, until suddenly Adam stopped outside a particular house with blue ceramic plant pots dotted around its white walls.

- "Bienvenida a casa guapa!"

- "Which means?"

- "Welcome home, beautiful!"

- "Oh wow it's adorable! Have you rented it for our stay?"

- "Well I would have done, and then I thought what's the point?"

- "How do you mean?"

- "Well, what with me owning it and everything."

- "Oh my God Adam!"

They went inside, Adam would show her the rest later, but for now he led her gently up the two flights of stairs to the roof terrace. As they came out onto it, it hit her. The sweeping, whitewashed houses forming the foreground to a panoramic background of rolling hills on either side, framing a stunning mountain range as its centrepiece. Lorelei could do nothing but burst into tears as it washed over and into her.

Chapter Fifty Six

Having failed to find him at home in order to arrest him for assaulting Kelly; the police had not launched a nationwide manhunt, although the warrant remained active. Consequently when he returned from his nice day out at the seaside, he was able to arrive home unimpeded, and feeling fairly satisfied with his day's work.

Kelly was determined that the sense of urgency must not be lost. Having managed to get hold of Debs, the two of them, along with Lorelei's borrowed medical records and old phone, went to see WPC Whitworth, who operated under no illusions.

- "We'll press ahead with charges regarding your case Kelly, although no doubt he'll deny everything; but we're going to need Lorelei fully on board to really get anywhere meaningful. These medical records paint a bleak picture, but without her statements, we're where we've always been. The big question is, will she do it? We know she hasn't before, understandably of course."

- "Right now I can see her wanting to move on with her new found life, but once she realises *he*'s already on her trail; hopefully she'll think again."

- "What about you Debbie, what do you think?"

- "Sadly she knows only too well what *he*'s capable of, and knowing her; she'll want to protect Adam and Kelly more than herself."

- "Okay now look, these incessant text messages are further evidence of his relentlessness; but sadly he's not been stupid enough to actually incriminate himself in any of them. At worst they represent harassment. If we can get that far; 'no further contact' can be included in the terms of an Injunction. First things first; we need to get hold of her."

- "Well worryingly, she's not shown up as online on WhatsApp for a couple of days; neither has Adam." said Kelly, "and their phones say 'out of service'.

- "Okay well I'll have a colleague from Sussex go to their address just to be sure there is nothing untoward, and in the meantime, we'll all keep trying to get hold of them by whatever means we can think of."

The following day a Sussex Policeman duly visited Adam's flat. He did manage at least to ascertain from the neighbour who was kindly watering the plants and feeding the cat, that they had gone abroad for an unspecified period.

Chapter Fifty Seven

For those lucky enough to experience it, there comes a time to a relationship when every associated feeling is simultaneously at its glorious peak. The thrills, tingling anticipation, physical desire, moments of doubt, relief at the quelling of such, delights of discovery and of a mutual experience, of falling in love; turn into the time when both parties are fully in love, with its optimism, its sureties, it's intensity, its sensation of having reached an impossible height, and consequent impossibility of ever coming back down.

Isolated from all other things, this time was Lorelei and Adam in their purest form. They delighted in the mere sight, the mere presence of each other, the merest touch. They made passionate, insatiable love to each other at a second's notice, where no physical act could actually fully portray the intensity of emotional or physical desires. They were ravenous at a banquet.

On days when they were at home, their recovery time eventually moved from the bed to the roof terrace, where the constitution of the feast changed to local olives, avocados, bread, toasted almonds, cheese, red wine, and mangoes.

On other days they went off exploring the surrounding area. They went to Málaga's old town, with its stunning Cathedral, its rabbit warren like narrow cobbled streets, and its tucked away tapas bars. They took the wonderful, slow and scenic train journey to Rhonda, and stayed so long that they had to stay there overnight. They went to Granada, to its breathtaking Alhambra Palace and surrounding gardens, and to its old town, to Córdoba, to its Moorish Mezquita, and its winding Judería.

Then they visited another planet on the outskirts of Nerja. At least that's what it felt like as they explored the vast length and depths of its caves, with its staggering stalactites and stalagmites, formed drop by drop, undiscovered and uninterrupted over millions of years.

There were always challenges though to being that in love in public. Not just due to the sheer strength of their desire to make love, sometimes they felt jealousy at the thought that anyone else could even set eyes upon the person they wanted to be exclusively theirs for the rest of time. That anyone else could see that smile, that look, that beauty, hear their voice, their laughter, even be near them.

Almost every trip out ended in exactly the same way once home. They showered together, slowly gliding a soft sea sponge over ever contour of each others bodies, like they were washing away every look, every brush, every single thing that had touched them before in any way; to cleanse completely so that they could give themselves to and experience each other, in their purest, unsullied form, so that when they reached the bedroom, every taste was their taste alone, every touch the only thing that was touching them, could touch them, or be felt by them.

Chapter Fifty Eight

- "Just look at those stars! So beautiful! Mind blowing really if you try to think about them! Do you believe in God Adam? I don't. Surely it all has to mean something though, this life we live?"

- "That's just it though, what if it actually doesn't have to mean anything? It changes everything."

- "Yeah I guess it would."

- "Totally. Here's how I see it. It's the understandable natural way of things that humankind looks for explanations, tries to make sense of it all, to progress, to make it less baffling, perhaps even a little more predictable, and therefore controllable up to a point, with some sense of purpose. That is not to say though that there actually is a purpose."

- "So we're all just here randomly? I'm not sure I like that idea."

- "Not many people do, that's the thing, but if you think about it, it's actually okay."

- "The world's religious communities disagree with you."

- "Absolutely they do, but I'm with Marx - Religion is the opium of the masses. It's the drug they need to get through. The thing is though, for all that each believes their religion has it right; only one actually could be right, if indeed any of them are."

- "Meaning at least 90% of them have to be living a nonsense!"

- "Pretty much."

- "That's one in the eye for them!" she laughed.

- "Yep, they're okay with it though. They all believe that they're the 10%, and all the time that they do, it serves its function."

- "I bet they'll be bloody furious when they find out they weren't!"

- "Yeah, best not to tell them, although by the time they do find out, they'll be dead anyway."

- "So it all works out!"

- "Yep. Sorted!"

- "So there is a purpose after all. The purpose is to get through believing that there is a purpose, so that when it turns out that there wasn't one it's too late and doesn't matter anyway!"

- "You're way more intelligent than you look, Lorelei! There was me thinking you're all just about the gorgeousness!"

- "You cheeky sod!" she laughed.

- "And look it's totally understandable that the cave people came out of their caves, saw a thunderstorm and feared that they'd angered some God or other. Then they tried to remember what they were doing immediately beforehand, so that they could try to avoid it in the future."

- "Like never again eat a potato on a Tuesday afternoon?"

- "Exactly! And equally, they looked for things to pacify the God, and make the storm stop. So when it turned out that Uggeth the Shepherd happened to be washing a sheep just as the storm subsided, the ritual began of always washing your sheep on a Thursday, which eventually became law."

- "So that's how and why religion started. We've totally cracked it Adam, and it only took us half an hour!"

- "I know! It does make you wonder, why they didn't just ask us before?!"

- "I do think that you and I have purpose though."

- "Which is?"

- "To love each other infinitely, and to give each other as many incredible orgasms as possible!"

- "Do you know what sweetheart, psychologically, even philosophically, I'm totally okay with it!"

- "Shall we head down from the roof terrace first though?"

- "It might be for the best."

Chapter Fifty Nine

They might have stayed there forever, but one month to the day since heading off, they arrived back at Gatwick, tired but fuelled by love's exhilaration.

England looked greener than ever from the train, contrasted with the stark beauty of dry and mountainous Andalucía. As the train slowed down to trundle into Brighton Station, Lorelei turned to Adam and said:

- "Well that was all a bit crap, can we go somewhere good next time?"

- "Yeah sorry, I really must do better."

He felt her embrace and her thank you whispered into his ear. He could also feel her tears, but he didn't want to let go.

They headed down the platform, through the ticket barrier and towards the exit; and there it was. Grubby and dog-eared, but unmistakably her, with *his* number to call if anyone sees her. They both looked at it, Adam a little taken aback at first, Lorelei looking horrified, Adam suddenly realising:

- "I should have told you I'm so sorry."

- "Told me what exactly?"

- "When we left the train at Gatwick, *he* was on it. I caught a glimpse of *him* as it pulled away."
- "Why didn't you say anything?"

- "Because *he* ruins everything, has ruined everything, will ruin everything. I just wanted….just needed….. something for us, something untouched by *his* poison."

-

-

- "It's okay, I understand." he said as he hugged her.

- "I tried to kid myself that it was just coincidence, but this poster does kinda blow that out the water."

They walked home, each with their racing thoughts, interrupted only by the need to tear down two more posters from café windows along the way. Once home, they put their phones on charge and turned them on for the first time in a month. Lorelei's phone especially, all but melted as it threw up the countless messages and missed calls from Kelly, Debs, and WPC Whitworth. Consequently it was not long before they were fully up to speed, and a trip to the coast was hastily arranged for Kelly and Debs.

- "Next time you suddenly bugger off, would you mind telling us!?"

- "Sorry, that was my fault Kelly, Lorelei didn't really know what was happening until we got to Gatwick."

- "So how was it?"

- "Oh Debs it was so ……"

- "It's okay, I can already see how it was!"

- "Right down to business. The moment has come Lorelei. It's comeuppance time and fucking long overdue it is too!"

- "I want it, I so do, but I'm terrified Kells!"

- "I know hun, we all do and are, but look, we've never been in this strong a position. *He* thinks *he's* so clever and untouchable, covering *his* tracks, but *he* properly fucked up this time!"

- "Plus hun, *he* doesn't know that we've all teamed up to join up the dots. I've your medical records from all the hospital visits and your old phone messages, we've the recent assault on Kelly, and now these bloody posters, the cheek of *him*! It will all tie in if you're prepared to give full statements, plus WPC Whitworth knows the score and is keen to nail him."

- "I'm so sorry Kells!"

- "It's okay hun, at least it will be if it leads to *his* conviction!"

- "What do you think Adam?"

- "It's totally up to you sweetheart, you have to go with your instincts, but we're all here to support you all the way, whatever you decide."

- "I want to make statements, really I do, I'm just so……..what if *he* worms out of it as usual?"

- "WPC Whitworth thinks we'll get *him*. Plus she said she'll throw in a conspiracy to pervert the course of justice for your so-called car crash, which she said will go down like a lead balloon with the judge."

- "Okay Debs, just….. just give me…. a little thinking time….plus I'd like to speak to that policewoman about a few things first."

The next day, Lorelei had a long, fairly informal chat over the phone with WPC Whitworth, in a bid to allay as many of her concerns as possible, the biggest of which being that there would be a her word against *his* element to the whole thing.

Whilst giving no guarantees, the WPC did exude confidence regarding the chances of a conviction, notoriously tricky though that can prove to be.

By the end of the call, one conviction had been secured, and rather than have to travel to London; it was agreed that Lorelei would go to Brighton Police Station to give her full statement, whilst PCW Whitworth was to take one from Debs at her local station, backed up by plenty of medical evidence.
Adam was very supportive and a great comfort, but he could not help thinking that he was just helplessly waiting in the wings, whilst trying his best to keep his nervousness under wraps for Lorelei's sake, as they went for brunch in one of their favourite cafés:

- "It's the right thing sweetheart, the best thing, really the only thing. You'll sleep easier once *he*'s safely locked up."

- "Yeah, let's hope it turns out that way."

- "It will. You, Debs, and Kelly make a formidable team. I wouldn't mess with you!"

- "Have you the vaguest idea how much I love you Adam?"

- "Well if it's even 6% as much as I love you, it's already a ridiculous amount!"

- "It could even surpass 6% by my calculations."

- "I'm happy with that!"

Chapter Sixty

Lorelei entered John Street police station at the appointed time. Although Adam had come along to lend morale support, when the time came to go into the interview room, Lorelei said:

- "If I'm to do this Adam, it needs to be alone; I don't want you to hear all this."

- "Okay sweetheart, but just know that I'm right outside if you need me."

Lorelei went in with WPC Brownley, who had been briefed by WPC Whitworth.

- "Thanks for coming in Lorelei, and well done, I know this isn't easy for you, but you'll feel better afterwards for having done it."

- "Let's hope so."

- "To make the process a little easier, I'm just going to let you talk, and Clara here will scribe everything, but don't worry, you can have a good read through before you sign it, okay?"

- "Okay, thanks."

Lorelei described the first time he hit her, six months into their relationship, after a night in a pub with friends. How he barely seemed to move, how she'd felt the blow land squarely on her lips, the searing pain, the sensation of blood, and the taste of it.

How in great detail, one year later, following a further five similar incidents, the car accident had unfolded, resulting in her losing her baby:

- *"Did you notice I was sick this morning?"*

- *"Yeah you never could handle your drink!"*

- *"I hadn't been drinking."*

- *"Dodgy take away?"*

- *"No I don't think so."*

His expression changed.

- *"Wait a minute, you are on the pill aren't you? You better fucking be on the pill!"*

- *"I told you I had to come off of it, it was making me feel ill."*

- *"Well you better not be fucking pregnant, that's all I need some kid weighing me down!"*

- *"Don't get angry, but I think I already am."*

He took his foot off of the accelerator.

- *"You stupid bitch! Well you better make plans to get rid of it then, I'm not having some brat hanging around costing me a fucking fortune."*

- *"I haven't decided whether I want to get rid of it yet."*

He pulled into the approaching layby and came to a halt. Her last words were still hanging in the air, as he got out, walked around the car, and pulled open her door.

- *"Oh **you** haven't decided yet? Is that fucking right?"*

How she only had time to utter "Please don't........" as he grabbed hold of her and dragged her out of the car, and onto the cold tarmac of the pitch black layby. Then he began to kick her. He kicked her in the face, then he kicked her in the stomach as she cried out in pain, then he kicked her in the stomach twice more, then he kicked her in the back as she tried to turn to protect her stomach, and then he kicked her in the back of the head. It was then that she lost consciousness, just briefly, but then he kicked her again which brought her round, but she feigned that it hadn't.

How he began to pace around the layby, seemingly unsure what to do next. She didn't move. A few cars passed by, but she was hidden from view in the darkness and on the far side of the car. Suddenly he made up his mind. He dragged her back into the passenger seat, propped her up, got back in the car, and drove off.

He waited until he was a good distance from the layby, veered off of the road sharply, and making sure her side would take the worst of it; crashed into a huge tree. She lost consciousness again.

How his subsequent story to the police about swerving to avoid an animal was a complete lie, but that she'd been too terrified of reprisals to speak up at the time.

How she'd ended up in A&E on Christmas Night with a swollen skull, numerous cuts and bruises, and five cracked ribs, telling Debbie who'd attended to her, and the police, that she fell down some stairs after drinking too much.

How three months later on a Sunday morning when he had been out until the small hours the night before, she'd crept about their flat trying her utmost not to make any undue noise, made herself a cup of tea, and sat down on the sofa to savour its reviving sips. Upon finishing her tea, she returned to the kitchen yearning for another. The jar was empty and so she reached up to a cupboard in search of replenishments. As she opened the cupboard door, the spaghetti jar came tumbling out with just enough velocity to crack on the edge of the worktop, during its journey towards the floor where it smashed upon landing, She took a sharp intake of breath and held it there; and then she heard him get up.

Within the few seconds it took for him to arrive in the kitchen, she had already snatched the dustpan and brush and was on her knees sweeping up the numerous pieces of glass. He grabbed her hair from behind, twisted it around with his fist, and with great force pushed her face down into the already half full dustpan, held it there for a few seconds, before dismissively letting go. He then took himself back to bed, without saying a word.

How he'd all but killed her, holding a pillow tightly over her face, how she tried to finish the job with the pills she'd become dependent upon. How she'd ended up in rehab, but really just needed to be anywhere away from him. How he had terrorised her every moment, if not with actual violence; with the threat or the prospect of it. How she had distanced herself from her family through the shame of it.

Where they had been direct or indirect witnesses, the statements of Kelly and Debs dove tailed perfectly with Lorelei's, and a further Warrant for his arrest for assault, conspiracy to pervert the course of justice, and insurance fraud, for good measure, was duly issued.

Chapter Sixty One

Warrant Officer Hill had a busy day ahead, which was nothing out of the ordinary in itself. He had eight arrests to make, some more concerning than others. In consultation with his colleague, Warrant Officer Hopkins; it was decided to leave his arrest until last. Given the nature of the allegations, it was felt that he may well resist arrest in a less than calm, possibly violent manner.

He had been planning to go home after work, briefly, before heading out to a pub. However around mid-afternoon his phone rang:

- "Hello?"

- "Oh hi, I'm ringing about your poster in the library……about your missing sister…..I think I may have seen her a few times."

- "Oh my god really?! Where?"

- "In my local café, Munch, it's in the North Laines. I can't be sure it's her, but it could be."

- "What's your name?"

- "Erm….Kirsty."

- "Thank you so much Kirsty, you're a lifesaver!"

With the seven previous arrests having taken longer than anticipated, it was 6.54pm by the time Warrant Officers Hill and Hopkins arrived at his flat. They rang the bell and waited patiently, but there was no sign of a response or any activity. After several more attempts they decided to call it a long day, and mark him down as the first job for the next morning.

He was greeted by the sound of seagulls as he came out of Brighton Station and walked down Queens Road that evening. It didn't take him long to find the Munch café, which by this time had closed for the night. He was pleased to note though that another café, Scoff, was situated diagonally opposite.

As Adam held Lorelei closely in bed that Friday evening, on a very rare occasion when they didn't make wild, passionate love; he was settling down nicely in his cosy single room, in a B&B very nearby.

Chapter Sixty Two

He was up bright and early the following morning, partly due the squawking of hungry seagulls, and partly due to his own hunger. By the time Warrant Officers Hill and Hopkins were paying their second unsuccessful visit to his flat; he was already ensconced at a table by the window in Scoff, enjoying a nourishing breakfast. As the minutes ticked past, breakfast moved on to just coffee, which moved on to another, as he bided his time with uncharacteristic patience. As coffee turned into lunch, he began to lose hope, but he wasn't for moving, not yet.

By 2pm, having already started to be regarded as part of the fixtures and fittings, he decided to call it a day. A day at the seaside in late summer - not too shabby. Perhaps he'd even give that Kirsty a call? He'd keep his eyes peeled though.

The following morning, there he was again, this time for Sunday brunch. He'd only been waiting a little over an hour when, is it..... could it be…...it is! Who the fuck is that with her though!? So much for the idea of sweet talking her back!

The urge to run over was strong, almost overwhelming, but he held it together, just.

- "What are you going to have sweetheart?"

- "Oh I think two bagels, one with avocado, tomato and olive oil, and the other with goat's cheese, caramelised onion, and pine nuts."

- "So the usual then?"

- "Yeah!"

They chatted over their brunch; something that Lorelei seemingly found increasingly difficult.

- "Are you okay sweetheart?" What's wrong?"

- "Nothing, I'm okay, I think……I just feel….it's probably nothing……ignore me."

- "Feel what though?"

- "Just a sense of….. something….. not being….quite right."

- "We'll make it right sweetheart, come here."

He paid his bill, so that he could leave quickly and unnoticed at any chosen moment. His view was somewhat obscured, but not so obscured that he had failed to see that hug. His fists subconsciously clenched repeatedly, his breathing shallowed. Eventually they got up to leave, he held back just a few seconds to see in which direction they headed, then set off. The street was just busy enough for him to hang back just far enough, unnoticed, following, seething.

Their address was not to be given away just yet though, as they appeared to be going for a stroll. They cut through the Royal Pavilion Gardens, and out across the Old Steine lawns. He had to be careful not to suddenly close the gap, as they stopped to wait to cross at various pedestrian crossings, and then quickly speed up again to catch the flashing green man lest he lose them. They cut through the coach station and out onto the seafront, he bristled at every hold, every laugh, every kiss, every touch; and headed towards the Palace Pier. With only one way back off again, he decided it was a pointless risk to follow them on there, so he held back near the entrance, resisting the thought of waiting until they were far enough out to sea, before accidentally tripping on a wooden slat, careering into her boyfriend, and knocking him over the railings.

After an hour's wait behind a large A-board, they reappeared amongst the increasing throng of locals and tourists, and headed back towards the Old Steine, this time going the longer way around, before meandering through the Pavilion Gardens again towards the North Laines.

Finally they made the shape of people nearing home, as their pace slowed, and keys were fumbled for. Not yet, not yet, got to time it just right, close the gap, wait for the key in the door, closer, closer, closer; go!

He sprinted as silently as he could, in not so much a red mist, as a volcanic fog, leaping up the stairs to their front door just as she turned to close it. He saw her see *him*, barely having time to express the horror as she tried desperately to close it before *he* got through it; but she was too late.

He saw the man turn from his position of having one foot on the first stair. He leapt over the already prostrate Lorelei whom he had floored as she attempted to close the door, and caught him a blow to the side of his head, swiftly followed by a second which landed squarely on the bridge of his nose, breaking it in dramatic, graphic fashion, as his nose released blood like a water balloon releases its contents, instantly changing the colour of his blue t-shirt. He felt the unsteady man try to grab hold of *him* as he unleashed another blow to his stomach, and watched as he fell breathlessly to the floor.

He felt Lorelei jump onto *his* back, grabbing *him* around the neck, and the piercing scream in *his* ear of "Leave him alone!" He smashed her against the wall repeatedly, until he felt her go limp and her grip loosen as she fell to the floor. He saw the man try to get up in a bid to reach Lorelei, which he curtailed with a kick to the side of his head before he was even on his feet. The man appeared to lose consciousness at which point he launched a frenzied assault of kicks and punches to any and every accessible area. Only his own breathlessness stopped him. Then he turned his attention fully to Lorelei. He slapped her around the face repeatedly until she came to.

- "What the fuck do you think you're doing, eh!? I told you, I told you, you can leave when I fucking say so! And who the fuck is that sack of shit? He doesn't look too pretty now does he?"

- "Just leave us alone……let go….I'd rather be dead ….it's over….. however many times you hit me….. it's over."

- "I'll fucking decide that, and you knew that you dumb bitch."

He began to punch and kick her repeatedly. Neither would ever know for how long *he* might have continued, because the nearing, distinctive sound of sirens interrupted *his* progress and *he* scurried out the door; but not before the kindly neighbour had a good look at his contorted face.

By the time the Police and an ambulance had arrived, and attempts were made to stem Lorelei and Adam's blood; he was already wending his way through the narrow streets towards Brighton Station, having turned his blood stained jacket inside out, ready to jump aboard the first train to anywhere else.

Chapter Sixty Three

He was frantic. He knew he had completely lost control of himself, and more importantly for him; the situation.

That there was already a warrant out for his arrest may have come as a surprise beforehand; but that there would be one out now, would not. He'd have to lay low for a while, a good while, but there'd be things he'd need in order to accomplish that; things that were at home.

With eyes nervously peeled at every stop, every passenger leaving or entering the train, he made his way back to London. Deliberately though, he approached London via a couple of diversions en route. The first train he had jumped on, happened to be heading east to Ore. He got off just before the end in Hastings, and waited the twenty five minutes for the next train to Charing Cross, this time getting off two stops before the end at London Bridge. From there he walked the thirty five minute walk towards his flat, trying to look natural, but failing as his eyes were everywhere at once. As he approached his street, he stopped just before the corner and slowly peered round. Sure enough, a police car could be seen parked near his flat. Bastards! Don't they have anything better to do? Deciding that they wouldn't stay there indefinitely; he slipped away through a few back streets, careful not to be on any obvious route to or from the police station, before finding a pub that he had never been in before, to have a few drinks, bide his time, and relax.

It was past 11pm by the time he abandoned the sanctuary of the pub. He had contained himself enough to not be too drunk, but had had just enough to feel nicely so. Whilst he felt some regret at the circumstances in which he had put himself; as he walked through the back streets, he couldn't help but smile at the thought of the punishments he had dished out; the vengeance he had exacted on that bitch and her prick of a new boyfriend.

As his road neared, he slowed his pace. He peered around the same corner as earlier, and just as assumed; the patrol car had gone. Maintaining caution, he briskly approached his front door and entered. Tempting as it was to fall into bed after his busy day, he quickly set about packing some essentials. A hidden stash of money for a rainy day, clothing, spare phone charger, headphones. He was just about ready to set off, when he saw headlights reflected upon the back of the curtains, heard a car engine, then a car engine stopping. The light, the light! He hit the light switch as quickly as he could, but it was too late. WPC Whitworth, having made a point of volunteering for the mission, and a colleague, having anticipated this scenario; had seen the light, and had seen the light go off.

He grabbed his duffle bag and set off at pace. Whether he could make it to the front door and off into the night before they got out of their car and reached it; he wasn't about to find out. The only other option was to head out from the back garden, and over enough garden walls until he could access a different street. The only problem with that was that only the occupier of the ground floor flat had any access to the garden. With neither the time nor desire for a polite knock on the door, he kicked it through on the fourth attempt. As no one was home, he met no resistance as he headed for the back door and let himself out just in time to hear the main front door bell ringing, and its door being knocked at quick intervals. By the time an occupier of one of the other flats had let the police in, and the kicked-through front door had been discovered; he was away into the night.

Via several back streets until he felt bold enough to come out onto a main road, he managed to flag down a black cab, and using the research already undertaken whilst in the pub; had the cab driver take him to St Pancras Station. From there he just made the 0015 to Derby, breathing a huge sigh of relief as it pulled out. It would mean four hours on a bench once there, until the early morning train to Leeds, and onto Edinburgh; but it was a long way from anyone who was looking for him, and nowhere anyone would especially think of doing so. As he settled down in his seat, and the adrenaline from the franticness subsided; a smile trundled away into the night.

Chapter Sixty Four

No one had been smiling during the intervening ten hours at the Royal Sussex County Hospital, where Lorelei and Adam had arrived in a hurry. Lorelei, in non medical terms, was in a bad way, but conscious; Adam was a lot worse, and was not.

Once the blood flow was stemmed in both, they were taken individually for x-rays and scans. It transpired that Lorelei had mostly suffered severe external and internal bruising, but with a fractured collar bone, a fractured wrist, five cracked ribs, and a fractured shoulder for good measure.

Adam had suffered 78 separate blows, resulting in a fractured skull in three places, a broken nose, a fractured jaw, lost five teeth, eight cracked ribs, severe bruising to his sacroiliac joint, and all over his torso, and internal bleeding in his kidneys so severe that emergency surgery was required to stop it.

After much attention, Lorelei was deemed to be well enough to be admitted to a normal ward, but Adam needed to be admitted to the Intensive Care Unit. He was still to regain consciousness at the point when a general anaesthetic was administered for his surgery, so Lorelei had an anxious wait for news. As painful as any movement was, she kept wheeling herself in a wheelchair to the ICU, and peering in through the glass in the doors trying to see him, only to be wheeled back to her ward again, told to rest and that she would be informed the moment there was any change to report.

WPC Whitworth was also anxious for news, and was free to be more proactive in her pursuit of it. She had orchestrated a press release, including a photo of *him*, supplied by Kelly, asking for the public to contact the police immediately upon any sighting. She had also circulated the photo to all national police forces, requesting immediate arrest and contact. If *he* was to be on the run; she didn't want it to be too easy for *him*.

She had figured that a train may well have been the best and quickest way out of Dodge that night, and so she spent the afternoon of the next day on a mini tour of nearby mainline railway stations, narrowed down to Euston, London Bridge, and Kings Cross/St Pancras; reviewing CCTV footage, figuring that with such a short window of time in question, she'd stand a chance.

It took a while, but there *he* was, boarding the 0015 to Derby, which also provided some still shots to circulate to colleagues nationally, as well as to those in Derby. Reviews later that day in Derby soon ascertained that he had boarded a train bound for Leeds at 0620.

That evening, from the comfort of a B&B in Leeds, he was relaxing in his room, when a news item on the TV jolted him out of such pleasant comfort. With his mind going into overdrive he gathered up his things at a frantic pace. Whether the B&B owner was also watching the news at that moment, and would recognise him if so, could only be ascertained once it was too late, and so he was out of the door and gone before the weather forecaster could clear their throat in preparation. Once outside he had to think quickly - nowhere with lots of people, stay in the dark, nowhere with CCTV, nowhere with a TV. With it now being past 11pm, options were narrowing - no train stations, the coach station maybe? Did they have CCTV too? Probably, too risky. How about the stop after the coach station? There's usually a stop or two as a coach heads out of town.

So with the hood zipped right up to the top, and his head down; he set off wandering through Leeds city centre. After a short while he came across one of those 'You are here' signposts, which enabled him to figure out how to get close, but not too close to the coach station, and the likely route north a coach would take out of town.

It was another anxious half an hour, before he reached what he figured was the first stop after the coach station, and examined the timetable behind the perspex. Lady Luck appeared to be with him again in the form of a 1.10am overnight coach to Edinburgh, being due in fifty minutes. He therefore removed himself from such a conspicuous spot, and hovered in the darkness of the back streets to wait out the time.

Sure enough, at 1.09am the coach approached and he boarded it, not just with no questions asked, but with friendly, jovial banter with the driver. He settled down in his seat, and as the adrenaline calmed in his veins again, he drifted off to sleep.

Chapter Sixty Five

Sleeping rather less serenely, Adam remained in the ICU, and was the cause of plenty of concern. His vital signs were steadily improving, but he had still not awoken despite the fact that the anaesthetic had long since left his system.

After much persistence Lorelei had achieved permission to spend time at his bedside. Whilst she was pleased about this change in policy, she could not help thinking that it was a sign that the doctors were failing in all their attempts at waking him, and were hoping as a last resort that he would respond to her.

They did not have to wait too long to find out, as no sooner had she touched him, caressed him, spoken to him, she sensed him respond, like he was trying to lean towards her, to be with her. His attempts to open his eyes were a mere flicker at first, his attempts at moving just a slight squeeze of her hand, his attempts at speaking just a faint movement of his lips; but there was no doubting it; he knew she was there and was yearning for her.

With her own injuries, it hurt her terribly to move, but nonetheless she leant over his bed and hugged him as best she could through the bandages, the plaster of Paris, and the tubes; and whispered in his ear:

- "I'm so so sorry my darling, I love you so much, please wake up now and be okay, please."

Very gradually the flickers turned into the opening of his eyes, the slight squeezes into caresses, and the faint movements into sounds.

- "Are you in there darling?"

- "I….. think..so. Am…..I. still..Adam?"

- "I bloody well hope so!"

Three days later Adam had improved sufficiently to be moved out of the ICU, and onto a small ward of six beds, laid out in two rows of three. With the binary gender policy a thing of the past, and thanks to a reconfiguration by a kindly nurse; Lorelei was occupying the bed adjacent to his. When she was not directly at his bedside, they were just close enough to hold hands across the intervening space and talk in whispers.

- "I never meant for you to get hurt too."

- "I always knew it was a possibility, sweetheart."

- "I know but still…."

- "If every blow I took meant one less for you, it was worth it."

-

-

- "You might be the best thing ever in the history of things Adam."

- "Well if I am it's only because you make me be that way."

- "What are we going to do…. about….. everything?"

- "We're going to send that sick pig to prison, and if every bruise extends *his* sentence, it will also have been totally worth it."

Chapter Sixty Six

Lorelei was discharged from hospital a week ahead of Adam, and reluctantly went home without him, although returned for daily visits.

Upon speaking with WPC Whitworth, and learning that *he* was still at large, she felt an almost paralysing sense of terror, only quelled, and only somewhat, by the arrival of Kelly, who did her best to reassure her that even *he* wouldn't be so reckless as to return to Brighton any time soon. It didn't stop them putting blunt instruments by the door though, and by their beds.

Whilst the circumstances could hardly have been worse, the week they spent together in Adam's flat, did provide an opportunity for them to spend proper time together for the first time since *he* had entered Lorelei's life with all the care and consequences of a Kansas tornado. They sat up long into the night, talking of their distant and more recent past, but could not avoid coming back to the present.

- "I'll never forgive myself for that fucking postcard!"

- "There is nothing to forgive, you didn't do anything wrong."

- "They bloody well better catch that evil pig soon!"

- "They will sooner or later…I hope. WPC Whitworth is confident that *he* can't run forever."

- "Where could *he* go? Who'd have *him*?

- "Sadly *he's* not stupid enough to go anywhere obvious. *He* was last traced in Leeds."

- "Let's hope *he* carries on north to that massive sea and keeps going."

Debs had managed to get a day off, and had called ahead to say she was on her way down to see them, thus avoiding the risk of a heart attack inducing sudden ringing of Adam's doorbell. She did first though pay an unexpected call to Adam, to see how he was doing personally and professionally. The staff let her browse through his notes, which reported all the initial grave concerns, and the subsequent improvements in his condition. Satisfied that there was nothing untoward that was being held back from the patient or their kin, as can sometimes be the case; she headed off to see Adam.

Although Debs was more than used to seeing such things, and worse besides; she was still taken aback by seeing someone she cared about so much, in quite the state she found him; professional distancing can only get you so far. Adam was drowsy from his pain killers, but that did not stop his extremely bruised face lighting up at the sight of Debs.

- "Well I must say Adam you've never looked better!"

- "Thanks Debs, yeah makes sense, I've never felt better."

- "I've warned you before about those Spanish Razor Clams; just coz they look like asparagus….!

- "I'll be sure to avoid them next time. How are you Debs?"

- "I'm grand Ad, how are you more to the point?"

- "I'm getting there hun. Please thank whichever one of your colleagues invented these painkillers though. Have you seen Lorelei?"

- "Not yet, I thought I'd get seeing you over with first."

- "It really is a blessing for us all that you chose nursing Debs."

- "I know, I know."

- "Please tell her how much I love her when you do, won't you?"

- "I will and when you're through malingering, you can tell her yourself."

- "All heart!.........I'm sorry I couldn't stop *him* Debs....to protect her....I tried.....it just all happened so quickly....so suddenly.....one minute we were having a lovely....."

- "Don't Ad please. Don't beat yourself up any worse. Everyone has been trying and failing to protect her from *him* for a long time now. *He*'s an animal, and a viscous, spiteful, venomous one. *He*'ll get *his* comeuppance, it's only a matter of time."

201

- "It's the waiting in the meantime though."

- "Yeah, I know."

- "I don't suppose there's any news?"

- "No *he*'s long gone, but hopefully the net is closing in, and any chance of Lorelei's previous accounts not being believed should be long gone too."

- "God I hope they catch *him* soon!"

- "Yeah and then that *he*'s sharing a cell with two 25 stone wrestlers with a penchant for swine."

- "Hahahaha ahhhh don't Debs it hurts my ribs."

- "Sorry Ad, couldn't resist. Right, I'm off to see your beloved. Let's hope she looks better than you!"

- "She usually does. Thanks Debs. Lovely to see you."

- "Lovely to see you Ad. Hopefully you'll make more of an effort next time; I'm really not sure about that gown on you."

- "I just threw on the first thing I could find. It was either this or that bed flannel."

- "I'll be grateful for small mercies then."

She kissed him on the forehead and squeezed his hand as gently as she could, before heading off. Had she turned around, she'd have seen Adam's eyes well up at the thought of her and Kelly; in stark contrast to the opposite influence they have to suffer. He began to wish that *he* was suffering, suffering terribly; and then he began to picture it.

Chapter Sixty Seven

In spite of recent events, Lorelei, Kelly, and Debs managed to enjoy an evening together, such was the irrevocable bond that had formed between them. They chatted long into the evening over wine and a grazing dinner, including large quantities of Spanish olives born out of Lorelei's new found love for them, and to where their taste took her back.

She went into great detail regaling them with so many wonderful tales of their time in Spain, how they had reached such a level of feeling, understanding, and connection, that words had almost become unnecessary, meaningless even, so that at times they felt no need to speak; just be. How the contrast from her first relationship to her second, was so stark as to have gone beyond ridiculous.

Eventually, inevitably, the subject of *his* still roaming free to poison life on earth with *his* bile came up.

- "It seems *his* heading north was just a random act as part of getting away then."

- "I guess so Debs, *he*'s no family up there as far as we know."

- "It's hard to imagine *him* having too many friends, anywhere!"

- "Wait…..unless……I can't quite…"

- "What is it Lorelei hun?"

- "There was this old school friend *he* used to mention, back in the day when *he* was capable of civilised conversation. John… James…Jimmy! Yeah, it was Jimmy I'm sure of it. *He* used to take the piss saying he'd ended up as a sheep shagger in the Scottish Highlands."

- "It'd certainly be a remote enough place to hide!"

- "Yeah Debs, and *he* has to be somewhere with someone. I can't see *him* putting up with sleeping rough."

- "Let's tell WPC Whitworth. Anything is worth a try. It wouldn't take too much detective work on her part checking old school records and that."

- "We'll call her in the morning, first thing, well first thing once we're up." said Kelly.

- "And had coffee." added Debs

Chapter Sixty Eight

They all felt a little better and more hopeful once they'd made the call to WPC Whitworth, who promised to act upon it with immediate effect.

Adam in the meantime, was just stirring again in his hospital bed for the second time, following the rude awakening at dawn endured by all inpatients, for no good reason he could think of.

Less than an hour later, she called back to inform them that she had found a record of a James Blay, a former pupil of Finchley Secondary School, who fitted the bill year wise; and it was now a question of awaiting a call back from her Scottish counterparts.

The response to WPC Whitworth came at its own pace, as the Scottish Highlands are not known for having thousands of Policemen roaming the hills. When it was received, it confirmed that a James Blay was indeed the owner of a Croft on a small Island next to the Isle of Skye.

It felt like a long shot, like it could be a hiding to nothing, but at the same time all of WPC Whitworth's instincts were telling her that *he* was there, and she wanted to make the arrest personally. Having sought permission from her superior officer, and on the strict condition that she go accompanied by Scottish Officers; she hastily arranged travel plans, involving a direct flight from Heathrow which takes 1 hour and 40 minutes, and a short boat ride.

Torn between wanting to give hope, and not wanting to falsely get hopes up, she decided to tell Lorelei simply that things were progressing well, and that she'd stay in touch. She set off for the airport with a steely determination in her stride, and the excitement stemming from the promise of bringing *him* in to face the music. Upon landing in Skye, she was duly met by two Scottish Highland police officers, one male, one female, the latter of which she had already given the rundown to over the phone.

It was only a short drive to the coast where they would take a small boat over to Rona and then go by foot to the Croft in question. McTavish had been running this small but essential service for as long as he could remember, and greeted the officers with respect and an affable smile. In a matter of ten minutes they were coming into dock at a small bay. They couldn't say how long they'd be, but McTavish assured them that he'd be back and forth like a boomerang all day, so they'd not have to wait long.

The officers made their way over the rugged, stark landscape, following a well trodden path, and WPC Whitworth was positively tingling with nervous anticipation at the prospect of seeing *his* face as they finally caught *him*, and the subsequent ability to call Lorelei and Adam with the news.

After traversing for 15 minutes, smoke could be seen coming from the chimney of the Croft house, a little distance ahead in a small valley. As it hoved into close view and taking no chances, the officers spread out a little to cover any back or side exits, and approached stealthily, with truncheons drawn.

WPC Whitworth took the initiative and tapped on the front door.

- "Just a wee moment!" came a voice from within.

True to his word, in a very short time, the bolts on the door could be heard drawing back, and a man opened the door looking rather surprised.

- "James Blay?"

- "That's me. To what do I owe this unexpected pleasure? I don't get too many visitors in my part of the world."

- "That's precisely why we're here James...."

- "Please call me Jimmy."

- "Okay Jimmy, we're wondering if you've a visitor staying with you right now?"

- "Just me and the sheep."

- "Would you mind if we double checked that Jimmy?"

- "Sure no worries. I'll not ask if you've a warrant." he replied as he stepped aside.

- "And I'll not ask what that suspicious smell is, emanating from the ashtray."

- "Fair enough."

Whilst her fellow officers kept vigil outside, WPC Whitworth went inside for a good mooch around. Nothing stood out as particularly telling, and it soon became obvious that *he* was not there. She was about to leave and resign herself to disappointment, and to a crisis of faith in her instincts, when she spotted it.

There looking innocuous enough, draped over the back of a chair, was a black jacket, all but covering another jacket, which upon closer inspection was in fact inside out. Upon even closer inspection, it soon became apparent that it was not inside out by pure happenstance - it had dried blood on it, lots of dried blood.

- "What have we here Jimmy?"

- "Err…. just an old jacket."

- "An old jacket which might just belong to a mutual friend of ours?"

- "And who might that be?'

- "Oh I don't know, someone wanted on several counts of GBH perhaps?"

- "Who's that then?"

- "I tell you what Jimmy, I'll remove this jacket and have the blood forensically examined. If it turns out to be sheep's blood, I'll bring it back to you personally, and dry cleaned; but if it turns out to belong to the victims of said GBH, I'll be back with an arrest warrant for you for attempting to pervert the course of justice. Deal?

- "Okay, okay, look I didn't want him here, he just turned up out of the blue. I'd not seen or heard from him since school."

- "And where might *he* be now?"

- "I don't know, he left."

- "And when was this?"

- "About fifteen minutes before you arrived."

The officers got back to the dock as quickly as they could, hampered by the terrain, and frustrated that there was no one to radio ahead to, but as suspected, the only person who could have possibly called ahead to warn of their arrival; had already left with his passenger list of one.

Chapter Sixty Nine

WPC Whitworth's Scottish counterparts initiated the next episode in the game of cat and mouse. They weren't about to close any borders for him, but by the time something meaningful had been put in place, there was no sign of him on the Isle of Skye.

When WPC Whitworth was left with no choice but to call Lorelei with the news; it felt like she was the perpetrator of another vicious blow. Lorelei promised to call her if she thought of anywhere else *he* might possibly go, however vague; and WPC Whitworth promised to keep searching relentlessly, however long it took.

A few days later Adam was finally allowed home. A home that now felt like a very different place, but one in which their love could do nothing but grow. The suffering and the post traumatic effects caused by such a major, horrendous event, could well have torn them apart, either quickly or in slow, torturous increments; but it bonded them all the more, and only strengthened their mutual desire to take care of each other. They even still found ways to make love despite their numerous injuries; albeit with a somewhat restricted repertoire. Artistic impression scores would have been well down on their extraordinarily high norm, but hugely offset by the increased scores for technical merit.

The weeks drifted by, still without news. WPC Whitworth, true to her word, worked tirelessly, accessing CCTV pictures where she could in the hope of a fresh clue. One morning during elevenses with a colleague, he joked that she would find him in the last place she'd think of looking, on the basis that at that point, she'd stop looking. Her face suddenly changed.

- "What? What is it?"

- "Or maybe the first!"

- "The first?"

- "Yeah all this time, *he*'ll have been assuming that we'd be thinking *he*'d never dare to go home, but maybe….. just maybe…….one daring trip to a 24 hour supermarket…..one taxi ride fully laden with longlife supplies at 4am……keep the lights off….. don't move the curtains…."

It didn't take too much work in finding out who the electricity supplier was, and having done so, she had an interesting conversation about average energy use at the property. Saying nothing to Lorelei other than asking to borrow her old downstairs front door key, and retrieving it from her; she gathered a selected team together, determined to do it right this time. A search warrant was sought and achieved to go along with the arrest warrant.

With everything set, the team set off at 0345 in plain clothes, and plain sirenless cars, with four officers per car, seven of them male, none of them in the best of moods given the time of the assignment. Two were to stay outside by the front door, two were to be stationed at the site of his previous exit, leaving four to perform the meet and greet duties. WPC Whitworth was determined to be one of the four.

In total silence the team gathered in position. The four stealthily let themselves in through the main front door, and slowly climbed the stairs to the first floor. They had no plans to knock and spoil the surprise, and had brought the appropriate blunt instrument along with them. Upon a silent finger count of three, the battering ram swung back and then through the door, breaking the door and the silence in equal measure. As the four poured inside, two shone very bright torches, illuminating the scene in an instant. Armed also with prior knowledge, they all headed for the one bedroom; and there he was.

By the time he had sleepily given countenance to what was happening, and even begun to reach for the baseball bat he had placed by the bed; they were upon him. In the ensuing melee, *he* received a brutally hard blow to the scrotum, thus ending any remaining resistance, occurring as WPC Whitworth landed flush upon it, knee first on the bed with all her weight; which the report would later go on to describe as 'an unfortunate accident in the act of the arrest of a known flight risk'. The report failed to mention though that during the agony, through the gasping for air, he had heard:

- "*So* sorry to have woken you, viscous scumbag, it's just that what with you heading off to prison for ages and everything; we wanted it to start as soon as possible, you know, the sooner you start….."

Lorelei awoke to a message on her phone, simply saying:

'Got *him*!'

Chapter Seventy - 4 years, 10 months, and 14 days until *his* release

Emily was becoming increasingly concerned about Adam. He only seemed to come alive when in pursuit of a perpetrator. At other times he seemed withdrawn, lost within. He would scour the newspapers, the TV news, in search of his next project, passing time. Once it got to the latter part of the evening though, and she had pulled him towards her in bed, she could physically feel the tension dissipate from his body, as every part of her touched every part of him. Any sense of the need for variety in the commencement of their love making, was non-existent. The variety came in any number of forms once things had progressed, with nothing out of bounds; but first there was to relax, to melt into him with her caresses, to feel the exquisiteness, the alleviation of her needs, all over her skin.

Adam was not the only one with an eye on an ever-reducing countdown - Jonathan was due out of prison in 18 months, assuming good behaviour. How compliant he would be with the Restraining Order that was to be put in place, remained to be seen, along with how he had taken his imprisonment. Then was the extra matter; Adam was now sleeping with his soon to be ex-wife in his stead.

She would broach it nearer the time with Adam, she did not want to add to the things already eating away at him. She loved him more than anyone in her life, more than she knew was possible, and was completely sure that he loved her an enormous amount. Whether he loved her more than he loved Lorelei, was another question, and one to which she could not know the answer, nor ever dare to ask. She was okay with that though. She would not, could not try to compete with her, and whilst it is a natural desire to want to feel like one is the ultimate love, the chosen one; that necessity within her was very much tempered by the circumstances. Her love for him was pure enough that all she wanted was to be able to give it to him, knowing how much he needed it, and for him to feel it. That he loved her in return, after everything, she knew was very far from a small thing; and that was surety enough.

Chapter Seventy One

Adam kept a keen eye on the activities at the Probation Service. From time to time security updates resulted in the need to contact Daniel again; but in the main, he could peruse their files and emails with little difficulty. One particular case had drawn his attention, and gradually it came to a head.

Gary Maybury had served 18 years of a 25 year sentence. His live-in partner of 5 years had disappeared, and following reports by the neighbours of repeatedly hearing the sound of violent altercations coming from his house; he had become the main suspect. The case had been far from straightforward though, as at first he had performed the unoriginal trick of reporting her as a missing person, and it was initially treated as such. However once no living traces of her could be found, the police began to suspect the worst, but then came the issue of trying to find her body.

Gary Maybury was a butcher, with his own shop in Reading, and therefore unsurprisingly, the police went down the film script avenue of believing her to have been placed in a deep freeze somewhere, perhaps even having been subject to butchering skills first; but Gary Maybury had more imagination than that.

The search had taken a full eleven months of police time, and was only finally solved when one of the detectives happened to watch a film set during the Spanish Civil War, wherein families hid their relatives to save them from execution, behind false walls, leaving the bare minimum of a gap so as not to noticeably reduce the room size.

In a room at the back of Gary Maybury's butcher's shop, behind a wall skillfully decorated to blend in with the others around it; there she was. Verity Dunn, died aged 26 from multiple stab wounds and blows to the head.

Parole had been granted, and set to begin in three weeks time. The halfway house allocated this time was in Oxford; not overly convenient for late night forays, but reachable enough from London.

Adam was more than comfortable enough with Emily to discuss it with her. He did not want to go into every detail, but being deceitful and slipping off to Oxford without her knowing the real reason why, was not an option. Whilst she had plenty of concerns, she knew that it would be futile to try to stop him, and also that it kept him going.

- "What do you have in mind for the charming Mr Maybury?"

- "I've not quite decided yet darling. I'm working through a few ideas."

- "It'll be something worthy, I don't doubt."

- "Well I certainly hope so. I'll try to do as much as I can from home and work, but I do expect to have to make a few trips to Oxford."

- "Promise me one thing, no, in fact two things."

- "Go on."

- "That you won't do anything too risky, too crazy?"

- "What's the second thing?"

- "That you'll make it back to our bed every night?"

- "The second one isn't just a question of wanting to, I *have* to."

- "And the first one?"

- "You know I won't promise you that which I can't darling; but I do promise to try to be as careful as possible, within reason."

Adam knew the address of Gary Maybury's new home before he did, and decided to run some reconnaissance. For the first trip he was more than happy to make it a lovely day out in Oxford with Emily, who had never been there before. Happy minus the painful memories it evoked.

It was agreed that they would first have a good wander around what was to become Gary Maybury's new neighbourhood. Adam had not been pleased to learn that it was in Cowley, an area traditionally full of students, and therefore perhaps not the best place, if there is such a thing, to put a violent, cunning, murderer of a young woman.

After familiarising himself with the particular street, it's surrounding back streets, local pubs, public gathering places, and the location of the Probation Service in St. Aldate's; he and Emily set off towards the river to try their hands at

Punting. With great hilarity, they found it to be one of those activities which looks simple and effortless enough, but very much is neither. After several near collisions with other amateurs, banks, moored boats, low bridges and the murky Thames itself; they made it back to their starting point at Magdalen Bridge.

Then it was on to tour some of the more famous pubs. They felt the history of The Turf Tavern which can boast having had an Inn on its site since the 12th century, and the tiny Bear Inn, delighting in its famed long held tradition of accepting Oxford University ties from all the various colleges, in lieu of payment, and displaying them all around the pub after the debt remained unsettled.

Afterwards they joined a guided tour of Bodleian Library in Divinity School, now even more famous for having been featured in Harry Potter, and then the grounds of some famous Colleges. As much as Adam was enjoying his day out, and time in close proximity to Emily, of which there was no such thing as enough; his mind was working away in the background.

They stayed late enough for dinner, returning to the beautiful old Turf Tavern, stooping to avoid its beams en route to their table.

- "Do you think we'll make it Adam, til the end?"

- "I do hope so. The thought of not feeling you every night is one of the most horrible thoughts there is."

- "Likewise."

- "I guess we better make it then."

- "Whatever happens?"

- "Whatever happens."

Chapter Seventy Two

Gary Maybury had been assigned to Parole Officer Daria Kaminski. Once released from prison, he was to report to her in person once per week as part of his conditions. He was far from the first such client she was to work with, but for all that professional experience; she could not help but feel disgust and a degree of fear after reading through his file. A certain nervousness had been displayed in her emails to colleagues. To what extent and in which ways does someone change, after being imprisoned for 18 years?

Daria steeled herself for a difficult day at the office whilst having her morning coffee and croissant, at Aromas, the snug little coffee shop around the corner. The day, 18 years in the waiting for Gary Maybury, had arrived. Would he be humbled by the experience, remorseful, or angered by it, and resentful?

As she sat there lost in such thoughts, a man whom she had noticed in there a few times recently, asked apologetically if he could sit at her table, in the absence of anywhere else to sit.

- "Sure no problem." she said, reducing the amount of space her things were taking up.

- "Thanks. It's a popular little place isn't it?"

- "Yeah it pretty much always is."

- "It must be the coffee. Being a no milk, no sugar, no frills, dull kinda guy; there's no hiding place if it's bad."

- "I wouldn't say that makes you dull, just easily pleased."

- "Haha yes maybe so. If only all contentment was so easily achieved."

- "Contentment huh? There's a word I don't spend too much time with!"

- "Sorry to hear that. Are you okay? Bad week? You were looking kind of pensive, a little nervous even, before I intruded on your breakfast."

- "Oh dear, am I that transparent?"

- "Well maybe not to everyone, but I must confess to a little insider information."

- "How do you mean!?"

- "Being as I am a Psychologist."

- "Ah I see. Well Mr dull coffee Psychologist, you're clearly quite a good one, things are a little tricky right now, but I'll be okay."

- "I'm glad, that you'll be okay that is. You can call me Adam if you prefer, Mrs Flat White with a touch of cinnamon."

- "Thanks Mr Adam. You can call me Daria, if you prefer."

- "Mrs Flat White with a touch of cinnamon it is then."

- "Nice to meet you." she said smiling. Perhaps I'll see you here again for my next check up?"

- "It's almost inevitable."

Daria walked the short walk to work, feeling a little better about life, and more specifically, the day in prospect. She had until 12pm to make final preparations, by which time she was almost as nervous as before.

- "Do please take a seat Mr Maybury."

- "Where to?"

She smiled cordially.

- "I'm Daria Kaminski, and as you'll already know, I've been assigned as your Parole Officer."

- "First bit of luck I've had in 18 years. Funny name though; where's that from?"

- "I'm from Polish descent."

- "Hhmmph, right."

- "Now Mr Maybury, fir…"

- "You can call me Gary."

- "Okay, Gary, first of all how are you? It must be quite something to suddenly be out of prison after so long?"

- "Quite something!? Yeah it's definitely quite something! A fucking great relief is what it is!"

- "I imagine it must be."

- "Have you ever been in prison Daria?"

- "Only as a visitor."

- "I thought so. So you can't imagine what it's like."

- "No, fair enough, but I can imagine the relief one feels when any ordeal is over."

- "I suppose so."

- "Now today is just by way of introduction. We'll meet here at the same time every week. I've arranged for you to have some weekly counselling to help you adjust."

- "I don't need bloody counselling! I just needed to get out of there!"

- "Nonetheless Gary, it's a huge change, it won't hurt to talk to someone about it, plus I need to remind you that it's one of your parole conditions."

- "Okay okay, I'll go to the poxy counselling."

- "Good, okay well that's it for now. I hope you settle into your new home okay and I'll see you next week."

- "I'm off to find a new local if you fancy joining me?"

- "Let's keep this appropriately professional Gary, shall we?"

- "If we must."

Gary Maybury arrived at his new home for the first time at 1.17pm. He left it for the first time at 1.32pm and headed for The Oxford Blue which was soon to become known as his local. At 1.41pm he ordered a pint of Guinness and a Streak and Kidney pie, telling the barman that he'd know if it was no good, as he did so. He seemed satisfied enough with it, and as the pints flowed he visibly relaxed in his manner, striking up conversations with anyone not far away enough to avoid it, unaware that the man quietly reading a book in the corner, was wondering how his presentation compared with that of his late partner, Verity Dunn, 18 years on?

Chapter Seventy Three

- "Morning Mrs….Daria. How's life in Dariaworld this morning?"

- "Oh hi Adam, back so soon? A bit better thanks. Are you here to experiment again with another exotic coffee?"

- "Yep, you know me - the more weird shite they put in it the better! You do seem a bit more relaxed today actually."

- "It's good to know I'm still so transparent!"

- "Yeah, don't go taking up poker for a living any time soon."

- "Especially not at a Psychologist's convention aye?"

- "Especially not there. So to what do we owe your more relaxed demeanour?"

- "A rather less daunting day ahead, that's all."

- "That's good, because I've not got time to take you through a relaxation meditation today."

- "Does that really work? It never really seems to on me."

- "Maybe it's all the caffeine, or the cinnamon? A known stimulant that cinnamon!"

- "Or maybe the meditation was just shite."

- "That is another explanation I grant you."

- "Well public duty calls, nice seeing you again Adam. Good luck fixing the minds of Britain today."

- "Public duty? Are you an undercover cop?"

- "Well if I were I'd have to deny it!"

- "Good point well made, so you still might be then?"

- "Nothing that glamorous or exciting I'm afraid. I'm a Parole Officer."

- "Well that's still pretty glamorous."

- "Yeah it's one debutante ball after another, interspersed only by all the champagne lunches."

- "That's exactly how I'd imagined it. Spooky!"

- "Haha I'd really better go. Take care Adam."

- "You too."

A little later that day, after some casual observation, the man in the corner of The Oxford Blue could not help but wonder, how Gary Maybury's relaxed demeanour, compared with those of the family of Verity Dunn, 18 years on?

227

Chapter Seventy Four

Exactly a week after their first conversation, Daria and Adam happened to cross paths in Aromas again.

- "If you weren't such an upstanding member of the Civil Service; I'd suspect you of stalking me."

- "How do you know I'm upstanding?"

- "A presumption on my part."

- "Well kindly cease being presumptuous Adam. In any case, you're completely wrong, I'm totally stalking you! My nearby job is a mere cover."

- "How are you?" he smiled.

- "A little apprehensive again, but I guess you've already deduced that?"

- "Well, yes. Tricky day in prospect?"

- "Yeah, just a certain client again that's all."

- "Ah, well I hope it goes okay."

- "Thanks. I think I just build it up too much in my mind."

- "I take it they are an unsavoury type?"

- "Unsavoury? Yeah you could say that! Let's just say he wasn't in prison for shoplifting the pick n mix."

- "Okay I get the picture; let's work on the assumption that he'll be on his best behaviour from now on."

- "Yes, that works for me. Well I suppose I'd better get to it. What are you up to today?"

- "I wouldn't dream of spoiling your stalking fix by telling you!"

- "Oh that's so thoughtful!"

- "I do try to consider others."

- "See you soon then."

- "Yeah, try not to make it too obvious."

- "Haha don't worry, I'll be like the shadow of the wind!"

- "I love that book!"

- "Me too! A topic for another day. Adiós!"

- "Hasta luego!"

At the allotted time, Gary Maybury arrived at Daria's office for his second appointment:

- "How are things Gary?"

- "Yeah great ta; I'm having a wail of a time!"

- "Really?"

- "Yeah really! What did you expect after 18 years inside?"

- "You're having no trouble adjusting?"

- "Do you mean like trouble adjusting to being able to go down the pub whenever I feel like it, coming and going as I please with no one barking orders at me, not having to look over my shoulder all the time? Nope! No trouble at all!"

- "Well that all sounds good. Now I see that you missed your first counselling session?"

- "Yeah sorry I wasn't feeling too well."

- "I see, well I must remind you of the consequences of missing anoth…."

- "I know I know and I won't."

- "And what about your accommodation?"

- "What about it?"

- "How are you finding it?"

- "Turn left out the pub, along a bit, then left again - easy!"

- "Yes, I'm sure, and you've settled in okay?"

- "Yep, happy as a pig in shit."

- "Right. Good."

On his journey back to London, Adam refamiliarized himself with Gary Maybury's case. He had shown no remorse at the time, and Adam suspected that he had only done so latterly in his bid for early release.

Over and over again, he pondered the prudence, and the rightfulness, of something he wanted to do - go to see Verity Dunn's family. To what end? Sympathy? Empathy? To make sure that they're okay? Useful information? Morbid curiosity? On the basis that he could not quite answer his own questions, and the family would be fraught with churned up emotions; he decided again that he would leave it; at least for now.

After seeing some clients of his own that afternoon, he went home to Emily - the balm that soothed the sorest wounds, without ever being able to heal them.

- "You do know, through all this, I'm not oblivious to issues surrounding your ticking clock, don't you?"

- "I know Adam, without asking."

Such brevity allowed for the moment both yearned for from the first second the last such one ended, to arrive all the sooner.

Daria had arrived home around the same time as Adam, relieved that her day was over. As she made something for dinner, and sat down to eat it alone, other than with her tortoiseshell cat, Benjy; she caught herself hoping to see him again soon, which, unlike the cat, did not sit well with her.

Chapter Seventy Five - 4 years, 9 months, and 23 days until *his* release

At every free moment, Adam kept himself busy, usually online, but on this particular morning he had other plans, and took a very early train to Oxford. As no morning there would be complete without a visit to Aromas, he made that his first port of call.

Initially there was no sign of Daria, but it was not long before she arrived, her eyes darting around as she came in.

- "Well it's about time you showed up! Minutes I've been waiting here! Minutes!"

- "I'm so sorry to have left you looking like a sad twat for so long, I feel just awful."

- "You really are too kind Daria!"

- "I know, I know. That's always been my weak spot."

- "A disgusting milky coffee with a cinnamon ball in it?"

- "That'd be lovely thanks."

- "So what keeps bringing you back here Adam?"

- "Oh I'm just working on a research project that's all; nothing earth shattering."

- "I see, am I allowed to know what it's about, or is it top secret?"

- "Well let's just say it's on a need to know basis. If it ever gets to that point; I'll be sure to tell you."

- "That's very considerate of you."

- "I thought so. So, Zafón's The Shadow of the Wind then? Have you read all four of the series?"

- "I have."

- "In English or Spanish?"

- "In English of course. Don't tell me you read them in Spanish, because that would just be showing off!"

- "Okay I won't."

- "But you did though?"

- "Yes."

- "I thought so."

- "Let's try a little experiment. Here is a pen and paper, write down the order in which you liked them best, without my seeing, and I'll do the same."

- "Haha okay…………right….. let's see……...done."

They both pushed their pieces of paper into the centre of the table; both read:

The Shadow of the Wind
The Labyrinth of the Spirits
The Prisoner of Heaven
The Angel's Game

- "And there I was thinking you were going to be a smart arse and write yours in Spanish!"

- "I didn't want to spoil the symmetry."

- "So what does this tell us, Mr. Psychologist man?"

- "That you're an intelligent woman of taste."

- "And that I see things the same way as you?"

- "In this regard at least, yes."

- "Time will tell I guess whether that extends to other regards."

- "It will."

- "I'd better get going, thank you for my disgusting coffee."

- "You're welcome."

- "I'll see you in here again no doubt?"

- "You will."

- "Are you going to continue to talk in such short sentences?"

- "No."

To her slight annoyance, Daria left Aromas smiling, with a spring in her step. Adam waited for a few minutes, and then headed towards Queen Street, and into the public Library, where he spent the next four hours before heading back to London.

Chapter Seventy Six - 4 years, 8 months, and 20 days until *his* release

A little more than a month later, things had continued to progress along these lines. Adam had become almost as familiar a face in the library, as he had in Aromas. Daria, in spite of herself, was increasingly pleased to see him, and from her perspective at least, things were beginning to get out of hand.

At each encounter, she just managed to stop short of asking him to meet her back there for lunch, round to her place for dinner, about his personal situation partner wise, for his phone number; but it was increasing in difficulty by the day.

- "Morning Adam, I took the liberty of ordering you a boring coffee, then I ordered you the dullest muffin I could think of, so here you go, plain and wholemeal."

- "You couldn't have chosen better, thank you, although this doyley is a bit fancy!"

- "Shall I see if I can swap it for a plain, white serviette?"

- "No, I'll put up with this upturn in excitement, just this once mind."

- "Admirable!"

- "Listen Daria, can I get something off my chest?"

- "It sounds rather ominous, but do go on."

- "I'd be a pretty crap Psychologist if I hadn't noticed a certain……..something………………..between us…..a certain….connection."

- "Yeah you would be!"

- "I don't want to use a load of cliches, and I should have said something earlier, it's just………"

- "You're married, gay, celibate, a eunuch, part of a hippy free love commune, in a relationship, completely unattracted to me?"

- "Just the second to last one."

-

-

- "I can't say I'm surprised, but I'd be totally lying if I said I wasn't really disappointed."

- "I'm sorry, truly I am. You'll have noticed I didn't confirm your last suggestion, it's just well…..I was single for such a long time…..incapable of being anything else……and then Emily suddenly arrived in my life…….and now, well I just can't be without her, I just can't."

- "So we even had that in common too huh? I haven't been with anyone for so long……can't be with anyone……I flirted with the idea that you could be…..well, my Emily I suppose."

- "I know this is just going to sound like something nice to say, but if I were still in that mode now…..in that place…..I would have let you in……you're so lovely, really you are, I wouldn't have been able to fight it."

- "I believe you Adam, really, but please stop now, else we're going to have one of those cliched scenes. Please excuse me for a moment."

- "Sorry, my brave face only lasts for so long. Just promise me one thing…..if Emily ever suddenly decides that you're a pig, and leaves you; that you'll call me immediately, well almost immediately?"

- "I certainly feel like a pig right now."

- "Well you're not, well a bit. Promise me?"

- "I promise."

- "Good, well I'm going to leave now whilst I still have a crumb of dignity, and try really hard not to blow it by tripping over someone's bag on the way out."

- "Yeah that would be bad!"

- "It would!"

- "I hope to see you soon?"

- "You will."

- "Good."

Adam, still feeling awful for not having spoken sooner, did not head straight back to work, nor home, but instead took a 22 minute train journey to Reading, to seek out a couple in their seventies whom he had never met before.

Chapter Seventy Seven

Adam arrived at Reading station and headed out into unfamiliar surroundings. Although there was a plethora of buses and taxis, he decided to walk with the aid of Google maps. According to which, his destination was 39 minutes away which afforded him yet more thinking time regarding how to play the scenario he was planning to instigate. The last thing he wanted to do was cause alarm or distress for their sakes, but also because he would be ushered out of the door.

Beating Google's estimate by six minutes, he arrived at 74 Braeburn Road. A quick observation confirmed his hope of finding the couple at home, and steeling himself, he headed down their front path and rang the doorbell. Within a minute a white haired man came to the door and warily opened it.

- "How can I help you young man?"

- "Good morning, am I addressing Mr Barnes?"

- "You are, who might you be? We don't want to buy anything."

- "It's okay, I don't wish to sell you anything. Please forgive the unexpected intrusion, it's just that I'd like to talk in confidence with you and your wife…..about your daughter."

Mr Barnes' facial expression changed dramatically, just before he quickly closed the door. Adam had expected such a reaction, and remained on the doorstep, patiently. A few moments later, the man returned.

- "Who are you? A reporter? A policeman?"

- "I'm neither of those things Mr Barnes, my name is Adam Mills and I'm a Psychologist."

- "And what have you to do with our daughter, may I ask?"

- "If you'll be so kind as to let me inside for privacy, and to hear me out, I promise not to take up too much of your time. If once you've heard what I have to say, you wish me to leave, never to return; I promise that will be the case."

- "Just wait there a moment please."

The man went back inside, spoke with his wife for a few minutes, and then returned.

- "Come in young man."

Adam was led into a cosily furnished lounge, and was immediately struck by the number of photos of a young woman on display.

- "I'm pleased to meet you both, thank you very much for agreeing to speak with me and for letting me into your home."

- "You're welcome, now please do tell us what this is about."

- "Okay, well, completely of my own volition, triggered by his recent release from prison; I've been doing some research into Gary Maybury's past."

Adam observed the look exchanged by Mr and Mrs Barnes at the mention of the name, and continued.

- "I've discovered that seven years before his conviction for murder, he was implicated, suspected......of having been involved with your daughter."

- "There was no doubt as to his having been involved with her." Mrs Barnes looked up at a portrait on the wall. "She was so beautiful….Hannah…..she deserved better."

- "I couldn't agree more on both counts Mrs Barnes, and I am deeply sorry for your loss. I don't imagine that 23 years on, the pain is any less. Of course when I say he was implicated, I mean in her tragic death too."

- "He was implicated alright; the problem was that with no evidence against him, no charges were ever brought. The police were satisfied that it was a suicide, and swiftly drew a line under it."

- "Indeed so Mrs Barnes; would it be fair to say though that like me, you both suspect that he drove her to it?"

- "We always suspected that he was violent with her, but we couldn't say for sure what went on behind those closed doors."

- "No, but I imagine we could guess. Did she ever let on, say anything at all, or was it always completely hidden?"

- "There were periods when we didn't see her, sudden cancellations with dubious excuses, but she'd never admit to it. She was too ashamed, we suppose."

- "Could I be so bold as to ask about her suicide?"

- "Where is all this leading to, young man?"

- "Well cutting to the chase, I don't like the fact that Gary Maybury is now free to roam. Initially I thought this on behalf of Verity Dunn's family, but now on your behalf too."

- "I see, and what do you propose that we do about it?"

That evening, as Adam gazed lovingly at Emily; he pondered the lottery of it all. Hannah Barnes' story could have been Ruth Jackson's; Ruth Jackson's could have been Verity Dunn's; Verity Dunn's could have been Emily's; Emily's could have been Lorelei's.

- "Are you okay Adam?"

- "As long as you are, yes." he said, holding her almost too tightly.

244

Chapter Seventy Eight

Adam had a long overdue coffee with Debs. He always felt bad when leaving it too long in between times.

- "How's your life treating you Debs?"

- "Like it caught me in bed with its husband, and I ran over its dog as I made my escape."

- "Haha that good huh?"

- "Yeah that good!"

- "How's you? How's Emily?"

- "We're doing well thanks, you know, busy."

- "Ahha, so what do you need Ad?"

- "Just to know you're okay is more than enough for me Debs, you know that."

- "Ahha, and what do you really need?"

- "Still on the ball I see. A favour."

- "Well colour me surprised. What's it to be? Something that'll put my glittering career in jeopardy again no doubt."

- "All in a good cause Debs, you know."

- "I know, you annoying, demanding, wonderful chap you. What do you need me to do?"

- "Head down into the dusty NHS archives of Reading, and borrow the medical records of a Hannah Barnes."

- "Borrow them?"

- "Yeah, just for a short while, just in case they turn out to be of interest to your favourite Psychologist."

- "Second favourite now, you should see our new one."

- "Thanks."

- "No worries, and what happens if they are of interest?"

- "Good things."

- "Okay, well I'll need some time, and any more details that you have."

- "Sure, and thanks as always Debs."

- "You're welcome as always. Are you sure this is a good idea though?"

- "Definite. Now tell me about this Psychologist you suddenly like even more than me….."

To no surprise whatsoever to Adam; within a week Debs had come up trumps, leaving him in possession of Hannah Barnes' hospital records from the Royal Berkshire Hospital in Reading.

It transpired that not uncommonly, Hannah had not been a particularly frequent visitor to their A&E department, but on the three occasions when she had visited, there were grounds for suspicion each time, especially if viewed from a certain perspective, and collectively; however spread out over a three year timescale, no one had joined the dots.

One incident described her arriving with a broken jaw, having slipped from a step ladder whilst painting the kitchen, and catching it on the worktop as she fell.

Another described the time when she arrived with broken bones in her hand and wrist, after having reached in to retrieve her handbag, her coat sleeve had become caught as she went to close the car door with her other hand.

A third, how she had suffered multiple bruises and hairline fractures in a nasty fall on a dry ski slope.

Adam also noted that her medication profile had gradually changed to include antidepressant, and anti anxiety tablets.

The following day, Adam took a trip to Oxford. He wanted to see Daria again, hoping that she was okay, and that it wouldn't be awkward following their last conversation.

- "Morning Daria, how are you?"

- "Hi Adam….. I'm glad to see you……it's been a week…..I was worried I'd scared you off."

- "I'm glad to see you too, I don't scare that easily, I've just been busy bollocks that's all, you know how it is."

- "Well, the busy bit at least; less so about the bollocks."

- "Hahaha, well I'm glad to see you're okay…….that we're okay."

- "Other than feeling like a twat, yeah I'm okay, and I hoped we'd be okay too."

- "You're so not a twat, I am if anyone is."

- "Yeah, let's go with that then."

- "Let's have cake with our coffees to celebrate, you know, really go mad!"

- "Do you mean a totally plain muffin?"

- "No, I mean actual cake."

- "Bloody hell!"

Later that day, Adam busied himself until after he knew that Daria would be finished with her tricky client, before heading to The Oxford Blue for a pub lunch, getting there ten minutes before he did.

From the furthest possible distance, Adam observed as he ordered his Guinness, observed as he made idle conversation, observed as he ordered a second, and then a third, observed as he laughed, how he laughed, as he read the paper, as he watched some sport on the television, ate crisps, leered at the female students, ordered another Guinness, bothered people, smiled, walked; breathed.

The following week, late one afternoon, Adam paid another visit to Reading. Things were coming into focus in his mind and there was purpose in his stride. He spent some more time with Hannah's parents at their house, and then, once darkness had fallen, made his way to another address, not too far away from there. He did not ring the doorbell, nor attempt any polite, apologetic introductions; but simply snuck down a side alleyway, before re-emerging a few moments later. Forty five minutes after that, he was aboard a train heading back to London, and home to the feel of Emily.

Chapter Seventy Nine

- "Daria, do you ever struggle with helping your clients? Beyond feeling understandably uncomfortable with them I mean."

- "In what sense exactly?"

- "In the sense that you may not actually wish to help them, perhaps not feeling that they deserve it, or should even have been released at all?"

- "Well there's a fine question for a Parole Officer on a Monday morning!"

- "Yeah, sorry. I think about it though....you know......the whole crime and punishment thing......only acting after the event......second chances.....if someone is lucky enough to be alive to be granted one that is."

- "Well since you've asked, I do struggle sometimes, depending on who it is, what they did....how they did it.....but then it's the system we have......I figure someone has to help them, hopefully help to prevent a recurrence. Perhaps it may as well be me."

- "Yeah, it's the system that we have alright. Aside from the morality of their enjoying life again, whilst their victims rot in their graves; does someone stop being capable of repeating a heinous act just because they've been locked up for a period of time?"

- "That's where you guys come in, and psychologically assess them before they're released though."

- "Yeah that's all well and true, but plenty of them learn to do and say the right things, and in any case, that only really helps for considering parole; eventually their sentence is up regardless!"

- "Are you okay Adam?"

- "Yeah…..sorry…..I…..just feel strongly about it that's all."

- "I can see. Well between you and me, many of them would never see the light of day again if it were up to me, but you know, I can only do so much."

-

-

- "Daria, could we perhaps continue this conversation later today, somewhere more private."

- "Errr…. like where?"

- "Your place maybe?"

- "Errm…okay…. what about Emily though?"

- "She knows."

With Daria having insisted on a little time after work to straighten up before allowing visitors, Adam was afforded a longer day to busy himself locally. He spent some more time at the library, and enjoyed a wander around the city, taking in the stunningly great architecture and the history, and their history there; feeling small against it all. There were any number of places to stop for some lunch, great pubs, cafes, and restaurants; but Adam drifted inexorably to Cowley, and into The Oxford Blue.

Gary Maybury was on particularly good form that day, very much enhanced by the fact that a man he wasn't familiar with was mug enough to keep buying him drinks as they chatted; something about a big win on the horses. As someone else was paying, it wasn't long until he moved on to the top shelf. One of those whiskeys might have tasted a bit funny, but he wasn't to notice, or care.

As he woke up at 4.11am, laying on his bed fully clothed, on his back, in the open casket at rest position with his hands folded across his chest, with a hangover of royal proportions; he couldn't really remember getting home, or even leaving the pub.

Several hours earlier, at 7.30pm exactly, a nervous Adam arrived at Daria's front door, and pressed the intercom buzzer.

- "Yes? Who the bloody hell is this!?"

- "Hahaha I'm touched that you've remembered!"

- "Oh it's you! Come up Adam."

Adam climbed the two flights of stairs and was greeted by Daria at the front door to her flat, and once inside, by a tortoiseshell cat, and the sight of a table laid for dinner..

- "Totally forgot I was coming huh?"

- "Yep, Benjy and I always dine together."

- "Well I think it's impressive. It isn't every cat that can use cutlery."

- "That's nothing - you should have seen him open the wine!"

- "Hahaha, yeah I'd like to have seen that!"

- "I'll leave the two of you to get acquainted, whilst I finish off in the kitchen. I'll be back in a few minutes to lay you an extra place."

Once eating Daria's pasta, and drinking the skillfully opened wine; Adam picked his moment:

- "Daria....."

- "Adam...."

- "I'm just going to lay this all out there, and hope to every God I don't believe in that I'm judging this right."

- "Erm...okay...."

- "I'm at the point where I could probably proceed alone, but I'd rather have you on board and not leave you feeling used."

- "You're scaring me a little here Adam...."

- "Oh God I'm so sorry... that's the last thing I'd want to... please don't be....just... hear me out okay?"

- "Okay."

Very carefully, selectively, Adam told her a little of what he'd been doing lately, and why; as Daria listened patiently, if rather open-mouthed.

- "I so know that you'll be feeling that I'm a total fraud, that everything I've ever said to you was just calculated, but please understand I had to get to know you a little...I could hardly have just blurted all of this out straight away. It is all in a.....wider cause."

-

-

- "Leaving aside the wider cause for a moment, can I ask you something?"

- "Yes, I totally did mean what I said about meeting you if I were still single. I absolutely promise you. I'm really not that callous."

- "And I really don't think that you are….but in the light of what you've just told me; that's quite a leap of faith."

- "I just wanted to get to know you, I wasn't to know that we'd……connect so well."

- "There was plenty I wasn't to know, it seems."

- "Well not at first at least, but I'm telling you as soon as I felt I could. Look I'm sorry, it's totally my fault, I'll just go and leave you be…..I really shouldn't have involved……"

-

-

- "What is it you need me to do exactly?"

Chapter Eighty

Having had a letter from Mr and Mrs Barnes to the Probation Service passed to her to deal with; Daria was making the relatively short trip in her car to Reading, with an uneasy feeling in her stomach. She had always been the play everything by the book type, so this was not sitting well with her.

She arrived at their house, and with trepidation, rang their doorbell. Once in their cosy, picture-filled lounge, with a cup of tea and a biscuit in hand….

- "Thank you for coming, Miss Kaminski. We'd rather talk with you than the police. The thing is, we've been having some therapy to help us cope with the loss of our daughter, Hannah. Even though it was so long ago, we've never been able to get over it."

- "I'm so sorry for your loss. I can't even begin to imagine how awful it's been for you both."

- "Thank you. The thing is, our Psychologist encouraged us to go through the rest of her things as a step towards trying to find some closure. We've never really been able to you see, they've just lived in our loft."

- "Has it helped at all Mr Barnes?"

- "Well …. not exactly….. we've spent all these years believing that our beloved Hannah had……but now…...well…..we've found this….."

Mrs Barnes carefully handed Daria a letter, and the couple sat looking at each other, and at her facial expressions as she read it:

December 6th 1995

I am writing this down now, in case I am ever brave or stupid enough to come forward, or in case anyone ever finds it, even if it is too late.

My life has become an unbearable cycle of violence and control at the hands of my partner Gary Maybury. I have been subjected to countless incidents of his brutality, under the threat of much worse to come should I ever tell anyone. On the three occasions so far that I was permitted to seek medical attention, he forced me to lie as to how my injuries came about.

In March 1993, my jaw was not broken by a fall from a stepladder in the kitchen - he broke it when he kicked me in the face for not answering him quickly enough.

In June 1994, the injuries to my wrist and hand were indeed caused by a car door, but it had nothing to do with my sleeve catching in it by accident - he slammed the door on my arm deliberately as we got home from an evening out, where he had not liked the way that I had behaved.

In July this year, my multiple injuries had nothing to do with a nasty, tumbling fall down a dry ski slope - I have never been skiing in my life, on a dry slope or otherwise. They came about during a picnic in a quiet spot in Lousehill Copse, when I had dared to speak up about my life with him. He offered to help me end it there and then.

He often says to me that any attempt to leave him will result in my death, which he won't have to pay for, because he'll make it look like I've killed myself, by leaving a note I once left him saying that I simply couldn't take anymore, and didn't want to go on; by my body.

If I am dead by the time anyone reads this, my guess is that he used a form of strangulation. Perhaps one of those plastic straps, that once you've pulled them tight, you can't undo them again. He often likes to strangle me as a punishment for varying lengths of time, sometimes it isn't even as a punishment; he has a real thing about it, always has done.

I'd better stop writing now, so that I can hide it before he comes home.

I love you Mum and Dad, and I'm so sorry for everything I've put you through.

Hannah xx

Daria took a few moments to compose her thoughts and herself.

- "My goodness…I don't quite know what to say….. what a shocking letter to find!"

- "It certainly has been a shock!"

- "There will be many questions down the line I'm sure….but….for now….. can I just ask…and I'm sorry to but….. is there any doubt in your minds at all that….. Hannah wrote this?"

- "None whatsoever, see for yourself."

Mrs Barnes handed her a box filled with Christmas and Birthday cards, letters, little notes, school books, notes taken at university. The letter was a dead match.

- "Again, I'm so sorry to have to ask……but what was her method of taking her own……her cause of ….?"

- "Asphyxiation."

Chapter Eighty One

Daria spent the entirety of that Thursday evening at home, in deep thought, with Benjy providing more solace than input. Adam had been careful not to put her in too compromising a position, but she did know a little more than if she had simply acted upon the letter from Mr and Mrs Barnes. She only had to pass that letter on to the police, along with Hannah's letter, and let them take it from there, without the need for a single lie; and then let things run their course. Nonetheless, she felt very uneasy about it all.

The following evening, she rang the doorbell of another house.

- "Emily?"

- "Daria?"

- "How did you know?"

- "I was half expecting you, please do come in."

- "Is Adam at home?"

- "No, he is seeing patients still, but he shouldn't be too much longer."

- "Why were you half expecting me?"

- "Well, if I were in your position, you know, I'd want to…see if he checks out."

- "He's told you everything then?"

- "He has; he's always honest whenever, or as soon as he can be."

- "It's not common for a Psychologist to play detective."

- "He's not exactly a common Psychologist."

- "So I'm learning. So what's his story?"

- "I really can't say too much…. he has his reasons for wanting to…. help people."

- "Does that include you?"

- "I guess you could say that, although I like to think it's mutual. He's in a tremendous amount of pain."

- "He hinted at something, but mostly he seems okay."

- "Sometimes he hides it better than others. Would you like a glass of wine?"

- "I'd love one!"

They sat together in the lounge. Following a few moments of silence Daria said:

- "I'm sorry if I came across as a little hostile, or suspicious earlier."

- "It's okay, really, I don't blame you for one second. I would have been too, in your shoes."

- "Did he also tell you how attracted I am to him?"

- "He did; but I kinda would have assumed that anyway."

- "There is just something about him."

- "I know, you're preaching to the choir here Daria!"

- "And you're not threatened at all by that?"

- "No."

- "I'm not sure whether I should feel insulted!"

- "It's no reflection on you…..I'm sure in different circumstances…….it's just…..he's unbelievably loyal."

- "It's such a cliche, but I hope you know how lucky you are?"

- "Fear not, I totally do."

They both turned sharply at the sound of the front door. Adam came into the lounge, rather startled, if not totally shocked at seeing Daria.

- "Oh hi Daria, how did you…..what are you….?"

- "Adam Cole, Psychologist, Golf and Tennis Club memberships in the area, local woman called Emily with a husband sent to prison for repeated violence, likewise an estate agent - you're not the only one who can play detective!"

Adam turned grey and stammered:

- "I…didn't…….have you…?"

- "Don't worry, they don't link, and I've not left any trails. I just had to be sure about you."

- "And are you?"

- "I am now."

- "What are you going to do?"

- "Contact the police tomorrow and let them handle it from here."

- "To what end!?"

- "Gary Maybury's hopefully!"

With any tension on that matter gone, at least for now, and glasses of wine either topped up or placed in hand; the three of them visibly relaxed.

- "You'll stay for dinner won't you Daria?"

- "Erm if you're sure that's okay with you both?"

- "I'm sure; Adam?"

- "Yes of course."

By the time dinner had been prepared and served, a third bottle of wine was well underway. Once they had taken their time eating the dinner, the pop from the cork of a fifth bottle had long since been forgotten. When 1am ticked around, no one could claim to have noticed the pop of the sixth bottle, rendering it unmemorable even before it was consigned to history.

- "So I guess you'd better stay over Daria?" said Emily in her best trying not to slur but failing miserably voice.

- "Erm if you're sure that's……okay?"

- "Well you're certainly not driving home in your state!"

- "No I guess not!"

- "Best we have a nightcap then, where's the Legendario Adam?"

- "Yes, clearly we've not drunk anywhere near enough! I'll get it."

- "You'll like this Daria, it's sweet and yum!"

As can often be the case, the use of the term nightcap in the singular, turned out to be a grammatical error. When finally at some time after 3am, the time for bed arrived, they had each had three such caps, possibly even four, but certainly no more than five. The final stages of the conversation never would be remembered, and vision had certainly become an issue. Nonetheless, Daria made it to bed in a room that Emily had never made use of, and Emily and Adam to theirs.

At 4.06am, according to Emily's old clock radio, she was aroused from her stupor by the sound of gentle but definite sobbing, clearly coming from Daria's room. She untwined herself from a sleeping Adam without waking him, which was a first, and tiptoed along to Daria's room, tapping ever so gently upon the door.

- "Who is it!?" she said through the sobs.

- "It's me, are you okay? Can I come in?"

-

- "Yes."

Emily entered the darkened room, slipped into the bed, and held Daria closely to her, shushing her, stroking her hair, telling her everything would be okay; until she fell asleep. Daria waited a few moments, before slipping out from her embrace, the room, and along the landing to find Adam. She crept into the wrong room, then the right room, then into the bed, then into him.

At 5.38am, despite the fact that alcohol was very much still the dominant force, Adam stirred with the sense that something wasn't quite feeling right. By 5.44am he had somehow pieced enough together, and slipping out from the embrace of whom he assumed to be Daria; he crept out of the room and along the landing in search of the feel of Emily.

At 6.25am, Daria awoke, took a moment, before dazedly heading back to her room, slipped into bed and joined the sleeping embrace.

When Emily heavily opened her eyes, she saw her old clock radio giving the time of 10.14am, and felt the feel of Adam. Five minutes earlier, Daria had awoken alone in the place she had begun proceedings.

At a very hungover breakfast, even if anyone could remember anything from the scenes akin to a seaside farce, with any degree of clarity; no one broached the subject; not then, not ever.

Chapter Eighty Two

Detectives Rowson and Grant left the Barnes' house the following Tuesday afternoon, having listened closely to their concerns, and with the letter carefully sealed in an evidence bag. They then paid a visit to the Royal Berkshire Hospital, before returning to the Police Station.

The following day they headed to another address not too far away, armed with a Search Warrant. They were however allowed to proceed without a demand to see such, as the couple now living there, were too alarmed to think, or be concerned about it, once they had heard even a little of the reason for the visit.

The Detectives went into the loft at first for a thorough search of anything that could remotely relate to the case, looking through old boxes and files for over an hour, but came out again empty handed. Then with further permission they headed to the garden, and into an old, run down shed. It was even harder to move about in than the loft, full as it was with very old, and long since used junk of various description. It was beginning to look like a waste of time, when behind a lawnmower, behind a folded misshapen wooden clothes horse, sticking out a tiny bit from under an old bedside table; there was a bundle tied up in old brown paper.

Later that day, Gary Maybury floated home from The Oxford Blue, coming down to *terra firma* with a bump upon finding two official looking men on his doorstep.

- "Who the fuck are you?"

- "Good afternoon Mr Maybury, I'm Detective Rowson, this is Detective Grant."

- "And?"

- "Might we come in?"

- "You might, if I let you, but why would I?"

- "Oh I don't know, to appear cooperative perhaps, or maybe because we've this Warrant?"

- "Fucking coppers, you can't leave me be can you, haven't I done enough time for you?"

- "Well that's what we're here to find out. Shall we....?"

- "Unbelievable! Right, well let's get this over with; I've nothing to hide anyway!"

- "It shouldn't take long then."

Gary Maybury sat cursing and scorning as the Detectives went about their search, which was far less arduous a task at this sparse venue. Within a matter of minutes, tucked away just out of sight behind the TV cabinet, was another bundle tied up in new brown paper. The ages of the two discovered bundles may have differed, but the nature of the contents inside did not - extreme hardcore, strangulation fetish pornography.

One week later, as Michael received a nice gift in the post of the finest of fine art pens; the parents of Verity Dunn were sitting down to breakfast, when they heard the arrival of the morning post. Mrs Dunn went to the front door to collect it, for a perusal over the toast. Amongst the usual uninspiring content, was a postcard depicting the Tower of London, which on the reverse simply read "You're welcome, with love and thoughts."

Chapter Eight Three - Two years, two months until her funeral

One year on from his capture, trial, and imprisonment, Lorelei and Adam had just about stopped looking over their shoulders everywhere they went, in the UK at least; stopped waking up in gasping terror; stopped the feelings of dread that something awful was to happen at any moment; stopped being unable to let the other out of their sight without a deep sense of panic enveloping them.

They had enjoyed a three month recuperation period in Spain, where their daily priorities had reduced again to the simple things; fresh bread, olive oil, Manchego cheese, wine, books. long, albeit sometimes painful, beautiful walks throughout Andalucia's stunning landscapes; and each other. Their mutual physical and emotional desires did not add together to make one vast sum; they multiplied together, to make a sum so astronomical, it warranted academic study.

They talked about everything and nothing, with only one subject ever off limits, but as before, often they did not feel the need to talk at all; just be. They took long train rides from Málaga to Seville, to Valencia, to Madrid, to La Coruña, to Santiago, to Oviedo, to Gijon, to Barcelona; partly for the desire to explore all these beautiful places together, and partly just for the simple shared pleasure of gazing out of the window at the ever-changing, breathtaking passing scenery. Everywhere they went, it was always the older quarters with their stunning architecture, and the discovery of hidden gems in the form of tavernas in charming little squares; that delighted them the most.

Communications with the UK were kept to a minimum - selected family members, Kelly and Debs. During the third of the three months, Kelly and Debs came to stay for a week. Although this ran the risk of feeling like an intrusion on their precious time; it never did so. They delighted in showing them their favourite places, and sharing their happiness with the two people they felt the closest to, and the most comfortable with in the world.

Evenings of tapas, drinks and authentic Flamenco at local bars, turned into late night chats and laughter on the roof terrace, with no need for any more clothing than shorts and a t-shirt.

- "Debs and I were looking at the flight ads when we were booking this trip, especially to New York. We found some for £500 round trip!"

- "Yeah then we looked at first class, you know, just to see, for a bit of comfort, £3500!"

- "Yeah I think the businessmen must get blown throughout the flight whilst another attendant gives a foot massage. I can't see how else they can justify it!"

- "Kelly! Hahaha! What do the businesswomen get then?" replied Lorelei.

- "I guess it's along similar lines. Debs and I have started saving up anyway!"

- "Hahahaha, let us know how it turns out!"

- "I will! In other news Debs has a new flatmate."

- "I do; let's see if they're better than the last one!"

- "Sharing your home can be so tricky."

- "Present company excepted darling?"

- "Por supuesto sweetheart! I was referring to my time at Uni, and one guy in particular. One morning he said to me "Oi Adam, have you been using my fucking spoon?" And I said, "You have a special spoon just for fucking?! No wonder my yoghourts have been tasting a bit off!"

Chapter Eighty Four

By the time the second year had passed, life was rather more settled; as far as it could be so, with a ticking clock; silent, not referred to, yet always present.

Lorelei and Adam had moved house. The happiness they had shared there in their early days together, had been tarnished, and always would be tarnished; by having to pass through the scene of *his* scene. They were now living in Oxford, where neither had any obvious ties. Lorelei had enrolled in a creative writing course, from which she derived great pleasure; often surprising herself as much as Adam with the ideas she came up with. Adam had managed to secure some lecturing and seminar work with under-graduates, whilst beginning to dip an increasing number of toes into private practice.

Their circle of friends gradually widened, and within it they were always referred to affectionately as 'the inseparable couple'. Any questions about painful looking movements they made, were always quickly attributed to a car crash they had suffered a while back which they would rather not talk about. Kelly and Debs visited regularly, and often stayed overnight. They also saw each other frequently, independently of Lorelei and Adam.

Life seemed as good as it could be, far better than it might have been with a looming shadow over it. Then it got better still - Lorelei was pregnant.

It was not planned in any way, yet neither were precautions always taken with precision - the price of spontaneity. Lorelei had always worried that it may never be possible again, and along with who the father was this time; she was left in not the slightest dilemma.

Adam hardly felt ready for fatherhood, but was aware of her fears, and in any case; the thought of something as precious with Lorelei left him in no dilemma either.

The first scan after 8 weeks showed as far as it can, that all was well, to their great relief. The second scan came at 18 weeks, and showed a perfectly forming, active baby. They agreed to decline the offer of knowing the sex in advance, yet were both convinced that it was a girl.

Four weeks later, Adam was startled awake by a terrified Lorelei bellowing his name.

- "Something's happening….. it's not right……it's……"

Adam reached for his phone and called an ambulance, whilst reaching his other arm around Lorelei. She was in a lot of pain, but her distress was overriding even that. He held her closely, searching for anything of use to say.

The ambulance duly arrived, he let the Paramedics in and they rushed up the stairs, covered her in a blanket and led her down them again, into the ambulance, monitors, cables, beeps, cannular, sirens, calming phrases, tears, pleading, the being rushed through, the "mind out pleases", the transfer to a proper bed, more cables, tubes, screens, numbers, changing numbers, more staff, "please stand back Adam, we've got this", alert tones, fluids into the cannula, too late labour has started, Lorelei beside herself, Adam determinedly beside her, labour is continuing, more drugs administered, labour can't be stopped, hope for the best, incubator on standby, staff entering and leaving, "try not to push", here's the head, here it comes, so small, not breathing, not moving, attempts at resuscitation…..Stop.

Chapter Eighty Five

There can come a time when there is an event, a scenario, that goes so far beyond inconceivable, that even as one is there witnessing it at close range; one still cannot process it.

Attendees were deliberately kept to a minimum, and four of that small number spent that evening in a flat in Oxford. Alcohol was served, but only for its numbing qualities. The baby, Hannah, had not been planned nor expected, nor especially yearned for right then at the point of conception; but she had entered their consciousness, their vision of the and their future, something that would be a manifestation, an enduring proof of a beautiful love for all to see, that would have been cherished as much, and for as long as humanly possible. Sometimes, the absence of something, can be as profound as its presence.

Lorelei did not bounce back quickly, nor was she expected or pressured to do so. She deferred her place on the creative writing course until such time she felt she had anything to say, or could say, even if she did. Amongst the many feelings she was not so much wrestling with, as at full scale warfare with; was the sense that she had been cheated. Had everything she had been through, they had been through, was to have led to Hannah, it would have been worth it; she would have signed for it. Instead, the tacky game show of life had pulled back the curtain and said "And here's what you could have had!"

Adam doted on her more than ever, and Lorelei still gave him all she could, feeling his pain too. None of it really needed any discussion, it was all there in how they held each other, how they were together. He threw himself into work as far as he could, but could never get back home quickly enough.

Neither Lorelei nor Adam had directly asked the doctors whether her prior miscarriage, had anything to do with the fate that befell Hannah, and they would have expected a non-committal reply had they done so; but the intuitive belief that it very much did, hacked away at their attempts at recovery, like a pickaxe at a coalface. Healing to whatever extent it can and will be achieved, is a process of time; if one is fortunate enough to be afforded it.

Chapter Eighty Six

Despite the length and gravity of the list of charges brought, and the intent behind them; no previous offences, claims of crimes of passion, promises of anger management; all factored in to provide him with a prison sentence determined at just six years. With such determinate sentences qualifying for parole at the halfway point, the three years were flying by rather more quickly for Lorelei and Adam, than hoped they might have been for *him*.

Lorelei had not even felt the first pangs of the beginnings of recovery from her latest ordeal, when he was released back into civilised society. That his parole conditions included a Restraining Order to stay away from her and Adam, provided her as much comfort as one of *his* beatings. Whilst she did not doubt that *he* would have hated prison, and be in no hurry for a return; she did not fancy the chances of that holding out and winning the day, if it were ever to be pitted against *his* hateful viciousness, in the heat of the moment, should such a moment ever arise. She also knew that in the putrid sickness of *his* mind, everything had been her fault. *He* would have spent the last three years mulling that over.

Adam was labouring under no illusions either. What he had been mulling over were the relative merits of taking them both back to Spain for more recovery time and a sense of safety; versus staying put so as not to be feeling they were being controlled and dictated to, but with the side effects of impingement and danger that that would bring.

The dilemma came to quick resolution in his mind however, once he saw the changes in Lorelei within the first forty eight hours of *his* release. His own stress symptoms were palpable enough; but they could not compete with hers. She could barely eat, sleep, talk, keep still, breathe steadily, nor stop from shaking; and those were just the visible symptoms.

They flew from Birmingham, and so were able to head off without retreading any old ground. Never had "doors cleared for takeoff" been met with such tangible relief, as Adam felt her all but turn into a ragdoll snuggled into him.

Within a week of being in the sanctuary of his Spanish house; both were beginning to feel like they could sleep again, breathe again, function again, live again; although it was several weeks before they were not startled by any unexpected noise. Adam began to see patients online to maintain his practice, and Lorelei even began to do a little writing, when not reading, in bid to ensconce herself in another world.

Following this steady improvement however, Adam suddenly began behaving and presenting oddly one Tuesday morning. He was irritable even with Lorelei, which she had never seen the remotest flicker of before, he was lethargic, nauseous, began vomiting, his head throbbed, his neck became stiff, patches that looked like bruises appeared on his skin, he struggled to cope with light. Lorelei tried desperately not to panic, as the symptoms increased, seemingly by the minute; she had read about this. In her broken Spanish she attempted to summon an ambulance:

- "¡Quizás meningitis! Quizás meningitis!!"

The ambulance duly arrived quickly, but could only park a five minute wheel away, due to the narrow labyrinth-like streets of Torrox Pueblo. The paramedics did not enter immediately, waiting instead until they had donned their full personal protective equipment. Once they had entered, they were left in little doubt upon seeing and quickly examining Adam. It would have to be confirmed, but it did indeed very much appear to be Meningitis.

With Lorelei as yet at least, presenting no symptoms, they sufficed with taking a blood sample from her, and instructing her to stay at home for the time being. Adam by contrast was carefully whisked away to the nearest intensive care unit, although not before enduring a juddering stretcher ride over the cobbles, to begin a period of isolation and undergo specific tests.

Feeling like it was almost surreal, Lorelei suddenly found herself alone in the house with no idea what to do other than wait, and terrified as to the potential outcomes that lay in store. Any number of possible scenarios whirled around her mind; none of them good. She rang Debs, who did her best to calm her, to reassure her that one of the keys was catching it early, which she had done well to do and act quickly upon.

It was eight long, lonely hours before Lorelei heard anything at all, via a kindly Spanish doctor, Doctora Linnes, who spoke to her in English. First she delivered the good news - Lorelei's full blood count showed no sign of anything untoward. They would have to wait a few days for the results of her blood cultures; but for now at least, Lorelei appeared to be fine. She would just need to stay at home alone in the meantime.

Then she was struck with the bad news - Adam showed every sign of Bacterial Meningitis, which is potentially fatal, and contagious despite being bacterial rather than viral. They had already started him on steroid treatment, and an educated guess as to which antibiotic, which may be changed once his blood culture results were back. He was to remain sedated and isolated indefinitely. The doctor then reiterated Debs' point about early action being key, and told her how lucky she could consider herself, if indeed she hadn't caught it, given her closeness with Adam.

Lorelei felt many things - devastated, terrified, panicked, utterly alone; lucky did not make the list.

Chapter Eighty Seven

Adam's stimulation in its various forms was kept to a minimum, but no amount of darkness, sedation, or Meningitis, could prevent his desperate concern and yearning for Lorelei, nor could any medication calm that pain. Communication was maintained by Doctora Linnes, who went beyond just the medical specifics, in passing on messages of love between them.

By the fifth day, the situation began to improve somewhat. Lorelei's blood cultures were somehow negative, and following results, the doctor's instincts about which antibiotic to begin treating Adam with, had proved correct. It was now just a question of anxiously waiting and hoping, whilst trying to cope with the psychological torture of it all.

Sometimes, just when one is wondering if one can cope, will cope, with life's latest offering; it throws something else into one's path to intensify the contest, for a bit of extra interest. Sure enough just as Lorelei was starting to feel a little more hopeful, able to nip out for bread and provisions, to read again on the roof terrace to pass the time, to believe that Adam would make it after all; Kelly phoned:

- "It's your Dad Lorelei…..he's really poorly……he's…..not going to make it…..they're moving him to….palliative care."

-

- "I know you're not……exactly close…..haven't been for some time……but….you know."

- "Are you there hun?"

- "I'm here."

- "Maybe you should come over and……you know……say your goodbyes……make your peace…..He's been asking for you."

- "I……I can't leave Adam."

- "I understand, I do, but well…..you can't see Adam anyway….hopefully by the time you're back you'll be able to."

-

-

- "What about…….*him*?"

- "I doubt even *he*'d have the audacity to show *his* face now, but in any case, Debs and I won't leave your side, not even for a second, from Arrivals to Departures. You won't even be able to pee in private!"

-
-

- "I don't know Kells…..I'm really not sure……let me think about it okay?"

- "Okay but look.....you really haven't got long to decide hun."

- "I know."

Lorelei wrestled all that night with one of the great dilemmas of life - to do something or not to do it; which would prove to be more regretful? Could she live with herself after turning down his last request and not hearing what he had to say? Maybe.

The next day, by the time Kelly called again, Lorelei gave her flight details for her arrival the following day.

Lorelei informed Doctora Linnes of her situation and plans, but was told in no uncertain terms that were such information passed on to Adam, it would have a highly detrimental effect on his chances of recovery. As much as Lorelei hated the idea of keeping anything from him, she knew far better than the doctor, the effect it would cause. It was agreed that Lorelei would keep in regular touch from afar, and that Doctora Linnes would simply keep up the loving messages as before.

Chapter Eighty Eight

The following morning, with a lump in her throat, a mini Boa Constrictor in her chest, and some kind of expert sailor's knot in her stomach; Lorelei set off on the 0730 bus to Málaga. Her feelings of being a foreign outsider were amplified by those of detachment, of alienation, from all the other passengers who were seemingly just going about their normal day.

As the bus approached the city centre, wending its way along the seafront road, those beaches and palm trees forming the foreground to that blue Mediterranean; never looked so beautiful, or harder to leave behind.

Upon arrival, she made the now familiar enough walk across to the train station, across the concourse, ignoring the evocative enticements to go instead to Barcelona, and onto a train bound for the airport. The organised chaos of and at the airport never seemed less enticing, but she went through the motions largely within the confines of her own headspace, until finding herself in seat 11A. Thankfully she had a window seat; she needed a window. She had never been quite so conscious of that surge going right through her, as the engines ramped up the power for take off. She felt she wasn't so much changing countries, as universes.

The plane though, two hours and twenty minutes later, did duly land in the familiar surroundings of Gatwick airport. Never could there have been a more welcome or relieving sight to behold, than the smiling faces of Kelly and Debs to Lorelei's anxiously searching eyes in Arrivals. The three way hug was in danger of being moved on for obstruction.

As they eventually went to make their way into London, Kelly and Debs imparted their carefully thought out plans. The three of them were to stick together at all times come what may. They were to all stay at Debs' flat as *he* had no knowledge of where that was, nor that she was even still in the picture. It was to be airport, Hospice, Debs' flat, airport; military precision, no deviations.

The term relaxed could not have applied at any stretch, but Lorelei did at least feel slightly less anxious with the confident determination and company of her two friends. She could do this; she would do this, and soon she'd have the feeling, the sensations as the Spanish would say, of heading home to Adam.

The designers and the staff of the hospice did their best to make the environment as pleasant as possible, but there is only so much one can do to disguise and soften the fact that people have come there to die.

One of Lorelei's anxieties was quelled at least, when she arrived there to discover that her father was still with us. The degree to which he was managing to hang on in there in order to see his daughter, is hard to measure. She was greeted outside the door to his room by a long embrace from her mother, whom she had been equally estranged from, before she, along with Kelly and Debs, let her enter alone.

- "Hi Dad."

He stirred and turned towards her.

- "Lori...you came…..I said….I said you would…your Mum wasn't…so sure."

- "I couldn't not come Dad. Dumb question….how are you?"

- "Oh you know….. terrific."

- "Yeah I can tell."

- "I'm sorry….I wasn't….there for you more….. wasn't….a better father for you."

- "I expect you did your best Dad, like most people do. I'm sorry too. . that I….shut you and Mum out so much."

-

-

- "This Adam fella of yours……does he take care of you…..love you….like he should?"

- "He doesn't just love me Dad, he adores me."

- "I'm so glad darling…..hang on to him won't you?"

- "Oh I will Dad!"

- "Tell your Mum we've….made our peace won't you? She'll be…..so pleased."

- "You can tell her yourself in a bit Dad."

The conversation had been no more in depth than she had expected it to be under the circumstances; but she was glad they'd had it. Taxi back to Debs' place, wine, take away, taxi to the airport, homeward to Adam.

At 0512, a little under an hour before the alarm was due to go off, a message came through on Kelly's phone from Lorelei's Mum - her Dad had slipped away. The funeral, already half arranged in anticipation, was to be in three days' time.

Chapter Eighty Nine

Adam, still sedated, but not quite as heavily as before, was roused slightly by the sound of a nurse milling about outside his room whilst talking on a presumably portable phone. Consequently she kept coming in and out of earshot. Despite that and his only being able to hear one side of the conversation in any case, he gleaned enough of it to realise to his horror that Lorelei was not only in England, but also upon hearing "Que descanse en paz", that her return had been delayed due to a death.

The nurses and doctors desperately tried to calm Adam for the sake of his illness, and reassure him that Lorelei was okay, not alone, and would be back in three days time.

Adam tried to impart the seriousness of the situation, that they didn't understand the danger she was in; and ascertain if he was still in fact contagious, or just ill?

Upon learning that it could not be ascertained as to which, without awaiting a series of further tests results, cutting off Adam's attempts at immediately discharging himself at the pass; he broke down almost uncontrollably until the extra sedation quickly administered kicked in. By the time he was compos mentis again, it was already the day of the funeral.

Lorelei had remained inside Debs' flat whilst awaiting the funeral. She had been desperate and tempted to return to Adam as planned, having already said her goodbyes; but her mother "would not hear of it," and she would not have heard the end of it had she gone.

The morning finally arrived, along with a taxi to take her, Kelly, and Debs to her parent's house, where they were to proceed to the cemetery in a funeral car. To the annoyance of Lorelei's mother, but at the insistence of Kelly and Debs, they all travelled together in that vehicle.

Amid the grieving, the condolences and the tears, three pairs of eyes kept a sharp look out for any highly unwelcome attendees. In fact there was a fourth pair discreetly doing so too, after Kelly had invited WPC Whitworth, who had slipped in at the back of the prayer hall, out of uniform.

The party then moved solemnly from the hall to the burial site, with Lorelei flanked on both sides for the entirety of her father's final journey, and as he was laid to rest and covered in earth. At no point at the post-funeral drinks and food in the private room of the nearby Coach and Horses, was she left alone either, not even to pee, as promised.

WPC Whitworth even saw them safely into a mini cab before bidding them farewell, to much gratitude from all three. During the ride back to Debs' flat, Lorelei was glad she had stayed behind, but was itching almost uncontrollably to get back to Adam in the morning, whom she was assured had been sleeping peacefully.

They got out of the car, paid the driver and arranged for a pick up at 6am. They waved the driver off just as they slipped inside the doorway and closed the door behind them, amidst sighs of relief. Lorelei got a message to Adam that all had gone well, that she would be back in the morning, and that she loved him even more than she'd thought.

At 5.50 am a car could be heard outside with its engine running; up and ready all three headed downstairs, in spite of Lorelei's protests that she'd be fine from here.

As Debs' head even began to emerge it was coshed before it could take anything in. As she fell to the ground, Kelly's emerging head suffered the same fate as did her body. Lorelei's attempts at closing the door in panic were thwarted by her two unconscious friends. Whilst the scream was still forming in her throat, *he* had trodden over Debs and Kelly, and coshed Lorelei too. Almost in one movement, *he* dragged Debs and Kelly inside, slung Lorelei over *his* shoulder and headed to the waiting car, shutting the front door behind *him*, threw her in the boot, and drove off. Five minutes later, the minicab driver cursed his luck as he received no reply to his repeated presses of the doorbell. Two minutes after that *he* had pulled into a dark alleyway, opened the boot, tied and gagged the still unconscious Lorelei, before continuing on their way.

Chapter Ninety

Kelly first, then Debs, still dazed and in pain, were roused by the sound of a phone ringing inside Lorelei's small suitcase. It was Adam. By the time Kelly had gathered her wits and fumbled around for the phone, the call was missed. It rang again immediately, and divining what pin number Lorelei would use, she was able to answer it.

- "Sweetheart, you okay!?"

- "Ad...it's me, Kelly."

- "Is everything okay? You sound....strange!?"

-

- "Kells!?"

- "I'm not quite sure .....what happened.....We were just leaving for the airport.....we were hit.....and now...."

- "Where's Lorelei!? Where's Lorelei!!?"

- "She's......I don't know...I'm so..."

Adam reached for his notes at the foot of his bed. Desperately scanning them for his latest test results. "No longer contagious, but in need of at least another 7-10 days of treatment and recuperation."

He disconnected himself from every cable and machine, removed his cannula, stuck some surgical tape over the puncture point, and frantically got dressed. There were very few staff around at that early hour, but just enough so that one came into his room to check on the warning beeps of the machines, before he was out the door.

The conversation in Spanish that followed was as fast as it was brief:

- "What are you doi..."

- "Emergency emergency have to go have to go!"

- "But you can't!"

- "Sorry, no choice!"

Weak and increasingly dizzy, he rushed from the room, from the ward, from the building, from the grounds; and into the first taxi on the rank. By the end of the twenty five minute journey home he had managed to find a flight at an exorbitant price leaving in four and a half hours. Taking no chances, he asked the driver to wait whilst he rushed in for his passport and a few grabable items; and within ten minutes he was on his way to the airport,

Travelling can be stressful at the best of times, but as anyone unfortunate enough to be far away from where they desperately need to be, at the time of learning of a grave emergency can testify; it can reach the realms of pure psychological torture. Every person, every slightest little thing en route, or of procedure, every word; is another obstacle thrown into one's path to be overcome, cruelly extending the agony. Adam would have run the distance if he could, just for a sense of some semblance of influence and control.

He, on the other hand, was feeling rather pleased with himself after a busy few days. He had heard of the death of Lorelei's father, and figured that from wherever she was; she was bound to go to the funeral. How clever they thought they all were sticking close to her at all times. Even that bitch copper was there, going over and above the call of duty. Such vigilance! Not vigilant enough though to notice that old man with a thick grey beard, in that innocuous car, stolen from people who wouldn't know it was missing for a week or two; who'd kept towards the back of the procession of cars heading from the cemetery to the pub; and just back far enough from the minicab that left the pub, yet just close enough at the last minute to walk by and hear the arrangements being made for the morning.

As a car with its elderly driver, made its way out of London towards country roads, an unseen, soon to be utterly distraught woman in the boot, slowly came to.

Chapter Ninety One

First came a throbbing sensation in the back of her head, then a strange sense of motion. Stranger still that upon opening her eyes, there was no change in the darkness all around her. Something was covering her mouth, intruding inside it. As she tried to move, she found that she could move neither her hands nor feet, not independently anyway, as she could feel something restricting her wrists and ankles. Then came the realisation, and the full horror that accompanied it.

Nothing could match the pain induced by the thought of the moment when Adam would receive the news, perhaps he had already, whilst helplessly laying in a hospital bed 1500 miles of land and water away. She could never rid herself of *him*, but had allowed herself to bring *him* inextricably into Adam's life too. He had allowed it knowingly, but she couldn't forgive herself for letting him, for making him want to.

The only thing that even came close to that pain, was the additional thought, the heartbreaking fear, that she may never see him again. She sobbed uncontrollably, yet somehow almost silently, so as not to give *him* the satisfaction of hearing her suffering.

Kelly and Debs were equally distraught. They had managed to reach WPC Whitworth after several tries, as the best starting point they could think of in those first few moments, cutting through many of the questions they would have faced with a 999 call. As much as WPC Whitworth knew of the background, there was actually little to go on, but she started every ball rolling that she could think of. Photos, descriptions, news bulletins, national police alerts, airports, ports, known associates, family members, potential addresses of refuge.

It was all very thorough; but it was nothing he had not gleefully anticipated. He was heading to where he had always planned to take her, if he ever saw her again. A scenario he had played out in his head, rehearsed to perfection a thousand times, during those long prison nights with little else to occupy the sickness of his mind.

Chapter Ninety Two

After a journey of seemingly biblical proportions, an exhausted Adam in every sense, fuelled only by the adrenaline of extreme anxiety; finally arrived at Debs' flat. The news updates that there was still no news, had done nothing to improve any aspect of his condition.

Kelly was still there to form a part of the threeway support team, but in reality no amount of support could do much to lessen the feelings of helplessness and fear in the extreme. No one dared to voice them; no one needed to do so. Phone screens were stared at, glared at even, as if somehow they could collectively will the arrival of news of her safe discovery. Woe betide anyone who contacted them about anything else.

Debs managed to use her professional experience to maintain some semblance of practically. She gently but firmly steered Adam into the shower, before insisting that he at least lay down on the sofa. She also arranged for a colleague to deliver some much needed medication for him.

Adam was hardly in a restful mood though. Finally he was compelled to speak:

- "Right, let's try and enter *his* putrid mind. *He*'ll know the avenues down which the Police will go, and therefore what and where to avoid. *He*'ll have known his face will get plastered everywhere, so it's safe to assume that *he* isn't going about looking anything like *his* true self. *He* can't be putting Lorelei on display anywhere either, so it's also safe to assume that she was, maybe still is; hidden in the back of the presumably stolen car *he* played *his* trick with. *He* would have had no more than three days' notice to plan this, beyond the three years in prison of course, and only a few hours to plan *his* exact route from here. So where does *he* go?"

- "*He* heads out of London towards the countryside by the shortest possible route."

- "I reckon so too Kells, but it's worse than that. I reckon *he* heads for the cover of plain sight - the M25. No one knows what they're looking out for, so *he's* not worried about traffic cameras. Then from there, *he* can head anywhere *he* bloody likes!"

- "*He* can't be on the road the whole time though. *He* has to head for some cover. An empty house maybe?"

- "Doesn't narrow it down much does it?"

They all knew what it meant - she either gets herself out, or she doesn't get out; no one's going to find her. They all stopped talking.

Around the time this desperate conversation was taking place, a car had slowly trundled down a distant, quiet country lane towards an old farmhouse. It was rare for anyone to have cause to visit it these days, let alone twice in three days. The driver pulled up by a run down haybarn, got out to pull open the creaky doors, drove inside, switched off the engine, and got out again to close and secure the doors from the inside. *He then opened the boot of the car.*

- "Out you pop darling, we're home!"

Chapter Ninety Three

WPC Whitworth and the wider forces at work were drawing blanks down and from every possible avenue. Occasionally a report of a possible sighting, even vaguely matching the descriptions and photos, would raise a flicker of hope; only to fail to endure closer scrutiny.

She cursed the parole system and the faith that anyone puts in Restraining Orders, which can only attempt to do anything effective after the event, so often making a fool of the hope that the deterrent factor will outweigh other motivations.

She and anyone else she could find to join in, spent every available extra hour gathering, scanning CCTV footage from anywhere and everywhere in the original locality, gradually expanding the radius, looking for anything even vaguely unusual. Nothing, nothing, nothing.

In the meantime, the one person who knew *his* exact whereabouts, was tied sprawled out in a star shape, in horrific psychological and physical pain, bleeding, with the vomit-inducing sensation of *his* sperm oozing out of her, and down her inner thighs.

He lit up a cigarette.

- "Ahhhh that's better! Three years inside is a long fucking time! I bet you missed me too aye darling!?"

-

- "Not saying much eh? Don't worry we'll have plenty of time to chat, you know, really catch up properly!"

On the second day, *he* raped her four more times, always face up. Every time she turned her face away from *him*, she received a slap, a punch, or had her face grabbed forcefully and held still.

By the third day, when the closest she had come to washing *him* away was when *he* had thrown buckets of water over her to 'keep her fresh'; she was already debating whether she actually wanted to survive.

It didn't matter what *he* did to try to force her; she would not speak to *him* even when *he* did remove the gag. Finally on the fifth day there came some respite. *He* opened the barn doors, and back in full disguise set off in the car, securing Lorelei, and the barn doors extra tightly.

As she heard the car drive away, she wept like never before, so pained and hopeless, and never saltier.

Chapter Ninety Four

Kelly sat bolt upright in bed at 3.31am.

- "The old man, the old man!"

Debs who was barely sleeping replied:

- "What? What old man?"

- "When we got out of the minicab that night……we'd had a bit to drink……I didn't think much of it at the time……an old man shuffled past."

- "You don't think….?"

- "Well how else did *he* know where we were…..or what time we were leaving…..it must have been *him*."

- "Did you see him get out of a car……or back into one?"

- "No…..but it's…. something….something to go on. Adam!"

Armed with this new piece of information, WPC Whitworth and any volunteer or conscript, set to work with a renewed sense of purpose and vigour, revisiting every inch of footage of CCTV they could painstakingly access. Traffic cameras, motorway cameras, speed cameras, high streets, car parks, supermarkets, petrol stations, supermarket car parks, petrol stations at supermarkets. Hour upon hour, with many a false alarm until, there!

A grey bearded old man, coming out of a big supermarket, loading up a car with a plentiful supply of provisions, looking a tad too agile for a grey bearded old man. The same grey bearded old man spending long enough at a petrol pump to be filling the tank to the brim. A clear sight of the make, model, and number plate of the car. She raised the alarm to every police unit in the country, and across the media, urging the public to call 999 upon any sighting of the vehicle.

He was rather enjoying himself. A nice drive out in the countryside before stocking up a few supplies, nowhere too close by just in case; and then a nice drive back again, before giving her a bit more of what he reckoned she loved really, and if she didn't well, serves her right, she should have remembered he'd be the one to decide when it was over.

He drove for twenty miles before pulling into a large out of town supermarket in Faversham. He had a leisurely stroll about the isles, finding many of his favourite snacks, before heading to the toiletries section, to buy a large sponge and some shower gel. It was about time she had a wash down, she's starting to smell, she'll enjoy a good rigorous bed bath!

As he just began to emerge from the big doors he stopped dead in his tracks. There, having a close look around his car, was a Policeman, already talking into his radio. He quickly went back inside, trying to stay calm. He headed into the toilets and quickly removed his grey beard, before exiting again, reuniting with the trolley, and emerged into the car park, feigning to be heading towards a different car in a different row beyond his one, watching the Policeman out of the corner of his eye the whole time. The Policeman now had his eyes firmly fixed on the supermarket exit, as he talked into his radio, calling again for urgent reinforcements. He had abandoned the trolley, he was stealthy, he crept closer little by little, ducked down behind the car, picked his exact moment and cosh! By the time the Policeman hit the ground he was already entering the car and starting the engine. He headed towards the petrol station, pulled up at the side of the car wash for cover, and waited. He did not have to wait long before numerous police cars began to arrive, heading towards his former parking spot.

At the point the first of them found their stricken colleague, he slowly emerged from the petrol station, and away he went, desperate to get just enough distance to get off of the main roads, and back towards the safety of Lorelei. A flaw in his plan quickly emerged though when he realised that other police cars were still appearing from all directions, and he had been spotted. Now he had a new mission; to get as far away from Lorelei as possible, and with a heavy foot, he set off on it.

Weaving in and out of cars like a demented racing driver, taking risks even the most experienced police drivers would not take; kept him ahead. Onto the A2 he went heading east towards Dover, further and further from her with every revolution of the wheels, with sirens blaring in alarm, sounding close, but not yet close enough. Near miss was followed by nearer miss, he could see the terror on the faces of other drivers, which only fuelled him further. Eventually the police cars closed in enough for the faces of their drivers to be visible. He waited until the last possible second before careering right across the carriageway to exit A2050. The manoeuvre all but worked, save for one of the police drivers, who having half anticipated it; managed to make the exit too. He got to the first roundabout and headed for the least busy looking exit, hoping to just slip out of sight and away in time, but the pursuing car kept track. As he took country bend after country bend at increasingly reckless speeds, he began to pull away again. Just as the words "fuck you coppers" were spewing from his mouth around the next blind bend, there it came - a perfectly timed stinger cast across the road. There was not even time to attempt a last gasp swerve. His tyres crossed the stinger and burst almost in unison, his speed though still carried the car on further until a large tree ended its momentum. He hit his head on the window, hard, but nowhere near hard enough. He jumped out of the car and began to run for all he was worth; so by the time he had gone three strides he was rugby tackled to the ground, and by the time he had even begun to squirm, four more Policemen were all over him like the illest of ill fitting suits.

Chapter Ninety Five

- "Adam? It's WPC Whitworth, we've got *him*!"

- "And Lorelei!!??"

- "No….not yet….we need *him* to tell us where she is….. assuming *he* knows that is, and she didn't get away."

- "What's *he* told you so far!?"

- "Nothing. *He*'s claiming *he*…. can't remember anything."

- "Fucking scumbag!!"

- "I know. At least we know one thing though - she isn't with *him* anymore!"

- "Yeah that's definitely something! I don't hold out much hope though for the 'she got away theory'….. surely we'd have heard by now?"

- "Well yes, but you never know…. she could be hiding somewhere too terrified to come out yet?"

- "Yeah, maybe….."

One long day later, in a formerly disused barn, 43 miles from where he was arrested, Lorelei was already starting to feel the effects of dehydration, in the form of an increasingly painful headache.

By the second day, she might have noticed having painful joints, if they weren't already so sore and bleeding from trying repeatedly to free herself from *his* shackles. Her ear was tuned to the slightest sound coming from outside. Beyond an unlikely rescue, there only seemed to be two possible outcomes - *he* comes back to torture her more with a glimmer of hope that *he* would let her go, eventually; or *he* never does, and therefore no one does. It was hard to say which was preferable. The former at least came with the possibility of seeing Adam, Kelly and Debs again, but could she even carry on, could they even carry on, so burdened by the weight of the pain? Could they carry on if she never made it out?

By day three her brain was swelling, her organs were starting to fail, she was losing consciousness "Adam……Adam…."

By day four she was having seizures, barely conscious in between them, with terrible stomach pain when she was so, and a swollen abdomen either way. She went into Hypovolemic shock, as her lack of fluids meant her heart could not pump enough blood around her body anymore.

By day five she was barely breathing; by day six, she was not.

Adam, Kelly, and Debs lived a horrendous existence wavering between anxious waiting and increasing hopelessness. No amount of threats of an increase in the seriousness of the charges, and the consequent length of the prison sentence;

could entice *him* to say anything other than *he* couldn't remember anything.

The police search teams combed areas at an increasing radius stemming out from the supermarket. It was six weeks before they got to the barn, with its new looking padlock seeming out of place.

The autopsy confirmed that she had died from dehydration, as had the ten week old foetus inside her.

Chapter Ninety Six

The next new day kept dawning, but the darkness never left. It was like having the least desirable companion imaginable, on the longest possible journey.

Adam wondered how much pain would it take for his brain to simply decide to shut itself down, to call it a day, to end the suffering once and for all, that being alive cannot possibly be worth this. How much? Life at any and all costs? Even like this? Seventy years of this would be better than the sweet nothingness of death? Why? Who or what would decide to choose that when presented with an alternative?

Nonetheless, in the absence of his taking the conscious decision to physically do it, and his brain refusing to override its most fundamental instinct; continue on he did. He had to at least get to the funeral, then review the position after that. He had already imagined that he would simply walk off afterwards, in the absence of anything else to do, or any other course of action to take. He could see no further than that though. Perhaps he would just keep going until he dropped down dead from exhaustion? He hoped so.

In the meantime, whether consciously or not, Adam, Kelly and Debs, did not, would not, let eachother out of their sights. Adam's previous sleeping spot on the sofa was changed, and instead he joined the other two in Debs' double bed. There may have been momentary losses of consciousness, but in the main the three lay awake, sometimes talking a lot, sometimes hardly at all, and sometimes in complete silence. An overwhelming sense of disbelief, does nothing to help along the act, or even the beginning of processing. Over the all but seven weeks, hope had been fading commensurately with the increasing surety that she would never be found alive; but until it was actually confirmed, there had been at least the tiniest gilmour of possibility, of some extremely unlikely scenario that no one had conceived of, arriving to save the day. Once that had gone, there was nowhere to go other than head full throttle into the abyss they had been staring at in horror all the while.

Debs had been the only one even vaguely capable of making any funeral arrangements, and even then only with help from colleagues. Adam and Kelly could barely bring themselves to get dressed, or get into the Hearse. When the darkest clouds would have been far more fitting, the forces at work contrived to make it a sunny day, with fluffy clouds effortlessly floating about an otherwise clear blue sky, in a deceitful attempt to claim that all was well with the world, that life goes on, and that it's a wonderful, beautiful, desirable thing to behold.

Before heading inside, Adam, Kelly and Debs did what they could to conform with the expected social norm of meeting and greeting the other attendees outside the prayer hall; but it was a token effort, even with Lorelei's Mother, there burying her daughter so soon after her husband.

They sat together holding hands, until such time as Adam was signalled to approach centre stage. After a final squeeze of his arms as an attempt at passing their last remaining strength and support to him; he approached and stood there, utterly alone.

Chapter Ninety Seven - Three years, three months and two days until *his* release

Emily and Adam had been rolling along with relative happiness. Adam kept his most obsessive thoughts largely to himself, but Emily was very perceptive in general, and especially where he was concerned.

Daria had become a firm fixture in their lives. Although the mostly innocent bed hopping incident had not been repeated; none of the three were under any illusions as to the degree to which Daria was in love with Adam. He was as sensitive as he could be around her, trying not to be too affectionate with Emily in her direct presence. Emily, rather than being in any way hostile, was increasingly fond and close to Daria, in a wonderful display of how humans can be with each other, once in the fairly rare scenario whereby everything is out in the open. In any event, a potentially more threatening danger was increasingly looming in the form of Jonathan's release from prison.

Emily had already achieved a divorce, and within the negotiated settlement of such, gained the house. However the thought never left her nor Adam, that losing a wife, albeit one that one likes to beat, is one thing; losing one to the man responsible for framing you into prison, is quite another.

That he should decide to slip away quietly, thus avoiding more prison time, was a possibility; whether it was likely, warranted plenty more consideration. Adam was not about to be complacent and simply wait and see what was to come to pass.

With little effort, Adam ascertained Jonathan's future address, in fact he knew of it before Jonathan did. Given the scandal, Adam was confident that he would not be showing his face at the golf club anytime soon, but he would need to occupy his time. He would be desperate to find gainful employment, but may struggle with the undesirable blot on his previously impeccable CV.

What might he have dreamed up during his time in prison? Dreaming something up is one thing, how far he might be prepared to act upon it, is quite another. Whilst both Emily and Adam did their best to reassure each other that he would be very foolish and unlikely to attempt anything drastic; neither was able to entirely convince themselves.

When the day finally dawned, Adam made sure that not only was he at home with Emily, but that Kelly was with them. Her role in the affair was hardly likely to have been forgotten either. They talked about the need for vigilance at all times, for charged phones, for making sure they always knew where each other would be, what time they were likely due back, and to give confirmation when they were back.

Jonathan had indeed passed much of his time deep in contemplation, cursing the day that Adam had appeared in his previously lovely life. However he was too euphoric at finally leaving the living hell that had been prison, to be planning anything that ran the risk of a swift return. His priority was to see if he could call in any old favours, and get himself back earning a good living in the City. Luckily for him, there is no club like an old boy's club, no misdemeanour that cannot be glossed over when required, and it was not long before he was looking every bit like a respectable businessman in a nice suit, travelling on the tube, with a briefcase and umbrella completing the facade.

By the end of his first month back in the world of high finance and splendid lunches, when his first salary payment had appeared in his bank account; the world seemed a bright place again. By the end of the third month he really had started living again in a manner befitting a Senior City Executive. On a Friday night out with colleagues for cocktails, he had even managed to persuade one of the younger staff members, after a cocktail too many, to take him home with her for the night.

He left her flat the following morning feeling extremeñy pleased with himself, and began to walk, hoping the fresh air would begin to clear his hangover. As he reached the end of her road and onto a main road, he realised where he was - only a few streets from his old house. The temptation for an innocent walk by was too much to resist; it couldn't hurt surely, just for old time's sake?

He was still five houses away when the front door suddenly opened; and there they all were, clear as day, the three of them laughing and hugging like butter wouldn't melt. He stopped abruptly, biding his time behind the cover of a tree and a window fitter's van, fighting the impulse to run and confront them. Once they had gone though, would he dare to go and see Emily? No you fool, remember you're still on parole! He remained in his spot, watching on quietly as the scene played out. When the single person of the trio said their affectionate goodbyes to the happy couple, and left, it was all he could do not to yell out in fury and incredulity. That conniving bastard!

Fuelled by the sheer indignity of it all, he found himself following Kelly from a distance as she headed away, fighting the impulse to run and assault her there and then and just about winning the day. She headed for the tube in her blissful ignorance as he followed just closely enough to keep tabs on her route. He sat in the next carriage with enough people around to maintain his anonymity, but not enough to obscure his vision of her. She changed trains and he repeated the exercise. When she finally got off and headed back up overground, he increased the distance between them again as far as practically possible. She looked round a couple of times but saw nothing of concern, before heading towards her front door and letting herself inside. Jonathan turned around and headed back for the tube station.

Chapter Ninety Eight

Two weeks later Kelly was arriving home from an evening out with Debs, phone in hand. As she approached the last fifty metres to her front door she texted the whatsapp group to say that she was home safe and sound, and was ready for bed.

As she turned her key in the door, something was suddenly placed over her head down to her waist, severely restricting her movement as well as her vision. As she went to scream she felt a hand cover her mouth with plenty of force, something sharp in the base of her back, then an alcohol fuelled voice whisper in her ear:

- "Keep very quiet and still. Anything to the contrary will result in this knife penetrating your spinal cord, then you'll definitely be quiet and still. Understood?"

Kelly nodded and mumbled her ascension as best she could, as her assailant guided her inside, closing the door behind them.

- "Lead on darling."

As they arrived at her actual front door, he snatched the keys from her, opened the door, led her inside, and then closed it again behind them.

He made her lay face down on the bed, still with the sack over her head and arms. He sat across her legs to prevent any possible sudden kicking movements, and kept the knife pressing into the base of her back, so that it penetrated just enough to hurt her and provide a constant deterrent.

- "Now the last time I saw you Kelly, hhmmm let me think, ah yes, you were to wait outside that pub, with the promise of a future shag! Shall we shag now? I've certainly waited my time, it seems long overdue."

As he said this last phrase, through her jeans he ran two fingers down between her buttocks to her vagina and kept them there. Instinctively she tried to move away from his touch, but was given a sharp reminder to keep very still.

- "You can go and fuck yourself you disgusting pig!"

- "Now Kelly, I really don't think you're in the best position to be insulting me, do you? Look, I'll keep my fingers here to keep you in the mood, but let's leave our pending shag, just for now, as I've a few questions for you first."

- "How thoughtful, whilst being utterly repulsive at the same time!"

- "Not lost your spunk I see, but you can have some of mine soon anyway."

- "I'd rather die!"

- "Are you entirely sure about that Kelly?" As the knife was pressed a little harder.

- "Yes!"

- "Okay well let's put that on the back burner for now. It does rather add to the excitement, I'm already as stiff as a board at the thought of emptying a few loads into you. You might surprise yourself and really enjoy it! Now, let's start the questions, and a nice easy one as a starter for ten. Who's idea was it to frame me?"

-

- "Don't make me draw blood Kelly!"

- "It was all of ours due to your being a violent wife-beating pig."

- "I see thank you, and at what point did your wonderfully clever, superhero friend start shagging my Emily? Long beforehand one supposes?"

- "You're wrong on three counts there genius. Adam isn't, or even trying to be a superhero; he just hates scumbags that's all."

- "You could have fooled me!"

- "Yeah I know, we did!"

- "Stop it Kelly, you're making me so hard! I guess it's deliberate! What are the other two counts I'm so wrong about then?"

- "Emily and Adam only got together long afterwards."

- "Hhhmmm really!? You must have been devastated!"

- " No, I was happy for them actually."

- "I highly doubt that."

- "No surprise there. It comes from wanting to see other people happy!"

- "How you wound me Kelly! What's the third thing?"

- "She isn't your Emily."

- "You really are a top class filly! Now keep still, sorry to move my hand from your inevitably soaking wet pussy, don't worry it'll soon be back; I'm just reaching for your phone. A quick borrow of your thumb, that's it, let's see now, WhatsApp, contacts, ah look you've a little group, how cosy! Well we don't really want the whole gang here do we, that could get messy, how about we just invite our mutual friend Adam? Perhaps he could watch me shag you; maybe even join in? Or perhaps I'll just watch as he shags you? We'll just go with the flow shall we?"

- "Adam help I need you right, now come quickly and alone."

- "I'm sure he won't be long in replying, ahh yes look!"

- "Are you okay Kells?"

- "No no clues, we'll just leave it there, that should have him over in a jiffy!"

- "I'll offer you a way out before it's too late Jonathan. Leave right now, and I'll never speak of this again. I'll make up some crisis to Adam."

- "Ha ha nice try Kelly, but we'd miss all the fun! You bastards owe me! In any case, do you seriously think I'd trust you again?"

- "Well I don't see this ending well for you otherwise."

- "You're so sweet to be concerned for my welfare Kelly! I'm touched, truly I am. Don't you worry, I've a little family card to play which is sure to prevent your going to the police, so let's just enjoy it!"

A long half an hour later, involving a fraught journey for Adam wherein he imagined any number of possible scenarios; Kelly's door buzzer sounded.

- "Ah and here he is, such a dependable chap! Let's let him in shall we? Up you get, nice and slowly, that's it, let's go to the door together."

With Kelly close at hand, he pressed the intercom button to release the door, put her door on the latch, and guided her back to lay face down on the bed at knifepoint to wait.

Within a minute Adam appeared, calling out as he did so:

- "Everything okay Kells?"

- "Adam hi! How great that you came over and how lovely to see you again! We were just talking about you!"

- "Kells are you okay!? Has he hurt you?"

- "He's already indecently assaulted me at knifepoint with the promise of worse to come, but I'm okay. So sorry you've been dragged here."

- "Oh come now Kelly, no pun intended, a little feel of your arse and wet pussy through your jeans? It hardly amounts to much does it?"

- "You hardly amount to much!"

- "Don't you just love her feistiness Adam? Talking of feisty women, how's my dear old Emily doing? Getting on your nerves yet?"

-

- "Nothing to say huh? Well I know better than anyone how annoying she can be. Anyway it's been great catching up, but let's crack on shall we? Adam, I'd like you to come over and very carefully, remembering that there is a knife on the point of paralysing dear Kelly here for life in an instant; make a hole in the sack so that her head can pop through. That's it, we want her to have a good view now don't we? Excellent, now move away, swift switch to her jugular, that's it, now back you come, undo her jeans, and slowly peel them down over her lovely arse, not the knickers yet, let's take our time and enjoy it. Wow Kelly that's quite the body you're packing, as Adam here already knows. Okay Adam, now run your hand slowly up between her legs, slower, that's it, stop just at her inner thighs, hmmm lovely. Now nice and gently rub up and down her pussy through her knickers with the back of your first two fingers, is she wet yet? I bet she is! Okay a little faster, not too much. That's the way. She'll be gagging for you by now I'll bet! Right let's see this cock that's been doing my Emily all this time. Slip out of those tracksuit bottoms and boxer shorts...excellent. Oh dear you're not very aroused are you? Right, we'll soon see to that! Start rubbing your cock up and down her arse crack, that should soon have you in the mood eh!? Nice! Okay slowly pull down her knickers... slowly Adam! I know you want her badly but don't rush these things! Throw them to me! Hhmmm you smell lovely Kelly, just how I'd imagined you! Okay Kelly, now your move. Very slowly open those thighs as wide as they'll go. Come on, you can go wider than that! Adam's about to fuck you, you'll want to make the most of it! Okay move in between them Adam, and really really slowly, slide into her, bit by bit, but all the way to the balls."

Just as the tip of Adam was at the very point of entering Kelly, Adam's phone sounded the receipt of a message.

- "You might want to get that Jonathan, I think it's something for you."

- "Nice one Adam, okay we'll delay a minute, it all adds to the build up! I'll stay here with the knife, while you get your phone and show it to me. Oh look it's something from Emily! How sweet! I'll bet she'll be extra sweet when you get home and tell her you've fucked Kelly!"

- "No it really is something for you, look!"

As Adam pressed play on the video message, a familiar scene unfolded before Jonathan's eyes - a complete rerun of the scenario since Adam's arrival, complete with audio. He watched on in horror, before looking mouth agog at the previously unnoticed pin on Adam's bag, left on the table since his arrival.

- "Now unless Emily hears from me otherwise, you've two minutes before that video goes straight to the police. That will of course involve another, rather longer prison sentence, but I don't want a repeat in a few years time, so you can go now, and if we ever see or hear from you again in any way shape or form, we'll send it then."

- "You fucking……!"

- "No time for fucking Jonathan, I calculate you've about 30 seconds left to decide, or it's decided for you."

- "Tell her it's a deal, tell her tell her!"

Adam typed "Deal, we're okay." into his phone and hit send, before showing it to Jonathan.

Still holding the knife, he ran from the room, slamming Kelly's door and then the front door behind him. Adam turned away to put his boxers and trousers back on, leaving Kelly time to get dressed, before comforting her on her bed, holding her close as she sobbed in terror and relief.

- "How did you know Ad?"

- "Well I've been fearing he might do something, and then your message seemed suspiciously worded, so I came prepared. When you just buzzed me up without a word, instead of one of your usual greetings; I knew."

- "Fucking hell Adam!"

- "I know Kells, I know."

- "You'd better ring Emily."

- "Yeah."

Having not wanted to leave Kelly there alone, after she'd taken a shower, she and Adam were soon heading back to Emily in a taxi.

- "Will she be okay Ad? It must have been beyond hideous for her to watch that scene!"

- "Not right away, but she will be…..I hope…..and that you will be too."

They rode the rest of the way in silence, cuddled up on the back seat. Unusually and not surprisingly, Emily was not waiting by an open front door upon their arrival. They made their way inside wherein there was no disguising the sound of sobbing coming from upstairs. Adam led Kelly into the lounge and poured her an extra large Spanish brandy, before leaving her curled up with it in an armchair and heading upstairs to Emily.

The time for deep conversation would come, but for now, he simply kissed her tenderly, took a quick shower, and then did his best impression of an Emily entwining under the duvet for the next half an hour or so. It was she who finally interrupted it, conscious of the fact that Kelly was downstairs and alone. They both headed downstairs and joined Kelly in person, and in the drinking of Soberano. Emily and Kelly embraced, apologising profusely to each other repeatedly through their tears. Adam deliberately left them to it whilst he prepared some snacks with which to soak up some of the alcohol.

Some snacking and more brandy later, they were all ready to try to get some sleep.

- "I don't want you sleeping alone Kelly."

- "I'll be fine in the spare room honestly Emily."

- "No Kelly, no. You're in with us - you need cuddling."

- "But…..won't it be a bit…..weird?"

- "I think we're well past weird don't you!?"

Chapter Ninety Nine - 6 months, 11 days until *his* release

That there is a storm coming is an overused analogy, but in Adam's mind the relentless, unstoppable thunder had been approaching for the longest of times. At each nerve jarring shard of lightning, he could not help but count the time interval until the inevitable, menacing, deep rumble. A little shorter in time lapse on each and every occasion, but always feeling like a minor earthquake, that was just that little bit less minor than the last one, and heading ever closer to the time when it would be so firmly overhead, it would be all there is to feel.

Imagining how that sky would look, when finally, the day of reckoning was upon him, led him to some dark places, until his mind resembled his vision of the final picture - a dense mass of leaden clouds, drawn down by their own sheer weight, so low that they envelope everything, and leave it all covered in poison.

Emily may not have been inside his mind; but she could sense all the changes in pressure nonetheless. During the night times, she retained a degree of control. She could hold him, comfort his darker moments, fulfil desires he did not even know he had, distract him with orgasms that were not of this planet, soothe his every fibre until she induced a floating off to sleep in post coital bliss. She could not though exercise any control over what he dreamed about later in the night, nor his thoughts in between the night times.

When he was not with a patient, or fully engaged in a project, he was left with a great deal of thinking time; maybe far too much. He could not sit still, he had to walk, to try not to get stuck in one place, in one thought, to burn off at least some of it; to do something.

It had not been discussed, it was not a topic for the dinner table; but Emily was under no illusions; whatever had gone before would be a spec in the cosmos by comparison to whatever it was Adam was planning for *his* release. She would not try to stop him, she knew it would be futile anyway; but she was going to have to live it, and live through whatever the aftermath would hold.

Her thoughts on the matter were bordering on obsessive, unhealthy, and unwelcome. Unable to talk properly with Adam about it, and only getting a "It'll be fine I promise, trust me darling", when she did try; she turned to Kelly, Debs, and Daria. They all shared her concerns, and the view that events would run their course no matter what. All they could do was be the support team, there whenever called upon, although they suspected Adam would attempt a lone mission as far as he could, in a bid to protect them.

What would be left of him afterwards, and whether he could finally really move on, remained to be seen; the prospect of which did nothing to subdue any of their nerve endings. The only certainty was that every passing minute brought the answer a little closer, like a tide inching its way back up a beach towards a lone figure watching on, with their leg trapped fast between the rocks.

Chapter One Hundred

One night over dinner, Adam announced the surprising news that he had set up and registered a building contractor company, called Judge and Jury Ltd. He was not a named Director.

- "This does seem a rather odd move for a Psychologist darling?"

- "Admittedly it does, however it will be highly selective regarding the clientele it works with."

- "I see. What sort of clientele will it be seeking, can I ask?"

- "It'll be focussed on social housing."

- "Okay, interesting, well do please keep me posted as to how it's getting on."

- "I will my darling. Now what's for dessert tonight?"

- "Well I thought we'd have me."

- "I bloody love this restaurant!"

The feel of Emily inside and out, the explosive climax it produced, the feeling of her entwined around him like only she can, until he drifted off to sleep basking in the afterglow; could not have contrasted more starkly with the imagery that entered his mind later that night:

A faceless creature, with no beating heart, was crying out in agony induced by immeasurable suffering. Although it made no discernable sound, its howls were deafening, penetrating, and shuddered through every fibre of anyone close by. The only person who was close by though was Adam. As he watched on, he felt not one ounce of sympathy, only utter contempt, and as highly unpleasant as the shuddering was, he never wanted it to stop.

When finally it did stop, he found himself bolt upright in bed feeling and hearing the soothing of Emily.

- "It's alright darling, you were just having one of your nightmares again. You okay?"

- "I'm totally fine. Just suddenly hungry, that's all."

- "Let me help you with that….."

The dreams kept coming, varying only in the strength of the silent howls of suffering, and Adam looked forward to them every night, feeling disappointed on the occasions when they failed to appear. It did not take a Psychologist to work out what they meant, and even though a colleague may have disagreed; Adam was convinced that they were a healthy outlet for his emotions. Gradually though, the images started to appear with increasing frequency during his waking hours, and not always of his own making. When patients commented that he appeared not to be listening to them, he would brush it off quickly by saying that he was deep in thought about their plight.

Emily was not so easily fooled though, and her need for reassurance that he was really okay, increased at the same rate as the strength of her belief that he very much was not. She was the one person he would and could open up to though, and when he eventually did, she gently suggested that perhaps he should speak to a colleague, and maybe get a prescription or two, just temporarily? He would not hear of that though, like a confirmation of the cliche that doctors make the worst patients.

He knew what it all meant, and he was happy to convince himself that it was all good psychological preparation for what was to come. He did not want medication, especially not antipsychotic medication, clouding his judgement nor preventing him doing what needed to be done - it could wait until afterwards.

The next day Adam had a coffee with Daria in Aromas for the first time in a while:

- "When the time comes Daria, I'd appreciate a little help in getting my new business venture off of the ground."

- "It's interesting that you're branching out into other fields. Would you like the job of refurbishing my flat?"

- "No thank you. I'm just hoping that you'll be able to assist in getting me the contract for some particular preparation work for….. the Probation Service."

- "You know I'm happy to help you Adam…..you know I'd……..do anything for you in fact…..but it's really not as simple as that; there are procedures to go through at every stage."

- "Yeah, I know, well I can imagine. I just need you to find out the email addresses of some of the key decision makers and well……..you can leave the rest to me."

- "Does Emily know, or will she know?"

- "I'll tell her as much as I can or need to, like always."

- "I love how much you two trust each other, and can know that underneath it all, you're always looking out for each other, always looking to protect each other. Not many couples truly have that, you're very lucky."

- "I wish you could find that too Daria, I really do."

- "Yeah I know, unusually though the three of us already know what I want, and I'm not for settling for any poor imitation."

- "I don't blame you for not wanting anything less, I just worry you'll remain alone, when you don't deserve to be."

- "It's no secret Adam, we all know that I'm waiting patiently, if not quietly in the wings, in case Emily suddenly takes leave of her senses and buggars off."

- "It could be a long wait, especially as she has 24/7 access to a Psychologist."

- "Perhaps you'll fall in love with the building game and lose your psychological skills?"

- "It's a possibility I guess."

- "Yeah and either way I don't completely lose out because I get to spend time with you, I just don't get…..the best bit at the end of every day…. not outside of my imagination anyway, which I must confess is extremely…..vivid!"

- "Okay well Miss Kaminski, best we end that there as our time is up."

- "Hhhhmph well I'll leave it with you to ponder."

- "Too kind."

Adam was soon at work writing, editing, and responding to Probation Service emails with meticulous attention to detail. The number of parties involved made the task far more complex than might have been imagined, but after three weeks they were delighted to confirm the offer of a contract to Judge and Jury Ltd, even if none of them could quite explain how they had arrived at that decision, or why a certain halfway house was due to be refurbished.

Phase two, with a fresh set of email addresses supplied by Daria, to determine exactly who would feel the benefit of such a refurbishment, could wait until nearer the time. For the time being the task at hand was to assemble a crack team of tradesmen, whose integrity could not be called into question, and for that he would need to call upon another old Uni friend - Sandy the Scaffolder.

Seeing Sandy in person meant another trip to Brighton, and the enduring of the painful memories that brought. However Adam was not to be deterred and instead decided it was time to take Emily there for a day out.

He was quiet on the train journey down, mostly spending it just gazing out of the window; but Emily, the master of anticipation and tact knew to simply leave him to it, cuddle up to him, and wait to see if he wanted to say anything at any point.

The meeting with Sandy in the beautiful grounds of Sussex Uni campus in Falmer, took place in one of their old frequently used haunts - East Slope Bar. Within an hour and two pints of lager, discussions had been concluded satisfactorily, affording Adam time to show Emily around, before they headed into the centre of Brighton.

He took her everywhere he thought worthy of taking her. He did not feel the need nor the desire, to point out whether a particular place held a specific memory, nor what it might be; with one notable exception. As they paused outside the flat he had lived in with Lorelei, he simply and quietly said:

- "That's where *he* attacked us."

Emily, as understanding as ever, just accompanied him everywhere, and only ever asked the kind of questions a first time visitor would ask. She knew that going back was cathartic for him. What can anyone do with such memories that refuse so stubbornly to fade? She knew that afterwards, she could only feel closer to him for having gone, and she was more than fine with that. She still wouldn't, couldn't, replace Lorelei, nor did she want to, that was not her role. Adam, like everyone, was who he was because of his past; change that and everything travels along a different path with a very different destination. She deeply wished that Adam and Lorelei had arrived at a different destination, even at the expense of her being without him; she wouldn't have missed what she had never known.

Here she was though, and here they were, giving him in particular a highly unexpected second chance at true love. He may well have been happier had the first time played out as it should, but on this second occasion, on a very different path, they had at least found each other, and a beautiful love; very different, with no shortage of pain to deal with, but no less beautiful in its own right.

Chapter One Hundred and One

Judge and Jury Ltd began the fairly sizable task of refurbishing a block of bedsits already somewhat familiar to Adam; where a certain Terry Stevens had resided. Sandy the Scaffolder, true as ever to his word, had assembled a highly selective, hand picked team, each of whom he trusted implicitly. Along with the obvious, the team was made up of plasterers, carpenters, electricians, plumbers, decorators, and carpet/flooring fitters.

With the existing occupants moved elsewhere temporarily, all the units were to be completely gutted and undergo a full refit, all to the exact same specifications. Sandy kept Adam closely informed as to progress along the way, and now and again Adam made a personal appearance. Whenever an unscheduled inspection visit was carried out by someone from the Probation Service; they always found everything very much to their satisfaction and on schedule, which promised to bode well for the future of Judge and Jury Ltd.

A little before the final touches were applied, Adam brought Daniel with him to consult on all things IT. As expected, his extra knowledge proved invaluable with regard to some of the finer details, and in avoiding some potential pitfalls. Once it was all finished, Adam invited Daniel round to give a tutorial at his house, and install some extra software and security gadgets. It was agreed that he was to be retained in a consultancy role if and as required.

With further attention to detail, Adam ensured that the room assignments were appropriate. As no one else had any particular interest in this matter, it did not take a huge amount of editing of emails and forms to make sure that the names and numbers came out to his satisfaction.

Adam was quiet, edgy. He felt like a coiled spring, one that physics had been gathering all its best forces within, ready for the big bang.

Emily was all too aware of the tension percolating within him. She was utterly terrified as to what might be to come, what was to come. She did her utmost just to be a supportive comfort, but unsurprisingly failed on certain occasions.

Adam tried his utmost to be sensitive to it all, but was drawn ever deeper into the sharp focus required to fulfil his hopes. They would get back to being them afterwards, if there was to be one.

For the first time since that first time, he was going to attempt to sleep without the feel of her, and even the prospect of it brought a very uneasy feeling. However such sacrifices would have to be made for the greater good, and he set off to go and spend three nights in a certain room of the newly refurbished homes Judge and Jury Ltd had so diligently worked upon. He needed to familiarise himself with all its aspects, and be satisfied that every feature worked exactly as it should. Nothing less than a five star review across the board would be acceptable.

To his great relief, he found that everything was just as he had designed it, and worked with precision in both timing and efficiency. Problems only arose when he finally attempted sleep. The absence of the feel of Emily was as stark as its presence. The lack of the comfort she provided brought commensurate discomfort to every sinew of his body. This engendered a proportionate psychological unease to the point of panic - how could anything possibly be okay?

He curled up in as tight a ball as he could, reducing the amount of himself exposed to any outside influence, to no effect. He listened to podcasts about his favourite interests, played gentle music next to the pillow, tried watching a little late night television, attempted to absorb himself in a good book in Spanish for the extra distraction factor; but sleep's sweet relief would not come to him. Nothing would come to him but highly uneasy wakefulness. He remained in this horrible state until the pre planned time of 9am, when having ascertained that a few more features were working well, he hurried on home to Emily for a desperately needed morning filled with nothing but the feel of her, and a few precious hours of sleep. Although he knew that the next two nights would simply be repeats of the first one; he was not for deviating and endured them both regardless, sustained by the promise of the comfort that the morning would bring.

As the days ticked closer, the other bedsits gradually began to be refilled with the paroled prisoners of varying kinds. A crisis sprang up when one of the tenants requested to be swapped into a certain room, on the grounds that it was empty and that he was there first. With permission initially granted Adam had to act quickly with some swift interventions along and within the email chain, to reverse the decision on the grounds that the dynamics within the building in terms of psychological profiling had already carefully taken place, in line with new guidelines from the Home Office. It caused some consternation that required satisfactory confirmation from higher up, but the decision was reversed. The stage was set.

Chapter One Hundred and Two - From 14 years, 11 months, and 19 days until *his* release, to 14 days, 11 hours, and 19 minutes, to 14 hours, 11 minutes, and 19 seconds

As the moment was finally fast approaching, and Adam's senses could not have been any more heightened, Emily was struggling to contain him and keep him tethered to even a semblance of normality during those final two weeks. Not even her night-time talents of loving comfort and other worldly love making, had any of their usual effects. The former could not stop his shaking, and the latter could not be sustained, if it could start at all.

Two nights before *his* release back into society, Emily thought it prudent to gather the troops; as much for reinforcements for herself as Adam.

Emily sensed the uneasiness around the table, as Kelly, Debs, and Daria joined them for dinner. It had been pre agreed that Adam was, as far as possible, to conduct a solo mission. Only when absolutely necessary would he call upon the others. The others however, as terrified as they were, had been far from happy with this arrangement and did not want to leave every burden on Adam's shoulders, but he had not been for negotiating; not then, not now. The most he had conceded was that he would call upon them at the merest prospect of a crisis point, as opposed to trying to ride it out alone until it was fully upon him.

They drank to Lorelei, they drank to Adam, they drank to their union, they drank to every good outcome they could possibly hope for; they drank to unconsciousness.

Chapter One Hundred and Three - 1 hour, 6 minutes, and 39 seconds until *his* release.

The morning was upon them, like no morning before. Breakfast was attempted as a kind of token gesture, but no one had the stomach for it. The knowledge that the person responsible for torturing and repeatedly raping one's pregnant girlfriend, before leaving her to die horrifically from dehydration, is being unleashed back into society; does nothing for the appetite.

One thing Adam could not resist though was one final check of *his* new home, this being no time for last minute hitches. All was as he had left it; it just lacked a welcome basket of fruit.

0 hours, 0 minutes, 0 seconds, *he* is released.

Despite all appearing to be well, Adam kept feeling the need to double, triple, and quadruple check everything in the room, satisfying himself, only to feel the compulsion to start the process again. He lost track of how many times he had done it, of where he was in the process; of time. Then he heard it pull up outside, and he froze to the spot. Van doors opening and closing, voices, items being unloaded, approaching voices, the front door opening, the front door closing, footsteps climbing stairs, ever louder voices, *his* front door opening, people entering, *him* entering; just as Adam was closing the fire escape door behind him as silently as possible. As much as he had wanted to see how much time and prison had worn *him*, had aged *him*; it would have to wait.

Adam headed home, leaving *him* some time to settle in nicely to *his* new home, to enjoy some of its refurbished comforts. He squirrelled himself away in his study which had also undergone a few changes of its own, and turned on the monitors. There *he* was. *He* was older, quite a bit older, looking gym -fit like someone who'd had plenty of time for exercise, pleased with *him*self; alive.

Adam felt his heart trying to beat its way out of his chest, he was sweating, and his stomach knotted so tightly until it formed a solid, heavy mass more akin to an anvil than a body part. Had he been able to, defying reasons of physics and his own state; he would have unleashed the most ferocious attack upon *him* there and then, sustaining it for as long as his body would allow it regardless of the state of *him* at any point. That though, as gratifying as it might have been, would have been far too quick an end to proceedings.

As *he* lay on *his* new bed, clearly approving of *his* new circumstances, Adam, desperately trying to calm himself, turned on the computer and opened the programs so carefully and skillfully installed by Daniel. He had only just begun to check a few things when he saw *him* jump up and put the kettle on. Using a tea bag from the box kindly provided, *he* made *him*self a cup of tea, and sat down by the window to enjoy its reviving qualities along with *his* new improved view. Life had finally taken an enormous upturn and it seemed *he* was not about to be slow to enjoy it.

After tea and biscuits, it was time for a tour of his new neighbourhood, familiar though some of it already was. He strolled around like he owned it, like someone who had not a care in the world; looking like a civilised, socialised, functioning member of human society. No one looking at him would have thought there goes an evil, raping, torturing, murderer; but rather such things as his clothes look a little dated, what a smiling friendly chap, how polite he is to let me pass first.

He strolled into The Forlorn Hope for a well earned first pint in fifteen years. Oddly he felt a little disoriented before he had even ordered the first drink, but he put that down to the excitement of it all. Halfway through the first pint, the edges of the tables and chairs did not quite seem right, like there was a strange fuzziness to them. In fact the edges of everything did not quite seem right, even those of people. He laughed at himself for being such a lightweight, but dismissed it as to be expected after such a long period of abstinence. When the barman spoke to him during the ordering of the second pint, there was a strange echoing quality to his voice, like it was coming through an effect on a guitar amp. Good value for money this drinking lark, he thought.

By the third pint things were decidedly worse, or better, depending on one's point of view. Nothing quite seemed within the bounds of its natural perspective, like there was a fourth dimension to each and every object and person. Whenever anyone spoke to him or around him, the echoing quality took on a greater strength until it was like hearing someone shouting from the bottom of a well.

Deciding that enough was enough for his first day of hard earned freedom, he headed for the door, which wasn't quite where he was seeing it, but close enough to navigate through successfully. Once outside again, the sights and sounds of the London traffic were not quite in proportion, with some vehicles taking on a greater or smaller size than one might traditionally expect. It is not often that a taxi appears bigger than a bus, but then it's not often one gets let out of prison after fifteen years. A nice sleep in a comfortable bed would soon have him feeling fine again, and he soldiered on towards that aim.

The front door was easy enough to find, but the lock seemed to float about as he tried to put the key in it. His initial reaction was one of amusement, but it quickly became bemusement as he struggled to marry the two simple objects together. At the 8th attempt he mastered the task, and made his way towards his very own front door, aware enough still to delight in the absence of guards, other prisoners and clanking great locks. With the edges of the bed not too clearly defined, he aimed for the middle and felt the relief of finding it. It too had a floating quality, but this actually proved an aid in helping him to drift off to sleep, albeit with an increasingly unpleasant sensation of dizziness.

The relief though was a short lived affair. Coming seemingly at once from nowhere and everywhere, was the faint sound of a voice, whispering in the darkness. At first he thought he was dreaming, but as he began to come to, taking a few moments to realise where he was, and where he very much wasn't; the whispering continued. He couldn't quite make out what was being said, but something very much was. It seemed to fade in and out in presence and volume, just as he was certain it had ceased, it returned. He put the bedside lamp on; there was nothing to see yet the whispering continued intermittently. Feeling dehydrated, he got up to get some water, still having vision issues, and still not entirely sure he wasn't having a vivid dream. The whispering had at least stopped.

Still feeling rather uneasy but relieved, he went back to bed and turned off the lamp. It was not long until he had drifted back off to sleep, nor before he was awoken again by the whispering. This time it was a fraction louder than before and there were moments when there were not any words to make out, just laughter; increasingly hysterical laughter. It mattered not how many times he turned on the lamp; there was never anything to see.

Day Two

By early morning, he had not had enough sleep, but he had certainly had enough. He decided to go for a walk in an attempt to clear his fuzzy head, which would have proved easier to do had he been able to see or hear clearly. The strange perspectives and echoes of the night before were back, nothing was as it should be, nor quite as it seemed, making even basic manoeuvres difficult to negotiate.

As the London traffic began to increase in both audible and physical volume, so did his disorientation. Sounds which are all around in London at all times, but which are usually largely filtered out, were all around him in disproportionate fashion, and with the addition of the peculiar and inaccurate vision he was experiencing; it all amounted to a disconcerting sensory bombardment. A passerby told him to mind out of the way, but the sound appeared to come from a different direction than the person in question, resulting in a collision as he turned in confusion. Such an incident would normally have elicited an aggressive response, but instead it was all he could do to avoid being hit by a taxi as he suddenly found himself on the wrong side of the curb.

He held onto a lampost trying to regain composure. When he could see faces clearly, they had disapproving looks on them, taking him for drunk at an unseemly hour. As much as he yearned to lay down, he was at least away from the whispers, and so with the pub not yet open, he headed for the nearest eatery. As he came through the door he knocked over a chair, then into a waiter as he tried to rectify the stumble. He was immediately asked to leave on pain of the police being called. As the voice didn't seem to come from the person saying it, but from behind him; he decided it would be best to leave quietly.

He had not strayed far from home, no more than a two minute walk, yet it took him over half an hour to find his way back again, as nothing looked familiar or right. The keys eventually found the locks again, and he made it inside his room, but only after holding the bannister very tightly to make it up the stairs in one piece. He was very relieved to make it back.

After a cup of tea which proved more difficult to make than he had expected, and as puzzled and concerned as he was about what was happening; he managed to fall asleep on the bed. After 25 seconds of much needed slumber, there came a very faint sound, incrementally increasing every 15 seconds, until it was just loud enough to wake him, and be discerned as the sound of a baby crying.

He opened his eyes in the semi darkness of the morning light with the curtains drawn, but there was nothing to see, beyond the fuzzy shapes of and in the room as before; then suddenly there was. A sequence of intermittent flashes at different points around the room, each of them showing a live unborn foetus at varying stages of gestation, followed immediately by a similarly developed one, clearly very much not alive. The crying started and stopped in accordance with whether the foetus was alive in each picture.

He sat bolt upright, he was dreaming surely, yet the crying was going right through him. He got up gingerly, it all stopped. He ran his fingers along the walls; nothing but smooth plaster and paintwork. The second he laid down again, it all started again as before. He turned over, burying his head under the pillow in a desperate attempt to shut it all out, but the volume increased commensurately. After several minutes it finally stopped, but there was no respite to be found within his own mind. There was strange shape after weird sound after moving colours; all meshing into a kaleidoscope of horror. Just as he thought he couldn't possibly take it anymore; the whispering started up again.

Day Three

By the next morning it was all he could do to function at all. He had to try to make it out though as he had his first and unmissable appointment with his Parole Officer that afternoon. As the appointment time approached, he started to notice that his vision and hearing were a little better, and by the time he had arrived, to his great relief, they were pretty much back to normal.

At the appointment, whilst perturbed by what had been happening, he wasn't sure whether he should say anything about it, concerned where it might lead.

- "How have you found your first few days of liberty after such a long time?"

- "Well, being out of there is great.....I couldn't wait of course..... it's not been.....quite as I'd expected though."

- "How so?"

- "I've been getting sort of.... dizzy spells when I'm out and about, and then at home.....my imagination's been playing tricks on me....and....I'm kind of....having nightmares"

- "That all sounds very common I can assure you. It's a huge shock to the system after so long in prison, you may well need a little time to adjust to your new surroundings and new way of life. I'm sure things will settle down for you, but don't worry, we'll keep an eye on you, and help you in any way we can if they don't."

The Parole Officer's report accurately reflected their conversation. By the time anyone read it however it stated:

"No initial problems reported, very happy with the new home and already beginning to settle and adjust to new surroundings."

He felt a lot better on the way back and called into The Forlorn Hope en route to celebrate the fact. This time the beer provoked a more predictable reaction, and quickly, but he liked that. He even treated himself to some chips on the way home to satisfy his lager induced hunger. Life was pretty good.

Upon getting home, it was not long before he had fallen asleep on the bed, nor been startled awake again, thanks to a sudden, loud noise. By the time he had realised that there was nothing to worry about, he had noticed an odour in the room. It seemed familiar, and it was getting stronger, yet he couldn't quite make out what it was, and it certainly did not seem to have any apparent source; then he realised - it was the smell of blood.

He jumped out of bed and opened the windows for a through draft, but it would not leave. It seemed to be everywhere, permeating everything in the room, it was all he could taste, it felt like he was breathing it in, swallowing it down, even his own skin began to smell of it. Finally it was all too much, and he just made it to the sink in time to throw up his cocktail of lager and chips.

He rinsed his mouth out with water, and drank some in a bid to at least be rid of the taste of vomit, even though it was debatable as to which was worse, before laying back down on the bed. The smell began to subside somewhat, and he began to feel a little better. He may well have drifted back off to sleep, had the whispering not started up again; amongst other things.

Meanwhile a few miles across London, Adam sat transfixed at the monitors in his study. He was shaking with adrenaline, yet unwavering. Emily sat downstairs, alone in the dining room, watching his dinner go cold, hoping that he would come down to eat, and against hope that it would all be over soon.

Day Four

It was 4.11am, he had still not managed to drift back off to sleep. Every time it appeared that the smell of blood had gone, it would appear again, just enough to make him feel nauseous. That was the least of it though. Nothing quite seemed right, the walls did not join to the ceiling in the traditional way, as if instead the ceiling was floating above them like a white cloud. If he stared too long at any point on a wall, the point got gradually bigger until it was the size of a small tunnel. When he went over to it, expecting to be able to put a hand right through, it was just a solid wall. By the time he had got back upon the bed, it was a tunnel again, each and every time.

The whispering became a little louder, he kept thinking he could hear his name, but he could not quite be sure, as much as he could be sure of anything. Then came something with a suggestion of clarity:

- "Hu ef m t d"

- "Hu lef me to da"

- "Hu left me to dah"

- "You left me to die."

- "You left me to die!"

- "You left me to die!!"

- "You left me to die!!!"

- "You left me to die!!!!"

- "You left me to die!!!!!"

- "You left me to die!!!!!"

He laid face down on the bed, desperately trying to hold the pillow over the back of his head to cover both ears, but it just got louder. It even began to sound like her voice, until there was no doubting it.

He jumped up from the bed and ran from the room, down the stairs and out into the London air, very much underdressed but anything was better than being inside. It was not all good though. A night bus passed by, more in the form of a jelly than a bus. He felt completely exposed by the looks from its weary passengers, which were even stranger than they might have been, even allowing for his boxer shorts and t-shirt attire. The sound of it still echoed in his ears, long after it had passed. He sat down on the doorstep of his new home, trying to make some sense of any of it through distorted vision, trying to get a grip of himself, trying to find the courage to go back inside; and failing miserably on all counts.

When finally, having spent over an hour on the doorstep, shivering with what he told himself was cold, he went back inside; all was perfectly quiet, with little discernible smell. He yearned for sleep. As he flopped onto the bed, its sweet relief came quickly and deeply; for a full eleven minutes.

Another hour later, there was a gentle tap on the door followed by a familiar whisper, as Emily slowly opened it and put her arms around Adam.

- "Whatever you're doing to *him* darling, don't do it to yourself too. Come on, come to bed now and feel the feel of me."

Adam, being too tired to resist, let her lead him into the bedroom, to the bed, pull him in to join her, and entwine him.

Day Five

There was no such balm available for him, but he did manage some sleep. It was far from quality sleep though; it was light, fraught, and fragile. When he was fully conscious again; it was the smell of blood that had woken him.

Such fitful rest had done nothing to clear his vision, nor restore the clarity of his hearing, and his thoughts were becoming increasingly muddled too. He made a cup of tea, which was surprisingly difficult to coordinate, downed it as quickly as he could, and went for a walk to get away from the lingering smell. He quickly became disoriented as his senses struggled to cope with the loud and hectic environment. Nothing looked or sounded as it should, again. After turning a few corners, he found it all too much, and tried to head for home. A few corners later he realised he was completely lost. Along, turn, along, turn, up, back, along, turn, down, along, right, along, back, up, left, back; nothing looked remotely familiar. He tried to seek help from passers by, but they scurried away as quickly as they could, if they acknowledged him at all. Eventually an elderly lady took pity on him, and stopped to listen.

- "Where are you trying to get to dear?"

- "Errm....I.... don't.....I...can't remember the name of..... the..."

- "Well that's not too useful is it?"

- "I.... can't........ think."

- "No. Do you have anything on you with your address on it?"

- "Sorry……. what?"

- "Do you have anything on you with your address on it? In your pockets or wallet maybe?"

Her voice sounded strange, like it was coming through bubbles.

- "I don't……no I don't think….. nothing."

- "Well I can't really help you dear. Perhaps it's a doctor you need? Good luck, have a sit down somewhere for a bit first maybe?"

He wandered around in bewilderment for another three hours, although he had no notion of timescales. Gradually his distorted senses began to clear, until finally his new address and his bearings came back to him. It took over an hour, but he did find a way home via a few calming drinks in The Forlorn Hope.

Upon his return all was quiet, and even the earlier smell had gone. He had something to eat and drink, turned on the television and soon fell asleep. Within ten minutes he was startled awake by a sudden change in the volume of the television. Far from the innocuous afternoon talk show he had dozed off to, there was now some sort of horror film with a barrage of brutal images depicting extreme torture. He quite liked it at first and he could not take his *eyes* from it, but then came the smell and the sensation that the room was beginning to revolve. He quickly tried to change the channel, again, again and again, but it made no difference; the images kept coming, the sounds kept coming along with the screaming. He turned the television off and laid on the bed, closing his eyes in the hope of making the spinning stop. No sooner had he done so, the television came back on with the same show. He turned it off again with the remote control as quickly as he could, and laid back down. Silence ensued, although internally he was feeling increasingly strange. Just minutes later the television came on again. He tried to stand up from the bed, but he was too dizzy, so instead he crawled across the floor and pulled the plug from the wall, before crawling back and onto the bed. As he laid back down the images started up again, this time intermittently on the walls, on the ceiling, seemingly all around him at intervals and then all at once. He closed his eyes trying to avoid them, but whenever he did so the volume of the soundtrack seemed to increase, until he opened them again. He struggled to his feet, barely able to see straight or balance properly, the smell got stronger still, the images yet more brutal when he could see them properly. He rushed out of the door holding onto every bit of wall, every bit bannister he could find, fearing he would fall at any second and very nearly doing so several times, until finally he reached the street, desperate to get as far away as possible from that smell, those images, staggering along using any railing or lamp post to sustain being upright, further and further and further, falling down in a daze, struggling back up again, further still; until he was utterly lost.

It was four long hours on the friendless streets of London before his senses had even begun to clear, and he had made it back home. People had taken him for drunk or drugged, and had done their utmost to avoid any kind of interaction. All was quiet and odourless, offering some welcome relief. He sat down with tea and biscuits, trying to take a moment to come to even the vaguest terms with what was going on, but nothing made any sense.

He laid down on the bed exhausted, closed his eyes and found sleep within seconds. Eighty two seconds later came the whispering, barely audible but incrementally louder every thirty seconds:

- "Hu mu t o m ba"

- "Hu murd to o my ba"

- "Hu murd to of my babi"

- "You murdered two of my babies"

- "You murdered two of my babies!"

- "You murdered two of my babies!!"

- "You murdered two of my babies!!!"

- "You murdered two of my babies!!!!"

He was frozen to the bed, staring at the ceiling with eyes fixed in terror. That the ceiling seemed to be moving, did nothing to quell the situation.

- "It's nice and cool up here but it'll be plenty hot enough where you're going. I've seen it, they show it to you, it's sort of part of the welcome tour. Kind of an aren't you glad you didn't qualify for that? moment."

- "Shut up shut up you're not real get out of my head!!"

- "I'm not in your head scumbag, that would be a vile, putrid place to be. I'm where you'll never be able to touch me, beat me, rape me, or murder me again. They know everything, see everything, you won't be coming to join me. The best bit though is that they let you go there to watch whenever and whoever you like."

- "Shut up shut up shut up shut the fuck up!"

- "There's a limit to the pain where you are now, but not here, it will never stop, it really is forever. You can't even pass out from it for a bit of relief. While you rithe and scream in truly unimaginable, ceaseless agony, I'll be in the gallery eating popcorn, maybe even some ice-cream for the non existent interval."

- "You're lying you're lying you're lying!"

- "Am I scumbucket? Are you sure? Hang on, they're just draining and boiling a fresh batch from some rapist who arrived in 323 BC, ready to put it back into him again. Oof it stinks! Stay there, I'll send you the smell again."

Within seconds the room began to fill with the stench of blood.

- "I reckon you believe me now huh? Oh fuck, they've started on his testicles again, I'd better go, I really can't watch this, not til they're yours."

He ran from the room like a startled hare, despite his sensory issues, almost tripping down the stairs en desperate route to the street. It was six hours before he dared, or was even capable of trying to find his way home again.

Day Six

The next morning he emailed his Parole Officer, begging to be seen that day instead of waiting for the next appointment. The reply came that he could go in at 4pm.

As the day wore on, ticking towards the time to leave, his vision and hearing began to feel rather more normal. No odours came and he heard no voices either. Perhaps he was finally calming down, perhaps it was finally over? Maybe he shouldn't tell the Probation Officer too much after all? He didn't want to end up in the nuthouse! Maybe he should make up an excuse for today? He mulled over these thoughts as he prepared to leave. Just as he headed for the door, there came a whisper:

- "Go l scu"

- "Goo lu scu g"

- "Good luc scumb g"

- "Good luck scumbag"

He left in a hurry.

- "So why the sudden urgency, are you okay?"

- "It's all getting worse! The dizzy spells, the confusion, I'm hearing things, seeing things, smelling things!"

- "What sort of things can I ask?"

-

-

- "Her"

- "Her?"

- "Her! Lorelei! Who do you think!?"

- "Okay let's try to stay calm shall we?'

- "Fucking stay calm!? She's haunting me!! That place you've given me to live is fucking haunted!"

- "Okay deep breaths. No one else in the building has reported any problems. As I said last time, there is bound to be an adjustment period."

- "An adjustment period! This is some adjustment period! It's fucking torture is what it is!"

- "How are you outside of your home?'

- "I can't see, hear, or think straight most of the time!"

- "Okay, so it seems that it's not just about being at home, it's about you, wherever you are. Perhaps you should see a Psychiatrist, just for a check up?"

- "A Psychiatrist? I'm not fucking mad!"

- "I'm not suggesting you are, but it'll be good to talk it through. It can't do any harm and hopefully it'll help you. They're just regular doctors first and foremost."

- "I suppose so….. okay."

- "There'll be a wait of course, but let me see what I can do."

The report was awaited with interest and in the end simply said:

"Seen two days ahead of schedule. There were a few understandable adjustment problems, but nothing of concern."

The referral to a Psychiatrist was duly made, but never arrived.

He went to The Forlorn Hope in a bid to relax. He found he was able to drink a little more, and like last time, the effects were the traditional ones. He even found a couple of people who would talk to him.

He walked the short walk home, stumbling only a couple of times, and arrived without incident. After a little post-pub supper, he laid down and soon drifted off to sleep. Two hours passed in relative silence before he gradually began to stir at some intermittent light. As he opened his eyes, there they were again; images of foetuses flashing around the room in the darkness, and blood, lots of blood, and the smell of it; and placentas, lots of placentas; and a whispering, young voice calling:

- "Daddy, Daddy here I am, here I am, or maybe there I would have been if you hadn't murdered me in Mummy's tummy?! How old would I be now? About 20 I suppose. It's okay though, I wouldn't have wanted a life with an evil pig like you for a Daddy, I'm up here with Mummy instead, far away from you. Mummy told me we're going to see you soon though, or rather, we're going to watch you soon, watch you get what you deserve…..watch you suffer….. watch you…. watch….you…. watch you…. watch you…………"

Day Seven

He had not slept for the rest of the night. Too terrified to run from the room and be disoriented and lost on the streets again; he had instead lain face down in the bed, pulling the pillow over his head with a vice-like grip. It only achieved a reduction in the sound though, nowhere near enough to block it completely; in fact sometimes it even seemed to get louder.

When eventually it seemed that calm had returned, and he braved the removal of the pillow; back it all came again within minutes.

- "We're all watching you scum of the earth, there is nowhere to hide, do you really think that pillow can protect you, that it'll save you? Nothing can, nothing will, it's all done, it's all been decided, it's all going to happen, it's all been set out, I've seen how it turns out, we all have, we all know, we're just sitting back now to enjoy it. Don't forget though all this is just the hors d'oeuvre, a few canapes to whet the appetite, and as utterly hideous as it's going to be, it's going to be summer picnic in paradise compared with the main courses and the infinite dessert where you're going to end up....."

It was a long night. The only improvement by the morning was that his vision and hearing seemed fairly normal again - outside of the auditory and visual hallucinations. By mid-morning though, other sensations were apparent. His mouth was still dry even after two cups of tea, in fact the more he drank of tea or water, the drier it got. He felt light-headed, progressing into full-blown dizziness. He began to feel increasingly nauseous, until finally he vomited. He laid down on the bed again, too drowsy and unsteady to remain standing. The room wasn't warm but he began to sweat profusely, all over his body. The room was spinning.

- "Enjoy the ride, scumbag" whispered Lorelei.

Faster and faster, more violently, turning over, spinning round, turning upwards, downwards, round, up and round, spinning within a spin in two different directions at once, like the world's least enjoyable and longest Waltzer ride. He just had time to experience throwing up all over himself, before passing out.

It was the afternoon by the time he had not so much woken up, as come to. The frequent smell of blood was absent, only to be replaced by the smell of vomit, without the need to doubt its tangibility. The taste in his mouth was disgusting. Once he had summoned the energy to get up, wash and change his clothes and bedding, brush his teeth, and have some tea and toast; he began to feel light-headed, his mouth was dry, he felt nauseous……….

Day Nine

This latest cycle had continued for the next forty eight hours, and showed no sign of stopping. He had no idea why he felt the way he did, or what to do about it; it was all he could do to get through the next spell of dizziness or vomiting. When he did attempt to leave the house, for some fresh London air or a break from the tormenting whispering and imagery; he could not last more than a few minutes outside, before needing to lay down again, or vomit, or both.

He considered calling for an ambulance, but along with his pride preventing it, he feared he would end up swapping a prison cell for a locked ward. He'd ride it out, it would all soon pass, surely, he must just have picked up a nasty bug from being out in the world again after so long.

As a bonus, he found himself constipated, which was doing nothing for the feelings of nauseousness; or rather, it was helping them along nicely. He also found that he had little appetite, and still could not quench that raging thirst.

As the day melted into evening, and he lay sweating on the bed; the hallucinations returned with a vengeance. The seeing of specs on the wall turning into tunnels, would have been welcome by comparison. He saw a hooded man locked inside a tight fitting cage in a medieval torture chamber, surrounded by instruments that left little to the imagination as to their purpose. He was being attended to by random women with battered faces, who were going to work on different parts of him all at once. The man was crying out for mercy, yet each time he did so, the intensity of their work increased. When finally after several minutes he made the connection and stopped his howling; the game changed immediately.

Now they went to work on him at a steady pace, stopping each time the man held his breath in a bid to endure the pain. Once he had realised that connection, he desperately tried to hold it for as long as possible, as the swollen, gleeful faces watched on eagerly, tools at the ready for the first sign of activity. The man's lungs almost reached bursting point each time before he finally had to let go and off they went again, inflicting serious harm anywhere they could.

Suddenly his hood was removed in a swipe, and there he was in all his glory. He just had time to see their delight before they went to work on his face.

He writhed around on the bed, it was so vivid, it was like he could feel it too. Now he was crying out begging, pleading for it to stop, that he couldn't take anymore, but they would not, not for a second. He again tried not crying out, tried holding his breath, but it made no difference, it was simply relentless.

After an incalculable period of time, it slowly faded away, and he found himself lying on the bed, panting, looking around. He tried to gather his thoughts and himself, but everything looked strange again in its perspective. After a few moments he heard an echoey tapping on the door, and a voice asking if he was okay.

- "Fuck off, fuck off, knock on my door again and I'll fucking batter you."

The footsteps echoed in his head as they faded away. Then the whispering started up again…..

Day Ten

After ensuring that *he* was highly unlikely to be going anywhere in his absence, Adam left the house for the first time since *he* was ensconced in *his* new home. The fresh air felt good on his face as he walked along the streets in the daylight. He was very tired, very overtired in fact, but adrenaline and motivation, along with the hive of activity in his mind; were more than enough to keep him sufficiently fueled.

Emily had felt enormous relief at seeing him finally break the cycle of living between his study and the bedroom, but it brought little comfort to her overall sense of anxiety. It was set to play out with or without her support, and she knew that, but she just yearned for it to be over, hopefully with enough recognizable semblance of Adam remaining.

Adam headed for the rendezvous point to meet with Sandy the Scaffolder in person. Travelling by tube would have been much quicker, but he needed to walk. The rest of London appeared to be going about its daily business, unmoved by the drama unfolding, which only added to his sense of detachment - how could they not know; how could they not care? Ultimately that was okay though; he didn't need their interest, in fact the more they stayed out of his business the better.

He arrived in Regent's Park a little ahead of schedule and had time for a stroll around the grounds before seeing Sandy's arrival at the agreed spot. After the heartfelt but brief pleasantries, they embarked on a conversation that lasted over two hours, before embracing and going their separate ways. Adam walked back home in only half the time of his outward journey.

He had spent another morning fighting nausea and dizziness, and losing, badly. He was still having terrible problems going to the toilet properly. Luckily, there was little left to pass after all the vomiting, but it was still causing increasing discomfort.

His physical state, as bad as it was, was of rapidly decreasing concern relative to his mental one. The sounds were increasing in frequency and variety. There were sudden bursts of sounds at such a high pitch that he felt his ear drums were about to burst from his head. There was often laughter when he vomited, or tried in painful vein to pass a stool. He heard babies crying, children crying out for help, he heard Lorelei telling him what was to become of him again. He even saw her clearly on a few occasions, standing in the centre of the room, but she could not be touched, his hand passed right through her each time. Most frequently of all though, came those whispers, incessant and incrementally terrifying.

He forced himself to go outside, just for a break from it all, but he could not stand the sensory bombardment, the weirdness of the sights and sounds, the dizziness, the nausea; until the doorstep became the furthest point he could manage. So much for freedom.

Day Fourteen

He was due to see his Parole Officer, but managed to cancel the appointment on the basis of having a nasty stomach bug. He was warned in no uncertain terms that this represented a breach of his parole conditions, but it was accepted on the condition that he appear for the next appointment, without fail, and with a Doctor's certificate confirming the illness. He had agreed; he would have agreed to pretty much anything at that point to avoid having to go anywhere in the state he was in.

When he was not in a sleeping nightmare, it felt like he was in a waking one. It was not hard to say which of all of it was the worst - it was hearing and seeing Lorelei. Not because he regretted what he had done, he regretted getting caught certainly; but because she had taken over, she now had control. It was becoming increasingly difficult to convince himself that it was just his imagination. It seemed real, it felt real, it looked real, it sounded real, it smelled real; it was real. She'd come back for him to compensate for him not doing so for her. She'd seen the future, she'd seen his future, she was to be in it, but only in an observing capacity, to watch him suffer in horrific fashion whenever it pleased her to do so. He really was going to hell, it was real, there was no avoiding it, she was just biding her time in paradise waiting for the day to arrive, he was going to suffer....... unimaginable pain......unimaginable, ceaseless pain……….. agony like nothing he'd felt before……...oh my God….. endless endless endless torture……. No parole.

Day Sixteen

His doorbell sounded at 11am. After much reluctance and many repeats, he answered it with trepidation. Following consultation with colleagues, his Parole Officer had decided to pay a visit.

- "Come to check up on me have you? Make sure I really am ill?"

- "Well I'd rather put it that I've come to see that you're okay."

- "I do actually finally feel a bit better this morning, since you ask."

- "I'm very pleased to hear it. What about the dizziness and the, well, hearing things? It certainly seems nice and quiet to me."

- "Nothing to report this morning."

- "Excellent, well hopefully things are finally settling down for you."

- "Yeah I bloody well hope so. I suppose I should offer you a cup of tea?"

- "That'd be very nice thank you."

A cup of tea and a twenty minute chat later, the visitor set off to go about the rest of his day. Feeling far from good, but

372

better than of late; he was soon out the door too. Just as he closed it, she whispered:

- "See you later."

Later that day, not long after returning home, the awful physical symptoms, the images, the voices, the laughter, the whispering; all returned.

- "There's no escape scumbag, wherever you go, I'll always be watching, listening, waiting…..waiting til I see you in hell."

Day Seventeen

The following morning, it was the distinctive sound of scaffolding being erected that woke him. He looked out from the window to confirm his suspicions.

- "What's all this in aid of?"

- "Just a quick job mate, sorry for the disturbance."

- "Great! More bloody noise!"

That night in the darkness, dizzy and drowsy, he suddenly sat bolt upright in bed. Something was appearing on the wall in front of his eyes, letters.... words....sentences....

- "How did you feel when you knew I was dying?"

- "Did you imagine my suffering?"

- "Did it make you feel good?"

- "Did you ever consider telling them before it was too late, or were you enjoying it too much?"

- "You're going to pay you raping murdering scumbucket!"

He went over towards the wall, terrified, unsure whether he was dreaming. He reached out to touch it..... nothing. He ran his hand over it..... completely smooth. He put an ear to it…….silence. He waited for a few minutes before going back to bed. He laid down again trying to gather himself, taking deep breaths to try to ward off vomiting yet again; and then the writing started up again. This sequence continued on repeat for the rest of the night.

Over the next three days, all the things he was experiencing were worse than ever. He was due to see his Parole Officer the following day. It was no use, he couldn't take anymore. He'd have to ask for urgent help, even if that meant a spell in hospital, even if it meant a locked ward in a psychiatric one. Just one more night to deal with…..so drowsy…….so drowsy……so…….

He woke up, he was in a great deal of pain; he was not at home.

Day Twenty One

He appeared to be alone, but not unaccompanied. There was the pain, like he had had some kind of accident, but highly accentuated. The realisation that he couldn't move at all came very quickly afterwards, along with the commensurate terror and confusion in the pitch darkness. He tried to cry out in desperation as much as pain, but he could barely produce a sound beyond muffled grunts. As time moved forward at whatever rate that was, the pain steadily increased. It moved past unbearable, and kept on going. He would have writhed in agony if only he could, cried for help, begged for mercy. Was this it? Was this it? Was this just the start of what Lorelei had come back to taunt him about? His imagination ran wild. His heart felt like it was galloping from his chest like a startled herd on a plain. Oh God oh God oh God oh God don't let this be it don't let this be it don't let this be it!!!

Then he heard a beep, and a soft whirr of a machine springing into action. There might have been someone there but he couldn't be sure. Then he felt a sensation in his arm, like cool liquid was entering it. Then came the hallucinations, visual and auditory. Lorelei's voice may have been in there, but amid the random, often horrific chaos and imagery; he couldn't really be sure.

He had been on the point of losing consciousness on many occasions; wanted to lose consciousness on many more occasions; but something kept bringing him back. When he was not hearing his own agonised, muffled screams, or worse; he could hear the screams of others all around - the pleading, the begging, the screeching cries, the searing pain. It was proving impossible to distinguish reality from hallucination;

but there was no doubting his own pain, simultaneously all over his shaking, yet restrained body. He had vomited and been forced to swallow it again, choking in the process, and he had soiled himself, as his constipation gave way in abrupt fashion.

He thought he could hear Lorelei's voice amidst it all, sometimes faintly, sometimes more clearly.

- "So glad you're finally here scumbag! It's about to be your turn, I'm here watching, front row seat, VIP section, huge bucket of popcorn at the ready. If it hurts a little more than it might have done; that'll be the Methadone withdrawal. You always did like cold turkey. Are you ready? It looks like they're about to begin….."

He felt something cold, hard and rigid pressing against his anus. He tried to wriggle away from it, but there was nowhere to go. Then came the click. It was a simple mechanism, just back and forth. The only possible variation was in its speed.

He felt it enter him, utterly devoid of any sensitivity, slow increments or subtlety. Along with the sudden pain, it felt like it wasn't stopping anytime soon, like it would keep going until it pierced all his insides, like it was invading his very being, whilst the sheer girth of it stretched him like he'd split at any second. It finally reached its limit, held itself there for a few seconds, before retreating right back out to its starting point, and repeating, and repeating, and repeating, and repeating, and repeating, and repeating, and repeating, and repeating, and repeating, and repeating; for five hours, nonstop.

After the first increasingly agonising hour, he had heard Lorelei speak to him again:

- "How is it so far? Oh sorry, I really should be more specific, I mean the raping. Ooh they've really gone to town on the selection of the cock, look at it! That's got to be a 12 incher! And the girth of it! The selection process clearly isn't based on the victim's own one, and definitely not in your puny case! It's not just about the size though is it scumbag? Although, well, I guess you might disagree right now; it's the sheer violation of the whole thing, you know, the lack of consent, free will, the pain, the humiliation, all that. Have they used any lube? No, doesn't look like it! Ouch that's gotta hurt though! You really are bleeding quite badly! I wonder what this dial does? Oh look it's going faster! Fabulous! I can't wait til they set up the ball machine! I bet you can't either?! Like I said before though, don't worry; they do say the first 100 years are the worst. Anyways, I've had enough of watching and listening to you being relentlessly pounded; I'm off to the spa for a nice soothing massage. See you later, enjoy! Oh by the way, don't worry if it does stop for a minute; sometimes they like to change cocks, usually for a bigger one. Bye!"

Day Twenty Two

The pounding had finally stopped. For him though, plenty else continued - the hideous, terrifying hallucinations, the voices, the screams of others, and the severe pain; were not for stopping. Nor was his own terror during moments of sufficient mental clarity to be aware enough of the situation.

So many things he had never believed in, were there to make a mockery of his views as to how it all worked. Hadn't he paid enough for his actions? He'd done his time! What sort of justice is this!? This for the rest of eternity, for the rest of eternity, forever more, never stopping, all the time, no end, ever, just pain and more pain, agonising insufferable pain. Then there was the actual feel of it....

At some point later, he again felt something cold and hard, but this time pressed against his scrotum.

- "Woo hoo they've attached the steel ball crusher! I've been waiting for this! Oh I so wish you could see it! Is it the spiked one? Oh no not yet, that'll come next - always keep a little bit back for later aye! Are you ready? I can't hear you; I said are you ready!?"

Click. The mechanism started as before, with its simple back and forth motion, at a slow, steady, even pace. Every impact was more painful, at the impact point, and in his stomach. He tried to scream in agony, to beg for it to stop; but it did not amount to much with the gag in place and his breath taken away; and then there was the vomiting, the swallowing, the choking.

- "Hang in there scumbucket! You can do it! Only another 4 hours 59 minutes to go! Oh there will be a little break of course, for that changeover! I told you before, you can't pass out! We wouldn't want you missing out on all the fun!"

There came the sound of a crowd cheering at every impact, laughter, champagne corks popping, air horns sounding, chants of:

- "Crush those balls! Crush those balls! Crush those balls!"

On and on it went, the impacts, the searing agony internally and externally, the feeling of asphyxiation; until suddenly the impacts stopped. There was a sudden silence, other than his anguished noises. Two minutes passed, then there was an eruption of sound:

- "Spikes spikes spikes spikes spikes spikes spikes spikes spikes spikes spikes spikes spikes spikes spikes spikes spikes spikes spikes!!!!!!"

Then silence. An unclicking could be heard, then a thud, then the sound of something locking into place:

- "Are you ready!?"

- "Yeeeeessssss!"

- "I can't hear you!!!"

- "Yeeeeeeeeeessssssss!!!"

- "What do you want!?"

- "Spikes!!! Spikes!!!"

- "When do you want them!?"

- "Now!!!"

- "What do you want!?"

- "Spikes!!!! Spikes!!!!"

- "When do you want them!?"

- "Now!!!!"

This continued to a frenzy for a full five minutes, before suddenly stopping:

- "Give me the countdown!"

- "Ten! Nine! Eight! Seven! Six! Five!! Four!!! Three!!!! Two!!!!! One!!!!!!"

He tried to rithe free for all he was worth, which amounted to very little. Click. He felt the first new impact on his battered scrotum, and numerous sharp spikes tear into it at the same time. Back and forth, relentlessly. The faster it went, the louder the cheers became, completely drowning out what sounds he did manage to make.

As the crowd were reaching fever pitch, his Parole Officer, having become increasingly concerned at the lack of contact, and response from his superiors up the chain, took matters into his own hands. Upon arriving at the property and receiving no reply from either the external buzzer or tapping on his actual front door; carefully let himself in. Everything seemed in order, aside from the notable absence of both him and his personal possessions. The only thing left behind was a handwritten note:

By the time you read this, I'll be abroad on a false passport, gone forever so don't waste your time looking.

Thanks anyway, no hard feelings.

Word travelled around the systems, ports and airports were notified, and eventually, the news reached the ears of WPC Whitworth.

Day Twenty Three

The only sound he could hear was his own agonised whimpering. He could feel the dressing that had been applied to stem the bleeding where his scrotum had once been. Lorelei had told him not to worry, as a bag of blood had been hooked up to his drip to replace the amount lost; and always would be.

If there was, or could be anything stronger than his pain; it was his hatred. Hatred for her, for causing him to have ended up here, for revelling in his suffering, for predicting it, for being right.

His prison sentence had an end in sight. There was always the hope, the promise, that things would eventually come to an end however long away it seemed; that things would change. Was this it? Was this really it!? However much you've reached the point whereby you simply cannot endure any more, however desperate you are to get out, to get away; it just carries on?

After an indeterminate period of time he heard Lorelei again:

- "Hiya scumbucket! How are those raping balls of yours doing? Will they be doing much more raping in the near future? Oof doesn't look like it! Fucking ouch! Now that HAD to hurt!"

- "Untng ugng itgh!"

- "Hahaha what was that? Anyways I won't stop, just wanted to say hi and let you know about the programme for later. You're quite the attraction, the hottest ticket in town, well, in hell at least. It's not that common to get the quadruple whammy of beater, raper, torturer and murderer; so you're down for the absolute lot! They're even allowing a vote for what folks want to see done next. It doesn't really matter I suppose as you'll be getting it all anyway, repeatedly; but you know, people like to feel like they have a choice. I voted for the blow torch, just so you know, but we'll have to see what comes out on top - it's very exciting! See you in a bit then!"

He lay in his pain-ridden, terrified state, waiting, waiting, waiting, for whatever unspeakable horror was to be done to him next. It felt like it was all he had ever felt.

Three long hours later:

- "Great news scumbag! The blow torch won the vote! I couldn't be happier! Looks like they're gonna start on your nipples, and just take it from there. If you suddenly feel your vile cock being held in kind of barbecue tongs, well, you'll know you're in trouble.... Personally I'm looking forward to the sizzle! Anyway, enjoy!"

- "Ukin itcks! Ukin itcks!! Ukin itcks!!! Ukin itcks!!!!"

It was the sound he noticed first. That distinctive, fierce, rushing howl of flame. It crept ever closer, until he just began to feel the warmth of it, followed quickly by the heat of it, followed quicker still by the searing, piercing burn of it. He tried to cry out, straining with every fibre to get away from it, but it was hopeless. Along with the unbelievable pain, in so many parts of his body, which was only added to as it moved on to a new bit, came the smell; the smell of his own burning flesh. His chest, his neck, his stomach, his legs, his feet; never knowing quite where would be next.

- "Burn that cock! Burn that cock!! Burn that cock!!! Burn that cock!!!!"

- "Really?"

- "Yes!!!!

- "Just a little bit? Just a light toasting?"

- "To a crisp! To a crisp!! To a crisp!!! To a crisp!!!!"

- "Oh alright then! Here we go!"

- "Yeaaaahhhh!!!!!"

He felt the cold metal tongs take a firm grip of his penis, then the slight, then increasing heat, then the unimaginable pain. The crowd were in such a frenzy, the noise was all but deafening. He tried so hard to pass out, for even a second's relief, but it just wouldn't come to him.

Day Twenty Five

He had lost all track of how long he had been there. He had lost all track of everything save for pain, fear, and suffering.

- "Good morning scum of the earth! Or is it afternoon? It's nothing really so who cares? How the devil are you? Oops ha ha ha!"

- "Uckof uckof itc!"

- "Me? I'm doing absolutely great thanks! Just had strawberries and cream whilst receiving a foot massage."

- "Unt!!"

- "What am I doing later? Well I've a booking with the God of Cunnilingus a bit later for a few hours, then I might pop back and watch your fun times for a bit; I'll see what mood I'm in, you know how it is. How's your day looking?"

- "Itcks!!"

- "Ah that's sweet! Well I can't stop, places to be, oh I nearly forgot, I do actually know a way out of here for you. I won't tell you though of course. Byeee!"

A little later he endured a long session of a thousand cuts to howls of laughter, encouragement, derision, applause, and chanting; but with the notable absence of Lorelei this time.

Her last words to him were churning away in his mind as far as they could, amidst the pain and mortifying terror.

The next day, if it could be couched in such terms, there was no sign of her either, as salt was quite literally rubbed into his wounds. Once he'd been left for a while for all that to soak in, he suddenly heard her voice again right by his ear:

- "Do you think you've had enough yet, scumbag?"

- "Umm umm umm."

- "I'm not sure I'd agree! You did murderer me brutally after all, and destroy my happiness in the process. And then there's poor Adam down there on Earth; you destroyed him too. Maybe I'll leave you a little longer….."

- "El ee, el ee, el ee, el ee!!!"

- "On the other hand, I am having a wail of a time up here, what with having whatever I want whenever I want and everything, and I've seen that Adam has moved on and is really happy; so I suppose I could tell you and save you from all this, but then, nah! See ya!!"

- "Ugin itc!!!!"

Day Twenty Eight

He lay in terror, in desperation, in agony. It really never was going to end. There was a price to be paid for his actions, a price on top of prison, regardless of the length of sentence served; and he was paying it, with indefinite interest. She'd never tell him, it was probably just a lie anyway, just another way to taunt him, to punish him, to make him suffer.

Someone should have warned him. Maybe they did but they'd not been overly convincing. He pondered his decision, not exactly for the first time, not to tell them where she was, risking adding murder to his list of crimes, in the forlorn hope that they'd not be able to prove the rest if they never found her. What a great decision that had proved to be! There is regret, there is deep regret, and then there is something 100 stops down the line past there to an uncharted destination. We live and die by our decisions; she certainly died by his, but it wasn't her death that he regretted.

Suddenly there she was again by *his* ear:

- "You don't deserve this Scumbag, but I've seen enough of your face, had enough of even the thought of your presence here, fun though the suffering has been to see. You've just one chance to get out, just one, do exactly as I say: blow it and you're here for the rest of eternity. Understood?"

- "Egh egh!"

- "Good. Right, I'm going to unchain you. I know you're in tons of pain but you can't make a sound okay? You can probably barely walk either, but you're going to have to try; the good news is we're not going far. I'm going to remove your blindfold, but it's pitch black anyway. Keep the gag on in case you cry out."

He felt the chains loosen one by one and the relief of their removal, although it did little for his pain levels.

- "Now slowly try to sit up, that's it, sssshhhh, no crying out! If they hear us we're fucked! Now try to swing your legs round, slowly, slowly!"

It was all he could do not to scream at the extra pain of every movement of his stiff body, but finally he felt his feet touch the ground for the first time since he could remember. He tried several times to stand, only to remain on the bed, until finally, very unsteadily, he managed it. After several minutes he could sustain it without the support of the bed frame.

- "Okay this is it, your one and only chance! Follow me."

He took uneasy, excruciating steps towards her voice, feeling his way in the darkness.

- "This way, through this doorway, keep going, we've not got long! Okay, you can remove the gag now. Listen very carefully, we're in the absolute depths here, the only way out is up via a series of ladders. Keep going until you've counted ten, then there'll be a doorway, step through it and you're home free."

- "Where will I be?"

389

- "Far away from here, in a much better place!"

- "It can't be worse!"

- "Exactly! Right now here's the first ladder, go! Good luck, you can do it!"

- "Thanks!"

- "It's okay, go! Ten remember!"

He began the agonising climb, feeling his way, every step more painful than the last, onwards upwards, one, onwards upwards, two, the pain, three, the effort, it'll all be worth it, four, anything but this five, anything but this, six, don't stop, don't stop, seven, not far now, eight, nearly there, nine, one more, ten! Exhausted and in unimaginable pain, he felt and reached for the door. This is it, just like she said, good old Lorelei! He stepped through.

Just as he did so, a voice inside his ear firmly said:

- "And now wake up!!"

At the same time a series of industrial spotlights came on to illuminate the scene, and he began to fall in what felt like slow motion.

The first thing he noticed was that all his pain had suddenly stopped.

Then he saw and recognised that old abandoned barn.

Then he saw a familiar, but older looking man, smiling and waving farewell.

Then he looked directly downwards towards his destination, which was an old, but full, farm sewage pit, looming ever closer, with its already overpowering smell.

He just had time to start to realise what had been going on, and tried to say something as he hit the surface; but it was never heard.

He felt the soft sludge cushion his fall.

He felt it engulf him.

He tried with all his remaining might to struggle up and out, but it was utterly hopeless.

The taste was beyond putrid. It filled his mouth, then his nose, then his ears; then into his lungs, then he felt it fill his stomach, then his whole being.

It seemed to be taking forever.

He felt disgust and blind fury in equal measure.

He felt suffocation.

Then he felt nothing.

Adam turned away, and walked off along the road. After a few minutes he saw a small convoy of vehicles coming towards him. He stepped aside and waved as it passed by. Several minutes later a police car approached and slowed down to a stop beside him.

- "Anything to see up ahead Adam?"

- "No, not anymore."

- "Anything I should worry about?"

- "No, it's all been taken care of."

- "I'm glad to hear it! Need a lift home?"

- "No thanks, I could use the walk."

The car slowly turned back around, and headed off into the distance.